no GOING BACK

JANICE WHITEAKER

No Going Back, book 3 in the Cross Creek series, book 7 in the Cowboys of Moss Creek world.
Copyright 2023 by Janice Whiteaker.
www.janicewhiteaker.com

All rights reserved. No part of this publication may be reproduced, stored in a retrieval system, or transmitted in any form or by any means electronic, mechanical, photocopying, recording, or otherwise without the prior written permission of the publisher and copyright owner except for the use of brief quotations in a book review.

First printing, 2023

TRIGGER WARNINGS

This book contains topics some readers might find difficult to read or hear about. These include spousal abuse, PTSD, and pregnancy complications. Please consider skipping this story if you are sensitive to any of these subjects.

ONE

DIANNA

"DAMN IT. I knew I should have come down here earlier." Mae Pace frowned at the mostly empty case in front of her, one hand resting on the slight swell of her tiny belly. "I really wanted cake."

"Come back in an hour." Dianna was already backing toward the line of second-hand commercial coolers spaced along the back wall. "I'll put one together for you."

Mae scoffed. "No freaking way am I making you stay late because I waited too long to get off my ass." She leaned down to look over the remaining items in the ca[se]. "How about the peach shortcake instead?"

Dianna frowned. "But you want cake, not a biscuit. The thought of Mae leaving with anything besides what she came for bothered the heck out of her. "It really isn't a big deal. All the cakes have to get put together eventually and I'm going to be here anyway."

Probably until almost eleven based on how much sold today. She'd gone through all her backup items and was now down to a couple dozen cookies and the final peach shortcake she'd secretly been hoping would remain after closing time.

"Nope." Mae shook her head. "I know what it's like to run a business like this and there's no way I would ever pile more work up on you." She smiled brightly. "I think that peach shortcake will be perfect. Sweet and juicy and creamy all at the same time.

Dianna stifled a sigh. The peach shortcake *would* be perfect.

"Peach shortcake it is." She snagged a small box from the pile stacked neatly under the counter and went to work folding up the sides. "Were you busy today?"

Mae owned The Wooden Spoon, a local eatery that dished out diner favorites and some of the best pies Dianna had ever tasted. The place was always packed and, from what Mae said, sold out of pies the same way she sold out of cake.

Mae sighed. "So busy." She leaned back to scan the empty cases again. "Thank God you're here too, otherwise I'm not sure I'd be able to keep up with this town's" Her brows pinched together. "Would that sweet teeth?" Her lips pressed into a thin line. "Doesn't sound right either."

Dianna huffed out a little laugh as she loaded the

shortcake into the box and carefully tucked the lid into place. "Either way, the cowboys around here definitely like their baked goods." She slid the treat across the counter to Mae, trying to keep the longing out of her eyes. "Which I'm grateful for."

She'd moved to Moss Creek a year ago expecting to crash and burn. Even after The Baking Rack opened its doors she was sure it would flop. It had happened before. It would probably happen again.

Instead, The Baking Rack was thriving. Thanks to hungry cowboys and women like Mae Pace.

"Can I get you anything else?" Dianna motioned at the basic coffee bar she used to offer her patrons the simplest of beverages to accompany their indulgences. "Maybe a decaf latte?"

Mae shook her head, grimacing. "Can't handle the coffee this time." She poked one finger at the slight swell of her stomach. "This one clearly likes making me miserable."

Dianna smiled even as an old longing settled into her gut, sitting heavy and sad. "Must be a boy."

Mae's head tipped back on a cackle. "Isn't that the truth?" She shook her head. "He would come by it honestly, that's for sure. His daddy has a history of driving me nuts."

Dianna laughed along with her. She'd met Mae's husband Boone a handful of times and the man did seem ornery as hell. He was also handsome as hell and completely devoted to his wife and their young daughter.

And she wasn't jealous. Maybe envious though.

Mae was kind and hard-working and had been amazingly supportive even though The Baking Rack stepped on the toes of The Wooden Spoon. She deserved to have a husband who adored her.

It was just that, even after everything she'd been through, Dianna couldn't help but wish she had that too.

Mae dropped a ten-dollar bill on the counter before scooping up the box. "Don't work too hard." She pointed at Dianna, her expression sharpening. "I mean it. Don't work too hard. You'll make yourself miserable."

She wanted to point out that finally feeling good about who she was and what she could do would never make her miserable, but Mae was clearly trying to help. "I won't."

Mae's mouth held its stern line. "And don't be afraid to hire help. I know it seems counterintuitive, but you might actually make more money with a second set of hands."

The smile on her face was suddenly tight to the point it was almost painful to maintain. "I'll think about it." The words were clipped and sharper than she intended.

But bringing someone else into the business—*her* business—terrified her.

Luckily Mae seemed oblivious to the change. "I'm always happy to help you narrow down applicants." She leaned closer. "I know who'll show up on time and who'll roll in hung over and wearing the same clothes they had on the night before."

The smile Dianna was struggling to hold came a little easier at Mae's offer. "Thank you. That's really kind of you."

It was the part of moving to Moss Creek that had taken the most getting used to. The people here were actually nice. They took care of each other and liked seeing others happy and succeeding instead of being competitive and cutthroat.

It was... Odd.

Mae rolled her eyes. "Anyone would do that for you." She lifted the lid on her shortcake, all her focus going to the treat inside. "It's just common decency."

"Decency isn't as common as you think it is." Dianna reached under the counter to snag a plastic fork free of the bin she kept handy for people who didn't want to wait to enjoy their treat. She held it out to Mae. "You want a napkin too?"

Mae beamed at her, looking happy and healthy and glowing. Like a woman who knew she was loved and appreciated. "Nah." She took the fork. "I don't plan on any of it missing my mouth." She gave Dianna another wide smile as she pushed out the door. "And I'm serious about helping. You just let me know and I'll be down here."

"I'll keep that in mind." Dianna waved as Mae stepped out onto the sidewalk, a forkful of peaches, whipped cream, and biscuit already halfway to her mouth. Mae paused as she took the bite, eyes rolling closed as she chewed.

Dianna sighed, turning away from the enjoyment that might have been hers, to scan the remnants of the day's supply.

There weren't many. Definitely nothing that sounded half as good as that shortcake did.

She checked her watch. There were fifteen more minutes until the closing time posted on the door, and since she did still have a little fresh coffee and a few options left in the cases, she decided to leave the sign on while she went to the back to get started on putting together the next day's lineup.

She'd gone overboard at the beginning, making all sorts of things that took an ungodly amount of time and effort to assemble and organize. Granted, every bit of it sold out, but she was running herself ragged to do it. It was amazing to see people appreciate what she made, but it wasn't sustainable.

So she'd started to streamline, narrowing down to the most popular items and then rotating through them in a schedule so everyone knew what was being offered and when. It was working well enough, even if she ended up being frequently disappointed when the treat she wanted most was gone by the end of the day.

Like today.

Dianna gave the tray that used to hold peach shortcakes a final glance on her way to pour the first cup of coffee that would get her through the evening. After adding a little sugar and cream she went to the back room and pulled out the packs of puff pastry that would be cut and baked into the Trifecta Strudels that sold almost as well as the custard-filled donuts she topped with warm chocolate ganache.

She had the pastry out and the ingredients for the sweetened cream cheese that would cover a third of each slice lined down the counter when the bell on the door rang.

"*I'm coming.*" Dianna worked off her disposable gloves, tossing them into the trash on her way to the swinging door separating the kitchen portion of her small bakery from the retail section, smiling wide in preparation to greet what would likely be her final customer of the day. "How can I help y—"

The question died off in her throat and both feet froze to the floor as she stared at the man waiting on the other side of the counter.

Griffin Fraley stared back at her in all his silver fox glory, looking relaxed as he leaned against the counter in a t-shirt that clung to a body she might have spent a few too many nights remembering since his hasty departure a few months ago.

"You're back." The words came out on their own, driven straight from her mouth by shock and no small amount of excitement.

Which was not good.

Griffin slowly smiled, one side of his mouth lifting a little higher than the other into a lopsided expression that edged toward a sexy smirk. "I'm back."

Dianna resisted the urge to smooth down the front

of her apron. To touch her hair. To do something to make herself look more appealing to a man who probably only dated twenty-five-year-olds with perky tits and tight asses.

And she hadn't been that... ever.

It took every bit of concentration and focus to move her feet toward him. "I'm sure Troy is happy to have you back."

Griffin straightened away from the counter, giving her a better view of his tall, muscular frame. "I'd like to hope so." He rested one hand on the surface between them.

The move dragged her eyes down the toned line of his arm, over the tight cord of tanned muscle and bulging vein, to the calloused skin of his fingers.

Never in her life would she have considered hands pornographic, but Griffin's absolutely were. They made her think, wicked, lustful thoughts involving her body and the things those well-worn hands might be capable of doing to it.

Which proved Griffin was just as much of a distraction today as he was six months ago when he walked into her bakery for the first time.

It took far too much effort to pull her attention from that hand and back to his face, but somehow she accomplished it, adding in a tight smile for good measure. "Is there something I can get you?"

Men were supposed to be the last thing she focused on here in Moss Creek. This move was about finding herself again. Picking up the pieces she had left and filling in the rest in a way she could live with. Proving she was so much more than she'd been told.

But Griffin made that a tough plan to stick to.

It had almost been a relief when he went back to Seattle, removing the distraction of his daily visits to The Baking Rack and the temptation to hope that maybe one day she could have all the things Mae had.

That maybe one day she could have someone like him.

Griffin leaned back, looking down the line of empty cases. "Looks like you sold out." He refocused on her. "Guess I'll have to come earlier tomorrow."

Her heart skipped a beat at the thought of seeing him again. Clearly it hadn't gotten the message she'd been beating into her brain since Griffin first showed up in Moss Creek, tilting her world and her goals. "If you know what you want I can set it aside for you. Or I could —" Dianna bit off the rest of the offer, stopping herself from continuing on.

It was still too easy to slip back into her old way of thinking. Into people pleasing and trying to earn attention and affection. It was what allowed her to be broken down and abused. Manipulated and controlled. It took her power and gave it away.

And she'd worked too hard to steal it back.

"No way." Griffin moved down the glass fronts. "I'm a grown man and I know the way things work around here." He paused in front of the single tray that still held cookies. "Those look interesting." He crouched down, eyes narrowing a little as he read the sign next to them. "Chocolate, Cherry, Macadamia Nut Chews." He lifted his gaze to hers. "I'm surprised you didn't sell out of these."

"It's the second time I've tried a chocolate and cherry combination." She finally gave in and smoothed out her apron, trying to flatten the front in a way that would hide the curve of her stomach. "It doesn't seem like cowboys like it as much as I do."

"I guess it's my lucky day then, because I love chocolate and cherry." Griffin stood up, all his attention zeroed in on her. "I'll take all of them."

It was difficult not to fidget under his gaze, so she crouched down to hide from it instead. "Sounds like the perfect dinner to me." Dianna retrieved a box from under the counter and worked on folding it into shape.

"I can't imagine you spend too many dinners eating leftover cookies." Griffin's eyes followed her as she loaded up his order. "You probably have all kinds of m—"

The bell on the door rang as a group of waitresses from The Watering Hole walked in, chatting and laughing until their eyes landed on Griffin. Then they all went quiet, smiling sweetly as they passed him, sneaking peeks as they moved around the bakery.

She couldn't blame them. Griffin was real easy on the eyes. He also seemed friendly and kind and respectful.

But lots of men seemed friendly and kind and respectful before you really got to know them. Then their true colors came out.

Dianna did her best to ignore the way the pretty young women watched Griffin as he pulled out his wallet and stepped to the register. She also did her best to ignore the way her foolish heart wanted to believe he might be different from the men of her past.

That maybe Griffin really was as friendly and kind and respectful as he seemed.

It didn't matter. Even if she was the kind of woman who would snag his attention, dating was off the table. It was a promise she'd made herself.

And she'd broken so many of those already. Too many.

So Dianna slid the box across the counter, forcing herself to treat the man on the other side as if he was any other customer. "Anything else?"

Griffin's eyes moved down the backside of the displays to focus on her beverage station. "Do you have any coffee made?"

"I do, but it's not as fresh as what you'd get down at Blue Moon." She tried her best to do for others what Mae did for her, sending people to the local coffee house whenever she could. Reminding them they could purchase the same coffee she made in bulk directly from the roaster, along with a whole lineup of specialty drinks instead of just the drip and lattes she made.

"I know you tell me it's the same stuff, but I like your coffee better." Griffin leaned against the counter again, looking unhurried. "You must have the magic touch."

She couldn't help but laugh. She'd been working hard to accept compliments when they came her way, but that one was too ridiculous to claim. "I think you just like boring coffee."

Griffin continued grinning as she pulled out a cup and filled it from the carafe. "I drank nothing but Folgers for years, so this is fancy coffee to me."

"Folgers isn't bad." She capped the cup and added an insulated sleeve before sliding it across the counter, intending to leave it next to the box of cookies.

Griffin reached for the cup immediately, his fingers wrapping around hers, lingering over her skin, proving they were just as deliciously rough as she expected. "But it's not as good as the coffee you make me."

The way he said it almost felt intimate. As if she put together the grounds and water just for him.

Unfortunately, tomorrow morning it might not be far from the truth.

As much as she wanted to think Griffin's reappearance wouldn't change anything, it absolutely would. Now she would always be looking for him. Waiting to see his silvery hair and crinkled eyes walk into the bakery. Hoping she might run into him on the street. That was what happened last time he came to Moss Creek and there was no reason to think this time would be any different.

Because as much as she'd been trying, change was hard.

But it had to happen. She couldn't go back to the way she used to be.

She wouldn't survive it.

Griffin spared the group of waitresses a quick glance as they moved to form a line behind him. "I guess I'll stop holding you up." He tossed two twenties down onto the counter before backing away, eyes staying locked onto hers. "I'll see you tomorrow, Miss Dianna."

TWO

GRIFFIN

*H*E'D ALMOST ASKED Dianna to dinner.

He'd given himself one rule when he decided to permanently move to Moss Creek, and he'd already come close to breaking it after less than five minutes in town.

Less than five minutes with her.

He wasn't off to a great start.

Griffin shoved the cup of coffee Dianna made him into the holder of the rental car he'd picked up at the airport, raking one hand through his hair as he set the cookies onto the passenger's seat.

He shouldn't have gone to The Baking Rack. He knew damn well what happened when he was around her.

But he'd done it anyway.

Not just done it, but driven over the speed limit the whole way there to make sure it would happen.

It had been almost three months since he'd seen her. Part of him was hoping his brain had embellished the memories he pulled up a little too often, making Dianna out to be sweeter and softer than she really was.

It hadn't.

If anything, his memories had dimmed, because when she came out of the back room, smiling like it was just for him, the sight of her nearly sent him back a step.

Like she'd been waiting to see him too.

"Shit." He started the engine and backed out, turning onto the road that ran through the center of town, unable to resist taking another glance into The Baking Rack as he passed. Dianna stood at the counter, laughing as she chatted with the group of women who saved him from himself, coming in just as he was about to self-destruct once again.

He wasn't here to find yet another woman to disappoint. He was here to figure out how to build the first functional relationship of his life. One that mattered more than any other—the relationship he hoped to have with his son.

Troy was the only thing that was supposed to matter right now. Getting to know him. Being the father he deserved to have.

They'd been without each other for almost thirty years. He wasn't going to fuck up this opportunity, no matter how tempting the town's dark-haired baker was.

And Dianna was definitely tempting. Full lips, wide

eyes, curves he wanted to sink his fingers into—the woman was a distraction that would test his limits.

His control.

His dedication.

But he couldn't fail at this. He'd failed so many people in his life. Troy couldn't be one of them.

Griffin forced his eyes from Dianna and her bakery, locking them onto the road as he drove through the little town he now called home, making his way to the small farmhouse he'd be sharing with Troy and his new wife Amelie until he managed to find a house of his own.

Buying a place in a town like Moss Creek seemed like it would be a simple process. He'd already sold his home in Seattle and was prepared to make a cash offer, which normally would have given him an edge over the competition. The problem was there was no competition to have. Most houses sold before ever hitting the market. Apparently everyone knew everyone around here and word traveled fast, making it easy for sellers to save themselves realtor commissions.

Good for them, bad for him and his plans of homeownership.

But he needed to find a place, which meant tomorrow he'd be looking at the only houses his realtor could come up with. Even if they weren't exactly what he was looking for. Because as much as he wanted to spend time with Troy, the farmhouse he lived in was a tight fit, and he didn't want to upend his son's life.

He simply wanted to be a part of it.

The scenery out the windshield looked a hell of a lot

different than it had the last time he was in town. All the snow was gone, replaced by lush fields filled with horses and cattle, making the drive to Cross Creek peaceful and serene. It would give him time to pull his thoughts from Dianna and put them where they belonged. Unfortunately, that was easier said than done.

He'd been single for almost two years after a breakup that resulted in most of his clothing being set on fire and his ego taking a hit that wasn't easy to recover from. Hearing you're the problem while your shit, and your life, goes up in flames fucks you up and makes you question your taste in women.

Which was what he was doing when he found out about Troy.

Finding out he had a son gave him something else to focus on. A new purpose in life. A sense of direction he'd never had. A direction that pointed him straight to Montana.

And straight to Dianna, offering up a test he wasn't willing to fail.

Being a good man hadn't ever been something he thought he was capable of, but Troy deserved a good father, so he was going to do whatever it took to make that happen.

The lights were all on in the small farmhouse when Griffin pulled in, catching sight of Troy and Amelie through the kitchen window as they laughed together in a moment of domestic bliss unlike anything he'd ever experienced. Knowing his son had that made him happier than he'd been in a long time.

He was barely out of the car before the back porch light flipped on and the door opened.

"Well look what the cat dragged in."

Griffin straightened to look across the top of the rented sedan at where Amelie's grandmother Muriel stood on the small deck at the back of the house. He shot her a grin. "Did you come over just to give me a hard time?"

Muriel laughed, head tipping back. "You know I did." She held the door wide as he rolled his suitcase up the steps and across the composite planks. "Couldn't miss out on a chance to see my favorite grandson-in-law's daddy."

He leaned in to press a kiss to her cheek as he passed. "How have you been?"

"Fair to middlin'." She followed him into the house. "I miss being able to order pizza, but that's about it."

Griffin paused. It hadn't really occurred to him that take-out and delivery might be a thing of his past.

He'd been toying with the idea of moving onto the mountain just past Cross Creek. Trying to buy a lot and build the house of his dreams. So far it had been what he considered his best option. But he'd lived in the city his whole life and maybe giving up all the conveniences it offered was a step farther than he wanted to take. "I might narrow my house search to places in town."

Muriel cackled again, patting him on the back as they moved into the kitchen. "Good luck with that. Not much comes up for sale down there."

"I've noticed." He'd been watching since his first trip

to Moss Creek, keeping his eyes open in case an opportunity presented itself. Because, even before he figured out how to work out the logistics of it, he knew he needed to get closer to his son. It didn't matter what it cost or what he had to sacrifice, he was going to be in Troy's life. "I was hoping something might come up when the weather got nicer."

It was how most housing markets worked. People liked to sell their homes and move while it was sunny and be settled before school started in the fall.

But Moss Creek was proving to be the exception to the rule.

"Hey there." Amelie, Troy's wife, came straight for him, offering a tight hug. "You hungry?"

"Sure." He held out the cookies he'd happily overpaid for. "I brought dessert."

"Ohhhhhh." Amelie stole the box away. "How'd you manage this?"

"Apparently chocolate and cherries isn't a great seller." He smiled as Amelie opened the box and took a deep breath, her lips curving into a smile.

"Their loss." She reached in and broke off a chunk before popping it into her mouth, eyes closing as she chewed. "Holy cow these are good." She held the open box out to Muriel. "Try these."

Muriel didn't have to be asked twice. She grabbed the remainder of Amelie's cookie and took a bite. "Maybe we can ask her to bring these to our next lunch date."

"If we can get her to come to lunch again." Amelie

went back to the stove where Troy was dutifully stirring the contents of a pot. "She keeps canceling on us."

He'd planned to leave his thoughts of Dianna in town, but like always, they seemed determined to follow him. "She's probably busy as hell." Griffin abandoned his suitcase and went to where Troy stood, patting him on the shoulder as he peeked into the pot. "The cases were all but empty when I was there."

"They're always empty." Troy stepped to one side as Amelie took over stirring. "She still sells out every damn day." He shook his head. "I can't imagine how late she stays there every night to get it all made."

Griffin lifted his brows, a little surprised. "She does it all herself?" He hadn't seen any employees at The Baking Rack, but he'd assumed they worked in the back. He'd been there first thing in the morning and seen just how packed the cases were. "There's no way she could be doing that all herself."

Running a business was hard work even when you weren't also the one making the product. If Dianna was the sole employee, she had to be working herself to death. Hell, he had a whole team of employees and managers who ran each location he owned, and running his auto repair shops still ate up the majority of his time.

"I don't know that I'd tell her that." Troy shot him a grin as he leaned back against the counter. "I've heard women don't like being told what to do."

Griffin smiled, the fact that Troy remembered his advice warming his chest. "I'll remember to keep my mouth shut then."

It was something that would be easier said than done. He already missed the hands-on aspect of running his business. He loved fixing things. Sniffing out problems and coming up with solutions.

And Dianna working herself to death was definitely a problem.

"How was Seattle?" Troy passed over a bottle of his favorite beer. "Everything go as smoothly as you were hoping?"

"Smooth enough." He didn't want to admit to his son that moving to Moss Creek had been a mess of epic proportions. "Hopefully I can find a place sooner rather than later so I can have all my stuff shipped over."

He'd planned to buy a house and move into it before selling his place in Seattle. When things didn't work out that way, he packed all his belongings into cubes that were now stacked in a warehouse, waiting to be shipped to their final destination once he found it. That meant he was once again living out of a suitcase.

At least this time it wasn't a less than amicable split that left him in need of a place to crash.

"I've been asking around and so has Evelyn, but so far we haven't heard of anyone looking to sell." Amelie switched off the stove. "But I'll keep asking."

"I appreciate it." Griffin tipped back a sip of his beer. "I'm meeting with a realtor tomorrow to look at a couple options she found, but they're a little farther away than I'd like to be."

His whole reason for moving was to be close to Troy. It was why he restructured his entire business, promoting one of his best employees to a general manager type position so he didn't have to be as involved anymore. No way was he going through all that to still be over an hour away from the son he desperately wanted to know.

"Too bad some sexy woman moved into Ben's old place." Muriel carried a stack of bowls to the table, wiggling her eyebrows as she set them down. "I bet she'd be happy to let you sleep on her couch though."

"Griffin doesn't need to sleep on your couch. He's got a whole bedroom here." Amelie dumped a collection of spoons next to the bowls before going to the fridge and pulling out cheese and sour cream. "One he can use for as long as he likes."

The way Troy's new wife embraced him was almost as unexpected as the way Troy did. Amelie was a little standoffish at first, but once she realized his intentions were good, she'd welcomed him into their life wholeheartedly. Going so far as to invite him to be one of the few witnesses at their courthouse wedding.

"I appreciate that, but you two just got married. You need to spend time together, not entertaining your third-wheeling dad." At least he assumed they did. He'd never made it to the point of a marriage, but it wasn't hard to imagine a man wanting his wife to himself.

Especially if that wife was like Dianna. Soft and sweet and gentle, with a ready smile and a body a man could easily never get enough of.

And just like that, he was back to where he swore not to be. Spending the time he should be focused on his son thinking about the woman he would never have. Not just because he'd sworn off women, but because he'd finally started to realize the problem in all the relationships he'd had stemmed from a single source.

Him.

And no matter how much he wanted Dianna, he would never do that to her. Even if Troy wasn't in the picture.

"I'm not sure how much time we're going to have alone together as it is." Amelie's gaze slid to where Troy stood and a slow smile curved her lips. "We're going to have a permanent house guest in about seven months."

Griffin opened his mouth, ready to explain he had zero intentions of staying in their house that long.

Then her words registered. "You're pregnant?"

Troy's grin was immediate and wide. "That sounds a whole lot like what I said." He wrapped one arm around Amelie's back, pulling her close as he pressed a kiss to the top of her head. "Except I was so shocked I said it about five times in a row."

He understood completely.

Finding out he was a father rocked his world, turning everything he thought he wanted on its side and tinting the way he viewed himself and the life he'd lived. It made him reevaluate all of it, picking apart the pieces of the future he envisioned before reassembling it in a way that took him out of the center, putting Troy there instead.

But now he wasn't just going to be a father. He was going to be a grandfather.

After missing out on everything in his son's life, it

was impossible not to see this as an opportunity to take back a little of what was stolen from him.

From them.

Griffin stepped close, grabbing both Troy and Amelie at once and squeezing them tight. He didn't know what to say. How to convey all he was feeling. So he didn't try. It was simpler to keep it in since chances were good he'd say it wrong anyway.

Amelie let out a little squeak, followed by a relieved sounding exhale. "I was a little worried you'd be bothered by the thought of being a grandpa before you turned fifty."

"No way." Griffin stepped back as the emotion of the moment came a little closer than he wanted. He raked one hand through his greying hair. "I already look the part. Might as well embrace it."

Amelie's eyes fixed on his face, a thin line of tears edging her lids. "I'm so happy to hear you say that."

His jaw clenched tight. Amelie had told him bits and pieces about her parents and the way they'd treated her and Muriel over the years. It wouldn't surprise him if their reaction to this news had been less than stellar. "I'm happy that you're happy."

It was all he wanted. For the people he loved to be happy. Happiness was easy to navigate and simple to handle.

But it was clear Amelie wasn't completely content. Not entirely. Her parents let her down. Again. It was something she probably wanted to talk about, but he would leave that conversation to someone better equipped than him.

Griffin pulled out a chair, handling Amelie's upset the only way he knew how. Redirection. "We should probably start eating. You've got a whole baby to grow."

THREE

DIANNA

THE MUSCLES OF her arm were on fire and the extended limb was beginning to twitch, but come hell or high water this was happening.

Snickerdoodle, the biggest of the squirrels that frequented her backyard, stood three feet away from the peanut pinched between her fingers, eyeing her warily.

"You know you want it." Dianna tried to keep her voice soft and soothing. "We could be best friends. I have so many peanuts I would give you."

She'd spent nearly every morning since the weather warmed sitting on her back porch, luring the herd of fuzzy beggars that loitered around closer and closer each day. It was a ridiculous quest, but one she was determined to pursue.

Her old therapist probably would have chalked it up

to her need for acceptance and validation, but she was pretty sure it was just because she wanted to pet a fucking squirrel.

Tik-Tok made it look so easy. Everyone and their brother seemed to have a raccoon or squirrel or even a fucking fox living in their house as pets.

She didn't even want the damn things in her house. She just wanted to be friends.

Snickerdoodle's little squirrel nose twitched as he took a tiny step closer, eyes locked on the nugget of goodness she offered.

"Stop being an asshole and just take the damn nut." Even though she said them in a sing-songy tone, her words were still sharp and demanding. Demanding enough that Snickerdoodle straightened up on his hind legs, gave her an indignant look, and bounced off to the far end of her tiny yard.

Because of course he did.

Dianna sighed, standing up and tossing the nut into the grass where Snickerdoodle, or one of his many cohorts, would likely come and retrieve it after she left for the day. She dusted off her leggings and adjusted the hem of her T-shirt, smoothing over The Baking Rack logo emblazoned down the front as she hurried inside. She'd spent way too much time trying to seduce Snickerdoodle, and now she was late.

The cowboys would already be lined up outside when she unlocked the door, ready for coffee and the sweet offerings she had for the day. Today was scheduled to be cinnamon rolls and cherry danishes, along with lemon bars and the dozens of cookies she baked every night, plus a few special-order cakes that were being picked up.

That meant being late this particular morning was extra terrible. Cinnamon rolls were one of her biggest sellers, and everybody showed up bright and early to make sure they got one of the cream cheese frosting topped buns.

Dianna snagged her keys from the counter, grabbed her bag and headed out into the tiny garage her small car barely fit inside. After carefully backing out, she headed towards town. Her shop was barely a mile away—close enough that she frequently chose to walk, using the quiet morning stroll to mentally gear herself up for the day.

But today there was no time for that. Today she had to rush, which meant she would already feel a little frazzled when she walked in, so the chances of her being overwhelmed before lunch were substantial.

"You will be fine." Dianna sucked in a deep breath and blew it back out. "You can do this. You are not dumb. You are not lazy. You are not always going to be a failure."

It was an edited version of the mantra the therapist she went to after her divorce recommended, but currently the best one she could manage.

It turned out it was more difficult to recover from years of emotional abuse than she expected. Apparently something like that affected you deeply enough that even three years later you still believed all the words that had been slung at you.

At least a little bit.

But the sun was brightening the small town she'd chosen as her home. And as she closed in on it, the sight of the quaint buildings of downtown relaxed a little of the tension tightening her shoulders. Today really would be fine. She'd see the same people she always did. The ones who came back time and time again because they liked what she made and thought what she offered was worth spending their hard-earned money on.

And at some point that needed to start counting for something.

Maybe today would be that point.

Dianna parked in her designated spot behind The Baking Rack, using her key to get in through the door tucked into the back of the building. It was the same thing she did every morning six days a week. Rain or shine. Sickness or health. She was here, proving at least one of the insults Martin loved to cut her down with was a lie.

She definitely wasn't lazy.

After hanging her purse on the hook beside the door and lacing her keys next to it, Dianna went to work flipping on the lights and the ovens, moving through a routine that felt like breathing at this point. She started up the warmers and went to work unwrapping the first tray of cinnamon rolls she'd baked before leaving last night. It had taken some trial and error, but she'd finally figured out the best process for every item she offered, toeing the line between offering the freshest food possible, while also allowing her time to sleep.

Occasionally.

It took about thirty minutes to get everything up and running on a normal day, but today she only had fifteen. Which meant by the time the doors were unlocked and people were filtering in, the coffee wasn't completely brewed and she only had two trays of cinnamon rolls warmed with the next round baking in the oven. But it would just have to be okay because there was only one of her to go around.

Dianna took her place at the register, plastered on a smile, and greeted the first person in line. Even on a day like today, where she was tired and running late, that first sale still held a special place for her. It meant she was succeeding. Accomplishing something she'd allowed another person to make her believe wasn't possible.

Unfortunately, an hour into the day that glow of accomplishment was starting to wear off. All the coffee she'd brewed up was gone and she was behind on the cinnamon rolls, forcing her to take a break from the register to refill the carafes and rotate out the trays of risen buns, pulling one from the oven before sliding the next one in. It was impossible not to feel rushed as the line of people continued to grow, filling the bakery before moving out the door.

That was when the thoughts she'd been learning to muffle started to creep back in.

Maybe she *wasn't* capable of doing this.

Maybe she *was* lazy. Maybe she wasn't as skilled of a baker as she thought. Maybe she wasn't good at multitasking. Maybe this business was destined to fail just like the one before it.

Maybe Martin was right.

"Hey."

A surprisingly loud voice pulled her from the cycle of thoughts still trying to rule her life. Dianna glanced up from where she was smearing the tray of freshly baked cinnamon rolls with icing, to find a woman a little older than her standing behind the counter. "Can I help you?"

The woman was pretty with full lips and strawberry blonde hair. She eyed the pan of rolls, using the hair tie around one wrist to twist her natural curls into a bun at the top of her head. "No, but I bet I can help you."

Dianna blinked, glancing from where the woman stood, looking effortlessly casual and cool in a pair of worn jeans and an old concert T-shirt, to the line of people still accumulating. "What do you want to help me with?"

The woman shrugged. "Whatever. I worked in a coffee shop before and I'm pretty sure I can spread icing on cinnamon rolls." Her smile turned sympathetic. "And I definitely know what it looks like to be overwhelmed as fuck, so put me to work."

Any other time she might have rejected the offer, but things were quickly getting out of control and the collection of people waiting outside certainly wasn't going to shrink. Not unless they walked away. And the fear of losing out on a possible customer was even greater than the fear of allowing someone else in her kitchen.

At least at this moment.

Dianna passed over the spatula. "I already added the full amount of frosting, it just needs to be spread around."

The woman hesitated. "I probably need to wash my hands real quick."

Dianna cringed inwardly. "Right." How in the hell could she forget something so simple? "The sink's through that door on the wall." She clenched her fists, determined not to miss something basic again. "Grab an apron while you're at it."

She finished up the frosting while the woman was gone, digging a server into one bun and loosening it from the tray so they would be easy to dish out.

By the time she was picking the pan up from the counter, the woman was back, tying on her apron with a smile.

"I'm Janie."

Dianna automatically smiled back even though her mind was spinning and her stress level was climbing. "Dianna."

Janie stole away the cinnamon rolls, taking them to the glass case. "I already knew that. I've heard nothing but good things about the magical Dianna who bakes the most amazing cinnamon rolls in town." She leaned down, sliding open the case before setting the still warm pan onto the trivet inside. "It looks like everyone else in town heard the same thing."

Dianna blew out a breath. "They do seem to be pretty popular." It was a good thing. It should be anyway. This was what she dreamed of. Doing what she loved most every day. Running a business that paid her bills and made her feel fulfilled and capable.

But the more popular The Baking Rack got, the less capable she felt. It was an outcome she hadn't foreseen and wasn't really sure how to deal with.

Janie closed the door to the case and clapped her hands together. "What next?"

Dianna's brain stumbled. So much of what she did was automatic at this point, and trying to explain it to someone else was overwhelming. It was also terrifying. She'd let another person into her business once and it had a devastating outcome.

But Janie wasn't in her business. She was just helping out for the day. Frosting some cinnamon rolls. That was it. It would be fine. *She* would be fine.

"The next tray of cinnamon rolls will be done in about five minutes. They need to rest for five more minutes and then they get frosted with two cups of cream cheese icing from the tub on the counter." Dianna stood a little taller, feeling slightly more capable after the explanation flowed smoothly. "Then put another of the pans in and set a fifteen-minute timer." She motioned to the line of rising buns down the counter. "After that, everything gets moved up in order and a new tray gets pulled out of the fridge and set at the last spot."

It was her version of an assembly line, one that had a fresh batch of risen buns ready to go in as soon as the pan before it came out of the oven.

Janie lifted her brows, propping both hands onto her hips. "You've got this shit down to a science, don't you?"

Dianna smiled, trying her best to believe what Janie was saying instead of what someone else tried to burden her with. "I try."

"You should probably try a little less." Janie nodded toward the line waiting at the register. "Otherwise you'll never be able to manage the crowds."

Six months ago Dianna might have thought that was a great problem to have. That a full bakery would finally undo the years of damage Martin did to her ego and her soul.

But that didn't seem to be true.

Janie pointed at the register. "You go handle them. I've got the cinnamon rolls."

"Thank you." The amount of relief she felt was unexpected and unnerving, but nothing she had time to dwell on because there were customers waiting to be served. Customers she wanted to keep happy enough that they would continue coming back.

Dianna gave Janie a quick smile. "Let me know if you need anything." She turned and went to the counter, greeting the next person in line with an apology that they had to wait so long.

The rest of the morning passed by in a blur of cinnamon rolls and lattes, most of which were crafted by Janie, who turned out to know her way around the espresso machine. By the time the afternoon lull set in, all the cinnamon rolls were gone, the day's cakes had been dispersed, the dirty pans had been scrubbed clean, and Dianna wasn't nearly as exhausted as normal.

Janie sidled up to her at the counter. "Is it always like that here?"

"Lately it has been." It was an admission she hadn't offered to anyone, not that she really had anyone to offer it to. She had many acquaintances in Moss Creek—people like Maryanne and Mae Pace, along with the rest of the women they socialized with—but admitting to them she was struggling felt like a form of failure. And she didn't want them to see her as a failure. This place was supposed to be her fresh start. Her chance to prove who she really was.

And she didn't want to be a failure.

"Well," Janie reached down to untie the length of apron string she'd circled around her body, "if you decide to hire someone to help out I'm looking for work."

Dianna studied the woman beside her, wracking her brain for anything that seemed familiar. "Are you from Moss Creek?"

Janie shook her head. "No. I just moved to town. A friend of mine lives here and loves it so I thought I'd see what all the fuss was about."

Dianna's brows lifted. "Really? Who's your friend?"

Janie pulled the apron over her head and passed it to Dianna. "Mariah Duncan. Do you know her?"

"I do. She works for Maryann Pace at The Inn." Mariah was great. She was sweet and cute and one hell of a great cook. She was also the kind of woman who tempted Dianna to make comparisons. Comparisons that resulted in harsh judgments about herself and all the ways she'd been told she was lacking.

But she was learning to be kinder to herself. Kinder to the woman still struggling to be fine even after all this time.

"That's her." Janie smiled wide. "We went to culinary school together." She tipped her head to one side, smile slipping. "At least until I dropped out."

Dianna couldn't help but be thrown off by the revelation. "Why did you drop out?"

If this morning was any indication, Janie seemed like one hell of a go-getter, so the fact that she quit school was surprising.

Janie lifted a shoulder and let it drop. "It wasn't really my thing I guess." She huffed out a little laugh. "Not that I know what my thing is, which is super depressing considering I'm almost forty."

"You know what they say." Dianna took the apron and hung it over one shoulder. "Forty is the new twenty." She rolled her eyes to one side. "At least that's what I'm telling myself as I get closer to it."

She'd expected to be someplace entirely different at thirty-seven. Someplace that included an adoring husband and a couple of kids.

Instead, she was divorced and the bakery was her baby.

It was what kept her up at night. Ate up all her time and stressed her out.

But it also gave her a sense of purpose and security.

Janie shot her a wink. "I'm putting that on a shirt." She snagged one of the cards from the holder on the counter and scribbled across the back with the pen

Dianna used to jot down orders, then held the card out between them. "Here's my number. Call me if you decide you'd like an extra hand around here."

Dianna took the card, glancing down at the number as Janie went for the door. "Wait." She patted the front of her apron, but her pockets were empty. "I need to pay you for today."

Janie waved her off with a smile. "Don't worry about it." She grinned. "I stole a cinnamon roll so we can call it even."

FOUR

GRIFFIN

"WHAT DO YOU think?" Nate gestured around the main floor of the house, a wide smile on his face. "Nice, isn't it?"

"It is." Griffin rested one hand on the smooth marble of the kitchen countertop, the snarled mess of his cuticles a stark contrast to the pristine surface. "I'm just not sure it's really what I'm looking for."

Nate had done his best with the limited inventory of homes available, spending their day together showing him houses in all the cities surrounding Moss Creek, but none of them had even come close to what he was hoping to find.

He wanted a house that fit him. One that suited his current needs.

And his current need was a project. Something to

keep him busy and occupy his mind so he wouldn't fall back into the same traps that always caught him.

And unfortunately, Moss Creek held one hell of a trap.

Nate's shoulders slumped the tiniest bit under the clean lines of his expensive suit. "I know, man." He shook his head. "I'm just having a hell of a time finding you a fixer-upper."

It was starting to look like Amelie knew exactly what she was talking about when she warned him houses got snapped up by someone who knew the seller before they even hit the market. That was a problem since he didn't know much of anybody around here. If it'd been back in Seattle, he could've had twenty houses by now. He'd run businesses in the area for so long his connections spread for miles.

But not here. Here he was nobody.

No. That wasn't true. Here he was the most important thing.

Here, he was Troy's dad. That's how everyone knew him, and he wasn't mad about it, because being Troy's dad was the most important thing he could be right now.

Which was why he needed a fixer-upper.

Nate raked one hand through his dark hair before tucking it into his pocket, looking exactly like the successful realtor he was. Every bit of him was clean-cut and high-end. He was well-dressed, well-groomed, and well-spoken.

Add in the fact he was at least a decade younger, and Nate was exactly the kind of man Griffin should be sending into The Baking Rack to solve his problem. If Dianna was taken, the temptation she offered would be gone.

But he couldn't make himself do it. The thought of anyone else touching her made him want to crawl out of his skin. The thought of anyone else pulling her close sent jealousy scrambling through his insides, clawing at his guts.

Because he was an asshole, just like so many of his exes had kindly pointed out.

"I really want something that needs work." Griffin straightened away from the counter, tucking his hand into his pocket. "This place is beautiful, but it's just not for me."

Nate tipped his head in a nod even though there was disappointment on his face. "I get it." He motioned toward the door. "From now on I'll limit our showings to houses that fit that requirement."

Griffin moved through the house, past the office with gorgeous built-ins and the light-filled formal living room. "I'm sorry for wasting your day."

"This is my fault, not yours." Nate opened the door, holding it wide as Griffin passed out onto the covered porch staged with expensive furniture and draped lights. "I knew your preferences, but thought I'd show you a few options outside of them. I'm the one who picked these places knowing they weren't exactly what you were looking for."

He couldn't fault Nate for trying to broaden his horizons. It was becoming pretty clear what he wanted was in limited supply and Nate was in the business of selling houses. He had bills to pay, and dealing with a guy who wanted what didn't exist probably wasn't high on his list of ways to spend his workday.

"I'll do a little more legwork. Let all my connections know I've got a client looking for a place that needs work."

"Tell them I can pay cash." Connections were great and all, but at the end of the day money talked, and he'd worked hard to be at a point in his life where he could say a lot.

Nate pointed a finger at him as they crossed the porch. "That will help." His eyes swung to the driveway. "I see you got rid of that rental car. That's a nice truck."

Griffin dug the fob to his new pickup from the front pocket of his over-worn blue jeans. "It was a hell of a lot easier to find than a house, I can tell you that much."

And also bought with the same intention. Trucks made it easy to help out at Cross Creek and would come in handy when he finally had the house he wanted.

"We'll find you something." Nate slapped him on one shoulder before heading to his sleek sports car. "I promise. It just might take us a little longer than we expected."

"Hopefully not too long." Griffin unlocked the truck. "Troy and Amelie say they don't mind having me around, but I'm sure they're ready to get their privacy back."

He'd been sleeping in the spare bedroom across the hall from his son and daughter-in-law for almost two weeks now, and while they'd never even hinted at him overstaying his welcome, he couldn't help but feel like he was invading the limited time Troy and his wife had left together as just a couple.

"I will do everything I can to find you a place." Nate opened the door of his car. "It'll happen."

"I like your positivity." Griffin slid into the seat of his truck, giving Nate a little wave before starting the engine and backing out of the driveway onto the road of the upscale neighborhood he would've always felt he didn't belong in.

Because even though money talked, it sure as hell didn't stop the past from whispering.

He might be worth just as much as the people who lived in this neighborhood, maybe even more, but that didn't change the fact he would never be one of them. He would always be that rough edged guy with dirty hands and a career most people looked down their nose at.

IT WAS WELL after lunch by the time he reached Moss Creek, and his stomach was growling. He angled toward the main drag, intending on going to The Wooden Spoon for an early dinner before heading out to Cross Creek. It had been a long and disappointing day, one that made him question if he was simply going to end up in yet another place where he didn't belong. An outsider looking in, finding out no matter how much money he had or how successful he became, he would never really be accepted.

Griffin slowed as someone pulled out of a spot, offering up the only vacancy on the street. He quickly claimed it as his own, managing to parallel park his new truck without too much trouble. It wasn't until he got out and locked the doors that he realized he wasn't quite as close to the town's most popular eatery as he intended.

Unfortunately he *was* close to another place. One he should pretend didn't exist.

But he was weak enough that the thought of Dianna's sweet smile lured him in, dragging his boots in the opposite direction of The Wooden Spoon.

There was no line when he arrived at The Baking Rack, which wasn't surprising. Dianna was only open until three in the afternoon and it was nearly two forty-five, so chances were good she'd already sold out of everything. Hopefully the door was locked and fate would save him from himself.

He pushed on the handle and it opened easily, but he couldn't bring himself to be disappointed as the sweet scent of the space immediately pulled his mind closer to the sweet woman who owned it. It'd been almost two weeks since he'd seen Dianna after stopping by his first night in town, promising to return the next day.

Two long weeks.

And it would be even longer since there was no sign of her behind the counter.

Griffin moved forward, peering over the edge to the space that ran behind the cases, expecting to find her crouched down organizing the boxes and cups she kept stashed on the shelving there.

But there was no Dianna.

His stomach dropped. She was always here and she never would have left her shop unattended like this. Something was wrong.

Griffin moved to the back of the bakery, reaching the open end of the cases that led to the space she usually occupied. He rounded the divider that always stood between them, ensuring he kept a safe distance from the woman he struggled to resist. "Dianna?"

Something bumped in the back room and a second later there was a loud crash, sending him racing toward the swinging door.

Before he could reach it, Dianna came rushing out, eyes wide, expression full of panic.

"Griffin?" She smoothed down her strangely damp hair. "What are you doing here?"

Griffin swallowed hard, unable to keep his eyes from moving down her waterlogged frame. "You weren't at the counter so I came to make sure you were okay."

She was definitely not okay. Dianna was soaking wet. The fabric of her white logoed T-shirt stuck to her skin, outlining the lush curve of her full tits. Her dark hair was clumped and dripping, clinging to the smooth skin of her face as it bled tiny rivulets of water down her cheeks. "What was that noise?"

"Umm." Her chin barely quivered. "I'm just having an issue with my sink."

"That would explain all the water." Griffin jerked his chin toward the swinging door. "Back there?"

Dianna sniffed and nodded.

He was supposed to be staying away from her, but there was no way he would abandon Dianna at a time like this. She needed help. She needed *him*, and that had always been his weakness. One he obviously still hadn't learned never worked in his favor.

Griffin pushed through the door, holding it open as Dianna followed. His boots were in a puddle almost immediately, making it clear Dianna had more than just a little problem on her hands. The amount of water he was seeing could quickly turn into a catastrophe. One that could shut her business down indefinitely and cost her a ridiculous amount of money to recover from.

Griffin rushed to the large stainless-steel basin that was currently spewing water like a geyser. A quick look underneath revealed the problem to be a busted pipe. He turned to Dianna, who was close behind him. "Where's the water shut off?"

She shook her head, blinking furiously. "I don't know." Her chin quivered and she sucked in a shaky breath. For the first time since he'd known her, Dianna looked something besides sweet and soft.

She looked scared. Upset to the point that if he didn't get this under control soon she was going to cry.

And he couldn't handle tears.

Griffin reached up, sliding one hand across her cheek

in a motion meant to comfort her, but might have also been a little self-serving. "Everything will be okay. I can fix this." He pulled his hand from the warmth of her damp skin and went to the electric panel at the back of the space. Crouching down, he peered behind the line of containers on the wall in search of the main shut off for the water to Dianna's bakery. He followed the path the main pipe took, moving everything in his way before finally finding the valve and shutting it down.

The sound of spewing water switched to a soft trickle before finally stopping.

"One problem down." He straightened and turned to the sink, forcing his eyes not to go near Dianna's shivering body, knowing full well the see-through fabric of her wet shirt would leave nothing to his imagination.

And his imagination had already provided him with plenty of ammunition where Dianna was concerned.

He scanned the room as he went to the sink. Everything was wet from about waist high down. The counters. Everything on the counters. The lower shelves. Everything on the lower shelves. The floors and any items stored there.

All of it was dripping.

He went down on one knee, bracing against the wet floor as he craned his neck to look over the damage. "What happened?"

Dianna sniffed again, the sound burning into his hide, fueling the desire to grab her and pull her close. To comfort her.

To touch her. To make her feel better.

To prove he could do it.

"The pipe has been dripping and at first I just put a bowl under it to catch the water, but it started to leak faster today and I thought maybe I could tighten it up and fix it." She sniffed again. "But it just came undone and started spraying everywhere."

"Why didn't you call your landlord?" Griffin gritted his teeth, bracing himself for the sight about to confront him as he turned to Dianna. "He's the one who should have been fixing this. That's part of what a landlord does."

Dianna had her arms wrapped around her middle, holding herself tight. "I didn't want to bother him for something little like that." Her chin trembled and she pressed her lips together, taking a sharp breath before continuing. "I figured I would just handle it myself."

"I admire your independence and willingness to take care of yourself, but that's what you pay him for." Griffin accidentally inched in a little closer. "A leaky sink is his problem. Not yours."

Dianna's dark eyes left his face to move over the mess around them. "It looks like my problem is bigger than his problem at this point."

"It does look like water and flour might not be a good combination." Griffin reached out to run one finger down the stainless-steel countertop closest to him, lifting it up to reveal the pasty white mixture that seemed to be covering nearly every surface. "You should probably call your employees to come help you."

Dianna ran one hand down her hair, smoothing it away from her face. "I don't have any employees."

"Why not?" He'd been hoping Troy and Amelie were wrong and Dianna did actually have people working for her, but apparently they were sadly well-informed.

She lifted one shoulder and let it drop. "It would take more time to train someone than it does for me to just do it."

He understood her line of thinking. He'd had a similar one before coming to Moss Creek.

"It's definitely not easy to bring someone in, but it's absolutely worth it in the long run." Griffin kept his tone gentle, hoping Dianna didn't think he was criticizing her. That's not what this was. "I hated the thought of not being in complete control of my business, but stepping away from it is the best thing I've ever done."

Not that there was a lot of competition for that spot. He'd fucked up more than he'd gotten right in his life.

But getting away from the day-to-day running of his repair shops gave him the chance to change all that. Now he could be close to his son. Do all the things he never had the chance to do.

Dianna's eyes widened. "I don't want to step away. I like running my business."

Shit. He was already fucking this up. "I didn't mean you should step away." Griffin struggled to find what to say next. "I was just saying that bringing someone in to help can be tough at first but might make your life easier in the end." He clamped his lips together, determined to keep them that way.

He never knew how to say things right. Especially when it came to women.

So he did the smart thing and learned to keep his mouth shut. Stayed quiet even when they screamed in his face and hurled everything he owned out the windows.

Luckily, Dianna didn't seem too bothered by his misspoken words. She gave him a sad smile, wiping at a line of water as it trickled down her neck. "It would definitely make things easier to have a second set of hands right now I guess."

Griffin pressed his lips together, fighting to keep control of the offer trying to spring free.

He couldn't do it.

Shouldn't do it.

He was supposed to be focused on Troy. On building their relationship.

Not on spending time getting close with another woman who would undoubtedly hate his guts one day.

But he'd never been able to resist the opportunity to pretend he could be someone's knight in shining armor.

"I can help."

FIVE

DIANNA

*T*HIS DAY WAS becoming a nightmare.

She thought it couldn't get any worse. Thought her sink exploding spontaneously and soaking down everything in a ten-foot radius was the absolute most terrible thing that could happen.

Then Griffin showed up in all his glory to bear witness to the mess she'd created and prove her wrong.

"You don't have to help." Dianna shook her head, keeping her arms across her chest so she wouldn't start shivering uncontrollably as the chill of the air conditioning sank through her drenched shirt and straight into her skin. "I'm sure I can get this under control."

She'd figure it out somehow. It might take her all night, but this place would be clean and dry when the first customer showed up in the morning.

Griffin seemed unconcerned with her protest as he reached down to lift one of the airtight containers off the floor, holding it up as water dripped from the base. "Man. It looks like everything is soaked." His blue eyes lifted to where she stood before drifting over her goosebump-covered arms. "Are you cold?"

Her teeth tried to chatter in confirmation so she clenched them tightly together. "I'm fine."

Griffin set down the tub before grabbing the hem of his T-shirt and yanking it over his head, baring his entire upper half before she had the chance to blink. He held the shirt between them. "Here. Trade me."

"Um." Dianna swallowed hard. It seemed as if every word of the English language fell out of her brain the second she was faced with Griffin's bared chest.

She knew he was attractive. There was absolutely never a question about that.

But part of her secretly hoped he was soft around the middle. Squishy in a way that would make it a little easier for her to cling to the hope that maybe one day Griffin might look at her as more than just the woman who sold him cinnamon rolls and coffee. It was an unlikely scenario, and one she didn't even really want.

But it was still fun to imagine.

Unfortunately, it didn't appear her cinnamon rolls were having any sort of effect on Griffin's figure. Every inch of him was solid and lean. His shoulders were broad and toned and his flat abs made it clear he didn't spend much time laying around letting calories collect.

Griffin's lips slowly pulled into a wickedly tempting smile. "Take it. You'll feel better. I promise."

Thanks to years of being conditioned not to argue, she automatically reached for the shirt. But then she just stood there. Holding it.

There was no way she was stripping down in front of this man. Not now that she'd seen how fucking perfect he was.

Griffin quickly solved her dilemma. Almost as soon as she took the shirt, he turned, putting his back to her as he continued talking.

"We should probably call your landlord and see how long it's going to take him to get down here to repair this. Then we can figure out the best plan for cleaning up this mess." He tipped his head, barely peeking her way over one shoulder. "Everything okay?"

He was waiting for her to change, and as much as she didn't love the thought of stripping down when he could turn around at any second, the temptation of pulling on a dry, warm shirt was a little too great. "Everything's fine." Dianna glanced around, looking for a spot to set Griffin's shirt while she peeled off her own. "I just need a dry place to set your shirt down while I get situated."

Griffin reached up to tap one shoulder. "Toss it over here."

Dianna pulled in a deep breath and inched a little closer, leaning forward to drape the shirt over the dark depiction of a wolf tattooed across Griffin's left shoulder. Then she turned her back to his, wrestling the sticky, wet cotton T-shirt over her head. She glanced down at the lacy bra clinging to her skin. It was just as wet as the shirt and would be horribly uncomfortable once it started chafing her skin.

Even more uncomfortable than going braless in front of Griffin, and that was saying something considering the size of her chest and the lack of perk it possessed.

She unclasped the garment, peeling it away from her skin before dropping it onto the counter. Then, using one arm to cover as much of her breasts as possible, she snagged Griffin's shirt, trading out hers before wiggling her arms through the gloriously dry cotton. A little of his body heat still lingered, warming her immediately as it settled onto her skin. Her goosebumps relaxed and she sighed in relief as the familiar scent of him surrounded her.

"Done?"

Dianna nodded even though he couldn't see. "Done."

Griffin turned to face her, taking the shirt she'd had on and wringing it out before shaking it loose as his gaze drifted down her front. "That looks better on you than it does on me."

A laugh bubbled out, riding a wave of nervousness and discomfort. "I highly doubt that."

His shirt was a little tight around her middle and didn't cover near enough of her ass, but it was warm and dry so she wasn't going to complain.

Griffin gave her the easy grin that had made her belly flip from the first time he stepped into her shop. "You shouldn't. It's the truth." He tugged the damp shirt over his head, working the fabric down his chest, sucking in a breath as it hit his skin. "Holy shit. This is cold."

She accidentally laughed again, managing her first full breath since that damn pipe split in half. "You want to trade back?"

"No way." He pinched at the fabric, pulling it away from his skin. "I was feeling a little warm anyway. I could probably use to cool off."

Dianna couldn't stop herself from reaching for her hair again. It was her favorite feature, the only one untainted by someone else's hateful words, and right now it looked just as bad as the rest of her, leaving her feeling completely exposed and more than a little self-conscious. "Stand in front of that open pipe for a few minutes. You'll cool right off."

"I would, but we've got a mess to clean up." Griffin braced his hands on his hips as he scanned the space. "Tell me where to start."

"Well..." She wasn't great at telling other people what to do. It was one of the main reasons she never called Janie. "We should probably start on the counters and work our way down."

"Smart thinking." Griffin immediately moved in at her side, his blue eyes sweeping the trays of tomorrow's baked goods lining the counter. "I'm guessing most of this is a lost cause."

Her eyes started to burn as tears of embarrassment threatened to leak free. "I shouldn't have messed with that damn pipe."

"Hey." Griffin's voice was soft as he reached out to

skim his fingers along her jaw. The touch was gentle and warm and something she'd never expected to have. Never expected to want after all she'd been through. "It's okay." Griffin stepped close, pulling her body against his. His arms were strong and solid where they wrapped around her, holding tight as one hand stroked down her wet hair. "We're going to get all this taken care of. I promise."

It was so strange to have someone comforting her after she'd basically fucked everything up. Maybe that was part of the reason she was so tense right now. Situations like this used to always result in hearing she was a failure. Inept. Stupid. Useless.

And even knowing she was none of those things didn't stop the knee-jerk fear built into her body.

"I'm actually really impressed you tried to take on that pipe." Griffin rested his mouth against the top of her head, his lips moving against her damp, frizzy hair. "Most people don't have the balls to attempt to fix a problem like that."

"Is it balls?" She sniffed into his shoulder. "Or is it just stupidity?"

Griffin was quiet, his hold on her tightening the tiniest bit. "You're definitely not stupid, Di." His hand slid up and down her back in slow, steady passes. "You've built one hell of a business in less than a year and you've done it all on your own. There aren't many people who could accomplish that."

Dianna closed her eyes, trying to let his words sink in. Hoping they might replace some of the ones she couldn't seem to rid herself of no matter how hard she tried.

She hated Martin. Knew he was an asshole and a piece of shit. Regretted the day she married him more than anything. But she still struggled to break free of the grip his abuse had on her, and that almost pissed her off more than anything else. That he continued to control her. Even now.

Especially now.

She tipped her head back, planning to thank Griffin and hoping to pull her focus from places she refused to let it linger.

It worked. The second her eyes met his it was impossible to think of anything else.

He was so close.

So warm.

So freaking handsome.

He smelled so good that her lungs sucked in a breath all on their own. She didn't even care that the dampness of the shirt he was wearing was starting to sink into the dry fabric of the one she wore.

"Thank you." Somehow she found the ability to speak, which was particularly impressive given the circumstances. "For helping me."

Griffin brought one of his hands to her face, the tips of his fingers dragging over her skin in a touch that was both rough and careful. "You don't have to thank me, Di." His calloused touch slid along her jaw before brushing over her lower lip. "I will help you whenever you need me."

It was the first time in longer than she could remember that an offer of assistance didn't make it hard to breathe. In her experience 'help' ended up being less about aid and more about a takeover.

Not just of her business, but of her life.

But Griffin's offer seemed different, which was confusing since there was actually nothing different about it. Nothing except the fact that it came from him.

Dianna swallowed hard, fighting through the yearning she'd been struggling to contain for nearly a year. "I'm okay. I've got it under control."

It was a lie. One Griffin could clearly see through since he was standing in the center of the waterlogged proof.

"I know you do." His thumb slid back across her lip in a slow drag. "And I know you could figure this out on your own." Another tortuously slow pass of his thumb. "I just don't want you to have to."

As much as she hated to admit it, neither did she. She'd been so very alone for so long. Even when she was legally bound to another individual she'd been by herself. No one else she could rely on. No one else she could trust.

That was the most exhausting part about all of this. Knowing the only time she was truly safe was when she was alone. It left her isolated and lonely. No one but the birds and the squirrels to keep her company.

Griffin's thumb made another glide over her lip and for some reason, one she didn't want to dwell on, her tongue flicked against it, teasing his work roughened skin.

Griffin's nostrils flared as his gaze locked on hers,

intense and utterly focused as he slid his thumb back against her mouth. Almost as if he was daring her to do it again.

What would happen if she did? Would it break the tension hanging in the air? Would it lead down a path she hadn't been on in forever and swore never to follow again?

Or would he laugh at her? Shake his head over how silly Dianna could've ever thought for a second he would be interested in a woman like her.

A woman with thighs that were too thick. A belly that was too soft. Goals that were too high and dreams that were too big. There was too much of her. Physically. Mentally. Emotionally. It'd been thrown in her face a thousand times, and no matter how much you don't believe what you're hearing, at some point it still sinks in.

Even if you know your thick thighs are beautiful and your soft belly is perfectly normal. Even when you love your dreams and are willing to work for your goals.

"I wasn't supposed to come here today." Griffin's voice was so soft she could barely hear it. Almost like he was talking to himself and not to her. "I was supposed to stay away from you." He traced her lip again, eyes locked on that slow pass of his thumb. "But I can't."

She should be upset that he wanted to stay away from her. Offended that Griffin was trying to keep his distance.

But instead she was relieved.

Because she felt the exact same way.

The last thing she needed in her life right now was

Griffin Fraley. She was supposed to be straightening herself out. Fixing all the parts of her that Martin messed up. Focusing on her business and herself.

But this man wasn't easy to ignore. Especially when his solid body was pressed tight to hers.

"Tell me to leave you alone." Griffin dropped his forehead to hers, eyes closing even as his thumb continued that same slow path. "Tell me to go."

It would be the right thing to do. For both of them. She had plans and Griffin was clearly struggling. But after months of telling herself she wasn't good enough for him, knowing Griffin wanted her soothed a part of her that had been raw and painful for too damn long.

Maybe that's why she was struggling to move forward. Maybe deep down she believed Martin was right when he said no one else would want her.

But Martin was wrong. The proof was standing right in front of her, looking at her like he was two seconds away from devouring her whole.

And the realization fed her battered and bruised soul.

A good woman would take that realization and hold it close while she sent Griffin on his way.

But maybe Martin was right about one thing.

Maybe she wasn't a good woman.

Dianna flattened her palms against the damp T-shirt stretched tight across Griffin's chest, sliding them up and over the swell of his pecs as she fell into a moment she wasn't strong enough to walk away from.

"I don't want you to go."

SIX

GRIFFIN

THEY WERE THE words he desperately wanted to hear, even though staying here with Dianna was the last thing he should do.

He'd done everything he could to stay away from her. Did his best to be the kind of man his son deserved as a father. But Dianna pulled him in. Her sweetness. Her smile. The sound of her voice. He couldn't get enough of it. Of her.

And that was before he knew how soft her skin was. How right her body felt pressed against his.

Unable to hold back, he laced his fingers into her wet hair. She sucked in a sharp breath as his mouth covered hers, whimpering against his lips as her fingers fisted in the fabric of his shirt.

Her shirt.

Offering her his shirt had been one of the many mistakes he'd made since walking into The Baking Rack. Seeing her lush curves draped in the worn fabric of his T-shirt was a little too close to one of the many fantasies he'd been holding about the small-town Baker. He'd imagined Dianna a thousand ways. Under him. Over him. Against him. On his bed. In his truck.

And right here in this fucking bakery.

But not a single one of those fantasies even came close to the reality of having Dianna in his arms. The feel of her skin was softer, smooth and silky under his hands. The taste of her mouth was sweeter, hinting at the sugared frostings she likely sampled and the creamy coffee she sipped all afternoon. She was too perfect to resist. Everything he'd imagined and more.

Too much more.

Her kiss was hungry and demanding and laced with a hint of the same desperation he felt, making him hope he wasn't the only one who'd been imagining this moment for months.

Suddenly she pushed against him, shoving him back a step and separating their bodies.

They stood in silence, both breathing heavy, eyes locked.

He should walk away now. Hire someone else to come in and help her clean up.

But the second Dianna came toward him he was right back in it, lifting his arms as she yanked the damp shirt up his chest and over his head, letting it fall to the puddles of water still covering the floor as her body hit his. Her hands were everywhere, sliding against his skin, warm and wandering as he claimed her mouth once again.

The levee had failed and there was no fighting the current dragging him under. Nothing to do but try to keep from drowning.

Griffin wrapped both arms around her, holding Dianna tight as he lifted her up and slid her ass onto one of the flour-covered counters. Dianna gasped, both arms tightening at his neck, eyes wide as she clung to him.

"I won't let you fall." He leaned into her, brushing his lips up the side of her neck. "I promise."

"You better not." Her hands came to his face, sliding over the rough stubble already making the skin around her mouth pink as her legs locked at his waist. "Because if I fall, you're going down with me."

He smiled, nipping at the fullness of her lower lip as he teased up the side of her ribs with the tips of his fingers. "Don't threaten me with a good time." He'd been way worse places than tangled with a beautiful woman on the floor of a bakery.

Griffin buried his face against her neck, breathing in. "God you smell good."

He was playing a dangerous game. One he had no business dragging Dianna into. But damned if he could stop himself. She was everything he'd never had, and no matter how hard he tried to stay away from her, he failed. She was like a drug he was sure he could quit after one last hit, but the addiction was too strong.

And he was definitely addicted to Dianna. To what she represented.

Now more so than ever.

She gasped as he raked his teeth over the lobe of her ear. "I run a bakery. I probably smell like cinnamon."

"Definitely cinnamon." He took another breath, finally getting his fill of the light scent that had been teasing him across the counter for months. "But something else too." There was the tiniest hint of something that wasn't a lingering byproduct of the pastries and cakes. He'd struggled to identify it, but now that he was close it was surprisingly simple to make out. "Do you wear men's cologne, Dianna?"

The scent smelled slightly different on her but was still clearly recognizable since it was the same one he'd put on every single morning for the past twenty years.

Dianna leaned back, just enough to look him in the eye. "Maybe. Is that weird?"

"Weird, no." He closed the tiny bit of distance she'd put between them, running the tip of his nose up the side of hers. "Intriguing, yes."

He thought he had her all figured out. Assumed the woman he'd been lusting after for months was just as sweet and kind and smart as she seemed. And she was.

But the woman in his mind would have worn some expensive perfume. Something light and floral. Not the same Cool Water he'd been buying off the shelf at the drugstore since he turned twenty.

Dianna's lips lifted into a hint of a smile. "No one's ever called me intriguing before."

"That's a shame." Griffin gripped the fullness of her ass, pulling her closer. "I would have thought the male population was a little smarter than that."

Dianna snorted, the grip of her legs tightening around his waist as her ass hit the edge of the counter. "You would have thought way wrong."

Griffin pressed closer to her. "Their loss."

Her laugh was throaty and a little husky, making him groan into her hair.

"I love your fucking voice." He ground the length of his cock up the seam of her pussy, looking for some relief to the ache building in his balls. "I remember the first time I heard it." Dianna whimpered a little as he thrust against the thin fabric of the leggings separating them. "You were back here and I was waiting at the counter."

It was probably what started all this off. What narrowed his focus where Dianna was concerned.

Griffin thrust against her again, groaning a little as she let out a soft moan. The sound made him bolder. Made him more forward than he should be with a woman like her. "Do you remember what you said to me, Di?"

She rested her forehead against his, breath choppy as he continued dry fucking her. "Yes."

"Tell me." He wanted to hear her say it again. Here. Now.

Dianna's lower lip pinched between her teeth as he dragged the line of his dick over her again, teasing them both with an eventuality that was too close to consider. "I can't."

"You can." He followed the line of the T-shirt she wore, tracing the edge of the hem before skimming under it. "Tell me." He smoothed over the soft skin of her belly, making his intended path obvious in case she was smarter than him and wanted to pump the brakes on all this.

But Dianna made no move to stop him. Instead she opened those gorgeous dark eyes and locked them on his. "I said I was coming."

He groaned again. "Fuck. It sounds just as good as it did last time. Maybe better." He curved his palm around the heavy fullness of her breast, dragging a thumb across one pinched tip. "Because this time I can make sure it's true."

Dianna was pure sex. From the fullness of her mouth to the slight huskiness of her voice, every bit of her was fucking irresistible. Which was why he was here now, unable to pull his hands away from her body.

Not that Dianna seemed to mind. She leaned into his touch, hips working her body against his as he rolled and pinched her nipple. "That feels so good."

"I can make it feel better." He sucked at the skin just below her ear. "Do you want me to make you feel better, Dianna?"

"Yes." The word rushed out on a breath. "Please."

"So fucking sweet." Griffin eased his hand into the waistband of her black leggings, working the tips of his fingers under the elastic of her panties. "Do you taste sweet too?" He dragged one finger along the line of her cunt, through the wet heat there, before pulling his hand free and bringing it to his lips. Dianna watched with wide eyes as he sucked the slickness of her body from his skin.

He knew she wasn't like the women he normally spent time with. That was part of the appeal. But it hadn't occurred to him that she might be a little sweeter than he expected. That she might find him too forward. Too crude.

Too vulgar.

"Oh." Dianna's chest lifted and fell with each sharp breath she took, eyes still locked on his mouth. "Wow. That was..." Her lower lip pinched between her teeth. "That was..."

He watched her expression for any sign she was bothered by what he'd just done. "That was, what?"

Dianna licked her lips before rubbing them together, hesitating just a second before answering. "Dirty."

That single word shot straight to his aching cock, making it strain even harder against the front of his jeans. "Does dirty bother you?"

Based on the way she was still wrapped around him, it didn't seem like it did, but he wanted to hear it from her lips.

It was one of many things he wanted to hear from her lips.

But if dirty bothered Dianna then he definitely wasn't the man for her. And maybe that would be for the best. They could part ways now and move on with the knowledge the attraction they clearly shared was only that and nothing more.

But Dianna barely shook her head, gaze steady on his. "No."

That single word was like waving red in front of a bull, daring him to charge after teasing and taunting him to insanity.

And that's what this probably was. Absolute fucking insanity.

"Good." Griffin slid his finger across her lips, pressing between them. "Then you can taste how fucking sweet you are."

The flash of surprise on her face barely lasted a second, moving across Dianna's striking features in the blink of an eye.

And then she was sucking on his finger. Stroking against it with her tongue as she pulled it deeper into the wet heat of her mouth.

"Fuck." Griffin pulled his other hand from her breast and laced it into her hair, gripping tight as he slid the finger free and pressed it back in, fucking her mouth, unable to look away from the sight. "You want to suck my cock like this, don't you, Dianna?"

She let out a little moan around his finger that made it damn near impossible not to consider the possibility.

But the floor was wet. No way would Dianna be getting on her knees. Not here.

Not now.

Griffin slid his finger free, dragging it down her neck and over the plushness of her body. "I bet you would do such a good job sucking my cock, wouldn't you?" He gripped the waistband of her pants, gathering legging and panties all at once and dragging them down, under where her ass pressed into the stainless steel before stopping at her knees. He gripped the collected mass and lifted, using it like a lever to tip Dianna back until her upper body was flat against the width of the counter and her bared pussy was positioned perfectly.

Then he gripped the backs of her knees, pressing her thighs toward the curve of her belly, pinning them in place as he leaned down to lick up her center, gliding his tongue along her slick slit until he found the hardened nub of her clit.

Dianna sucked in a breath as one hand went to the edge of the table and the other grabbed the back of his head, fingers lacing into his hair before twisting tight.

It was the kind of moment he loved. Proving all he was capable of. Gaining the validation he shouldn't still need, but continued to crave.

Dianna's body trembled under his tongue as he lapped against her clit, offering focused, consistent passes while she started to rock under him, chasing every touch like she never wanted it to end, feeding that part of him he tried to suppress.

She wanted him. Desperately. Completely.

And soon she would know he could give her all she needed. Anything she craved.

Almost.

He slid one hand between her thighs, dragging it along her core before splitting his fingers, letting them press along each side of her clit, the pressure pushing it higher. Exposing more of it to the stroke of his tongue.

Dianna's back arched off the table with his next lick, a string of unidentifiable words rushing from her mouth along with a ragged groan. Two more passes and she was coming, legs shaking, body quaking, that husky voice he loved so much calling his name as her wetness soaked his face.

He dragged his mouth away, running his lips along the satiny skin of her inner thigh as her hand slid from his hair, falling into the pasty layer of wet flour on the counter beside her.

Fuck. He'd shoved her right back into that. Laid her across the mess he was supposed to be helping her clean.

Instead, he was making a mess of his own.

One he'd swore wouldn't happen again.

But Dianna was different from the women who usually found their way into his bed. Those differences stacked up more every time he saw her, each one making him want her even more. Almost more than anything. Enough that he easily slipped right back into his old self-serving ways.

The realization was like a kick to the chest.

Griffin took a step back, carefully letting Dianna's feet fall to the floor as regret and guilt swept over him like smoke, heavy and smothering. "That was—"

Dianna straightened, her eyes going everywhere but him as she yanked up her leggings and panties. "A mistake."

His head tipped back a little in surprise. That was not what he was expecting to hear.

Dianna's hands went to her hair, smoothing it down

in jerky, aggressive strokes as she turned to face the mess of her kitchen. "I need to start cleaning."

Was she dismissing him? It sure as hell seemed like it.

It was a blow. One that shouldn't hit as hard as it did considering she was right.

This was a mistake.

One he'd been determined not to make.

But the fact she agreed cut into that insecure little part of him that refused to be eradicated. Not by money. Not by success. Not by power or connections.

And unfortunately, Dianna's rejection seemed to feed it, making it grow and press against his chest. "I should—"

"You should go." Dianna shot him a tight smile that didn't reach her eyes. "Thank you for showing me where to shut the water off." Her words were curt and polite, not a hint of the fact they now knew each other intimately showing in her voice.

Griffin raked one hand through his hair, the hair she just held in her hand while his mouth was between her thighs, unsure what to do next.

This wasn't how things normally went for him. Normally by now the woman would have her bags halfway packed with plans to move in. And deep down he loved it. Loved being wanted so much someone would turn their life upside down to be with him.

But clearly that wasn't the kind of woman Dianna was, proving yet again she wasn't like the ones in his past.

Unfortunately, he was still clearly exactly who he thought he was.

SEVEN

DIANNA

SNICKERDOODLE SAT BESIDE her, nose twitching as he chewed through the fifth peanut in a row. She'd worked so hard to make friends with the chubby squirrel and expected this moment to carry a little more impact than it did. It was one more thing to add to the list of disappointments stacking up around her.

Dianna closed her eyes, sucking in a deep breath of the warm midday air, hoping to force herself to enjoy her only day off. She used to look forward to Sundays. They were the single day each week she could spend a little time relaxing, even if it had to happen while she caught up on laundry and housekeeping.

But over the past few months, Sundays stopped feeling like a day of solace and rejuvenation and started feeling a little more... lonely. They showcased the fact she didn't even have enough of a social life to fill up one freaking day.

Sure, there were plenty of people around Moss Creek who came to see her at the bakery nearly every day. She even went to lunch with Mae and her sisters-in-law on occasion. But all that felt more like politeness. It just seemed to be the way things were done in a small town.

She opened her eyes to peek down at Snickerdoodle, who was finishing up the nut she'd just passed over. "You want another one?" Dianna held out another peanut, pinching one end of the shell to provide as much distance between her and the squirrel as possible. Instead of immediately grabbing it the way he had the ones before, Snickerdoodle shuffled backward before darting off, racing over the freshly cut grass of her backyard before scaling the large oak tree in the corner to perch on one thick branch.

Dianna sighed. "And I bet I never see him again either." She tossed the nut into the yard for one of the birds or other squirrels to claim and stood up, dusting off the butt of her shorts before turning to go in the back door.

She'd spent the morning scrubbing the tiny kitchen at the back of her cottage within an inch of its life, taking out all her pent-up frustration on the nineteen-sixties linoleum and metal edged countertops. They were the only reason she'd managed to snag this particular house out from under Nora and Brooks Pace, house flippers extraordinaire. While the finishings of her two-bedroom home were more than old, they were still in pristine condition thanks to the loving care of the ninety-five-year-old woman who sold it to her, and Brooks and Nora simply didn't have the heart to take it on as a flip.

That meant Dianna was able to claim it as her own and carry on the loving care it had been shown over the years.

Very little of the house had been modernized. The full bathroom down the hall was still done in seafoam green tile, and cedar lined all the closets. The only real upgrade was to the electric, and that was so a central air system could be installed—which she was ridiculously grateful for. Especially on days like this when it would be scorching before noon.

Dianna cracked open the fridge, bending at the waist to peer through the lackluster contents. For someone who made their living feeding other people, she sure had a hell of a time feeding herself. Probably because by the time she got home every night she was exhausted enough that a bowl of cereal and extra sleep was more appealing than spending time making something more involved.

But she had the time today, so maybe she should consider pre-preparing some items for the week. Not only would it give her more nourishing options in the evenings, but the activity would keep her mind off bothersome topics.

Topics like Griffin Fraley.

She slammed the refrigerator closed and stood straight, clenching her teeth as she willed his face out of her brain. His face and other parts of his body. Parts that she was too familiar with for her own good.

Or her own sanity.

Dianna grabbed her purse and keys and headed for the door to the garage, keeping her focus on the task at hand. She snagged her reusable shopping bags from their hook and went out into the tiny, attached garage, shimmying her way to the driver's door before squeezing in. Tossing all the bags into the seat beside her, she punched the opener, letting the morning sun bleed into the dark, windowless space.

It was one of the few things she didn't love about her little house. Sure, windows leading into the garage were probably a liability, but it would be so nice to have just a little sunlight coming in. Maybe she could hire someone to replace the entry door leading out into the backyard. Put one in with one of those small windows at the very top. Something so it didn't feel so closed in and claustrophobic.

Dianna was so distracted by the thought of the tiny upgrade, she almost didn't notice her neighbor's grandson standing at the end of her driveway. He was a little too close for comfort when she glimpsed him in the rearview mirror. Panic slammed her foot onto the brake, jerking her body forward and tipping her purse to the floorboard.

Cooper grinned at her in the mirror, waving as he moved from behind her car and jogged up the side. She rolled down the window as he leaned in, the smile still on his face revealing the hint of a dimple in one cheek. "Just the woman I've been looking for." He leaned one arm against the roof above her head, relaxing like he intended to have a lengthy conversation. "I didn't mean to scare you."

"I just wasn't expecting to see a police officer standing in my driveway so early in the morning." Dianna glanced at Cooper's uniform, taking in all the gear strapped to his shoulders and chest. "I thought you worked the night shift?"

"I do." Cooper reached one hand back to scrub along his neck. "I got off work and went to go see my grandma at the nursing home." His focus lingered on her face. "Then I came straight here hoping I might catch you before you got busy on your day off."

Dianna lifted her brows, surprised and a little concerned that Cooper sought her out. "Oh? Is everything okay?"

He shook his head, expression somber. "Not really. We were really hoping my grandma might be able to come back home, but it's not looking like that's going to happen."

Dianna's heart sank. Vera was feisty and opinionated and, even though she hadn't lived next door to her long, she'd grown pretty attached to her wild-haired neighbor. "I'm so sorry to hear that. I was really hoping we would be neighbors again soon."

Cooper nodded, his eyes dropping. "Me too, but it's just not in the cards." His focus returned to Dianna's face. "That's why I wanted to come see you. I wanted you to be the first to know we're going to be selling her house."

It was an unfortunate situation, but she understood completely. The house was in disrepair, beyond the point of being able to be maintained. The place needed a full overhaul, and letting it sit would only make that worse. "I'm sure she'll be sad to see it go."

Vera was fiercely protective of her house. To the point she wouldn't allow anyone inside, which was why it was in the sad state it was in.

"I'm not sure she even realizes what's happening." Cooper's lips pressed into a frown. "Her mind's most of the way gone at this point. That's probably why she's been so combative these past couple of years."

It was something Cooper and his mother had both mentioned to Dianna in passing but was never a characteristic she saw in Vera herself. Thankfully.

The only memories she had were sweet moments talking over the fence in the backyard while they fed the birds. Or when she was testing out new recipes and delivered the overflow next door. "I hate to hear that." Dianna glanced at the dilapidated house towering over her small cottage. "Hopefully it will go to someone who loves it just as much as she did."

"Unfortunately, it will have to go to someone with deep pockets and the willingness to deal with a complete renovation." Cooper shook his head. "That place is a wreck."

Dianna sat up a little taller as a thought occurred to

her. This was an opportunity to do for someone else what so many had done for her. "You should call Brooks Pace." Dianna smiled, feeling a little better for the first time in almost a week. "He and Nora take houses just like your grandma's and make them absolutely beautiful." She leaned closer to the open window and to Cooper, perking up at the possibility that maybe she was finally starting to feel like she belonged. Like she was one of them. "I bet they would absolutely jump at the opportunity."

Vera's house was gigantic, with two main floors, plus a walk-up attic and an unfinished basement. It had been built by one of the original arrivals to Moss Creek, so it was one of the oldest houses around, and the architecture reflected that. It was the kind of house she could only dream of owning, partly because she didn't have the skill set to fix something like that up, and partly because there was no sense in buying a house so huge for just one person.

But if Nora and Brooks bought it, she would get to witness its rebirth and also reap the rewards of an increase in her own property value.

Cooper clicked his tongue. "I'll pass your suggestion on to my cousin. He's a broker at a big real estate company in Billings and he's the one who will be handling the sale."

The word sale sounded so final and she couldn't help but feel a little disappointed that Vera was losing the home she was so attached to. "Hopefully she gets a decent amount for it." It wouldn't get Vera back in her old home, but at least it would help keep her comfortable in her new one.

Cooper straightened away from the door. "It doesn't really matter what it sells for. The government will get pretty much all of it."

Dianna frowned. "That's unfortunate."

Cooper shrugged. "It is what it is." He hooked his thumbs into the bulletproof vest wrapped across his chest. "And we all knew there wouldn't be much to be had, so it's not like anybody expected anything." He smiled softly. "We just wanted her to live her life and enjoy every bit of what she had."

Dianna returned his smile. "It sounds like she did that."

"I'd like to think so." Cooper was quiet for a minute, rocking back on his heels. "You have any exciting plans for the day?"

Dianna sighed, the weight of her to-do list quickly swooping in. "I've always got too much to do and not enough time to accomplish it."

It seemed to be the story of her life since moving to Moss Creek, but for the first time it was really working out in her favor. Being busy meant she didn't have time to sit and dwell on how easy it obviously was for Griffin to walk away from something and never look back.

It was technically what she'd claimed to want. She'd been the one to call what happened between them a mistake. The one to tell him to go.

But what she *should* want and what she *actually* wanted were turning out to be two very different things.

She expected to be farther along in her recovery from an emotionally and occasionally physically abusive relationship, but putting all that behind her was turning out to be more difficult than she anticipated. It was why she had to tell Griffin to go. It wouldn't be fair to shove all her issues to one side and bring another person into her mess. Not to the other person, and certainly not to her.

But it still stung a little bit that Griffin hadn't at least come in to buy a cup of coffee. Maybe a scone. Hell, even just a walk past the window and a wave would be better than his complete disappearance.

"It's a shame you're so busy. Doesn't give you much time for socializing." There was something different in Cooper's tone. Something she almost wanted to identify as interest.

But Cooper was at least five years younger than she was and exceedingly good looking. Certainly he wouldn't be interested in her. She was creeping close to forty and was what her mother considered pleasantly plump.

A sudden realization made her stop. Made her think.

Maybe she'd missed something. Maybe she'd been putting blame in one place when it really belonged in two. Maybe it wasn't just Martin's words that tried to control her sense of self. Maybe this went back farther than she realized.

Maybe the reason she was struggling to overcome the negative words dominating her brain was because they'd always been there. First fed to her by the person who was supposed to love her more than all others.

But that didn't make them less wrong.

One person's pleasantly plump might be another's curvaceous goddess. It was all about perspective, and her perspective clearly needed to change. Yet another reason she should be thrilled Griffin walked away from her.

But she didn't always want to be single, and today's light bulb moment made her feel one step closer to being whole again. One step closer to finally being able to move forward.

Dianna sucked in a breath, giving the handsome police officer her best smile. "Maybe someday soon I'll have a little more spare time for socializing."

She held her breath, waiting to see what Cooper would say next. Hoping she wasn't reading this completely wrong because it might give a little more weight, no pun intended, to the words and opinions she'd allowed to lead her life for so long.

Cooper reached into the front pocket of his vest, pulling a business card free and holding it out. "Give me a call when that happens. I'd love to have the opportunity to occupy some of that spare time."

Dianna took the card, a giddiness that was difficult to contain bubbling up. "Okay." It wasn't the most eloquent or flirtatious of responses, but she wasn't the most eloquent or flirtatious of women.

Maybe that could change too.

Cooper reached out to tap the roof of her car, his smile wider than she'd ever seen it. "You take care, Miss Dianna." He stepped back, giving her room. "Hopefully I hear from you soon."

Dianna held up the card, making it clear she had the

ability to contact him as she rolled up her window and then backed the rest of the way down her short drive. Cooper watched her go, giving her a single wave as she pulled away, excitement still fluttering in her belly.

Not necessarily because Cooper wanted to take her out, although hearing he was interested did give her cracked and fragile ego a little boost. What had her feeling hopeful had more to do with the revelation Cooper's subtle invitation spurred.

She'd kicked Martin out of her life. Legally, physically, financially.

But part of him still lingered, tainting this new start she was trying to forge. And that was because it wasn't just Martin who led to her floundering self-confidence. It was someone who'd influenced her since the first breath she took.

Her mother.

And while the intentions were completely different, the words were strikingly similar, always cloaked and twisted in a way that made them more palatable.

But still just as damaging.

And it was time for them to stop.

Dianna sucked in a breath, gripping the wheel as she drove, feeding herself a new set of words. Ones she chose.

Ones she might believe if she said them enough.

She wasn't chubby. She was gloriously curvy.

She wasn't fat. She was lush.

She wasn't big. She was fucking perfect.

A goddamned goddess.

EIGHT

GRIFFIN

*H*E MIGHT HAVE made a mistake.

Griffin stood in the foyer of his new home, hands on his hips as he stared at the space around him. It looked a hell of a lot different in the full sunlight than it had that night two weeks ago, when Nate called him with news they were selling his grandmother's house in Moss Creek.

It seemed like fate. That the stars had finally aligned and everything was falling into place.

But everything also seemed like it might be falling apart. Literally.

The house was a wreck. The roof had been leaking for God knows how long, leading to damaged ceilings and walls. The constant penetration of moisture meant floors were soft and spongy and peeling paint was everywhere. These were all things he knew and expected to see. They just looked a hell of a lot more overwhelming in the light than they had in the dark.

Griffin picked his way around the items left in the large front hall, rolling his suitcase past the curved stairway and toward the back corner of the large house that held the only room currently safe for habitation.

The large office looked the same way it probably did when Everett, the former owner's husband, died twenty years earlier. The walls were covered in real wood paneling, and built-in shelves stretched from the floor to the ceiling on two walls. The giant desk that was in there when he looked at the house was now gone, along with the stacks of papers and books that had filled the shelves and covered most of the floor. With all that cleared away, it was easier to see how large the room actually was.

It was flooded with light thanks to the large windows that took up most of the back wall, looking out over a backyard that was probably once manicured within an inch of its life, but now stood overgrown and littered with weeds. Someday it would make a great office of his own, but right now it was just a relief to see it would easily hold the king-sized bed being delivered after lunch.

Which left him six hours to clean out all the cobwebs and clear a path for the movers.

He wanted a project and it looked like he found one.

Griffin tilted his suitcase onto its base, leaving it in the room before going to the front of the house to start sifting through the items he'd told Nate his family was welcome to leave behind. The best plan of attack was probably to organize everything into two piles. One that would find its way into the dumpster arriving tomorrow and one of the items he would keep in the house as a reminder of the family who lived here before.

It was clear Nate and his cousins felt sentimental about the place, but none of them could afford to take it on. It made him even more determined to do right by the house. To make it the kind of home it deserved to be.

Even if it was just him that would enjoy it.

Griffin propped open the front door so he could easily carry in the tools stacked in the back of his truck. The neighborhood was nearly silent as he skipped down the steps, the only sounds coming from the birds in the trees. It was too early on a Sunday morning for anyone to be finding their way to church just yet, so he was the only one moving around outside as he went to work hauling everything in.

He was halfway through emptying the bed when a sharp sound made him pause, going still as he tried to identify what it was and where it came from. It didn't sound like an animal. It was too high-pitched and too shrill.

It almost sounded like—

A second scream pierced the silent air, sending a chill down his spine and his feet across the overgrown grass.

He'd heard plenty of screams in his life. Screams of excitement. Screams of happiness. Screams of pleasure.

This was none of those.

This scream was one of terror, and it was coming from the tiny house tucked next door to his.

The scream came again as he raced toward the little porch, taking the steps two at a time as he rushed to help the woman inside. He was surprised to find the main door open, the front screen providing the only barrier to his entry.

"Get out, get out, get out!" The pitch of the rushed words made them difficult to decipher.

Difficult, but not impossible.

Someone had come into this house. Someone who was trying to hurt the woman inside.

Griffin yanked open the screen door and stormed into the feminine looking living room on the other side of it, pausing just a second to glance down at his dirty boots before rushing across the pale carpet. "Hello? Where are you?"

Something crashed to the floor, the sound of the toppling item followed immediately by a strange scratching.

It was fast and sharp, but not loud. What in the hell would make that kind of—

He had his answer a second later when a fat, fluffy squirrel launched itself through the doorway in front of him, flying full tilt in his direction.

"What the fuck—" Griffin jerked to one side, barely managing to miss the rodent's grabby little paws as they scrambled for purchase. Instead of hitting him, it landed on the back of a comfortable-looking chair, barely pausing before jumping to the couch and scrambling up the curtains.

"*Snickerdoodle*. I swear to God, I never would've

been your friend if I'd known you were going to act like this." The woman of the house rushed into the living room, a spatula in one hand and a cutting board in the other. "Get out of my house you little asshole."

"Dianna?" Griffin stared, unable to look away.

It had been so long since he'd seen her. Three weeks of avoiding The Baking Rack and the woman who owned it had felt like fucking forever. But now that he was face-to-face with her, he knew it was absolutely the right thing to do. Because even after only two seconds with her, all he wanted was to figure out how to get his hands on her again. How to convince her to let him bury his head between those soft, creamy thighs a second time.

Dianna straightened, eyes wide. "Griffin?" She pressed the cutting board to her chest before crossing both arms over it, obscuring his view of her perfect tits through the thin fabric of her nightgown. "What are you doing here?"

That's when it hit him.

"You live here." He glanced around the space, taking in the full effect of his surroundings.

If he'd had to pick out what he thought Dianna's home would look like, this would be it. Everything looked comfortable and welcoming, from the overstuffed furniture to the plush blanket draped over a ladder style rack propped against one wall. The paint on the walls was the same pale, robin's egg blue of the paint at The Baking Rack, and the floral print of the curtains hinted at the design on Dianna's business cards. "This is your house."

"I know it's my house. I just don't understand why you're in it." She hugged the cutting board a little tighter, almost as if she was trying to hide behind it.

Hide from him.

"I heard screaming." It reminded him why he was there. He took a step to the left, blocking the path the squirrel would have to take if it tried to jump at Dianna. "I came over to see what was wrong."

Dianna's skin paled. "Came over from where?"

There was dread in her voice. Like maybe she knew the answer to the question before she asked it.

He'd spent the last three weeks trying to convince himself Dianna's reasons for pushing him away had nothing to do with him. That even if they did, it was for the best. He was in Moss Creek to focus on his son. That was why he restructured his business and sold his house. So he could be the dad he never had the chance to be. Not so he could fuck up another woman's life and ruin his best shot at finally having a family.

But the fear on Dianna's face still cut into his hide.

The only thing he could do was rip the band-aid off and hope the sting didn't last. "I bought the house next door."

"No." She stared at him, unblinking. "You're kidding."

Griffin shook his head. "We closed on it yesterday."

He'd been able to put in an offer and sign the papers in under two weeks thanks to his willingness to skip inspections and his ability to pay cash. The only reason it took as long as it did was because the family he bought it from had to move out everything they wanted to keep.

"I thought you were staying with Troy and Amelie." Dianna pressed one hand to her head. "Out at Cross Creek."

"I was, but I can't live with them forever. They have their own life to live and with the baby—"

Dianna's eyes widened. "The baby?"

Shit. "I shouldn't have said that. They haven't told anyone yet." This was why he was supposed to be focusing only on Troy.

He had a lifelong habit of royally fucking up every relationship he got into. It would take everything he had to make sure he didn't ruin the one with his son. He couldn't afford to divide his attention. He couldn't afford to risk it.

Dianna's expression softened, hinting at a smile. "I won't say anything." One side of her mouth lifted. "Grandpa."

And just like that the tension in the air snapped, breaking apart. "Now that was just mean."

Dianna laughed, looking a little more relaxed. But her laughter was short-lived. She sobered almost immediately, posture going stiff, expression tight. Like she remembered what had happened between them.

The *mistake* as she called it.

"Griffin." She whispered his voice before pressing her lips together.

She was going to send him away again. Kick him out of her life yet again.

At least one of them was smart enough to follow through.

But instead of kicking him out, she slowly lifted one finger, pointing it at a spot just behind his head.

He didn't have the chance to turn around to see what she was motioning toward. A second later something smacked into the back of his skull. Tiny claws grabbed at his hair as the squirrel he'd forgotten about fought for balance.

His natural inclination was to grab the thing and launch it across the room. But, as much as Dianna seemed irate at the small animal, she'd given it a name.

One it shared with one of his favorite cookies.

So instead of chucking the invasive rodent, Griffin stood still, wincing as it yanked on his hair and ears.

Dianna's eyes focused on where the squirrel was perched on his head. "Do you want me to grab him?"

"No." Griffin slowly backed toward the door. "I'm going to go outside. No matter what happens, don't try to grab the squirrel." Taking Dianna to the hospital to start a round of rabies shots was not how he wanted to spend this day.

"You've got about three more steps." Dianna watched as he moved through her house, guiding him with her soft, slightly husky voice. "A little to the left."

He angled himself to the side, following her directions.

"Not your left. My left." Her shoulders slumped a little. "Sorry."

"Don't be sorry." She didn't have anything to apologize to him for. "I'm guessing this is your first squirrel removal scenario."

Her mouth hinted at a smile. "Hopefully it will be my last too." She chewed her lower lip, stepping forward to follow him. "You're almost there."

The squirrel suddenly shifted around on his head and Griffin rushed the last bit, managing to get his upper half out the door just as the animal leapt, landing all the way on the other side of the porch. The second Snickerdoodle hit the grass he was off and running, scrambling up a tree before settling onto a branch to hurl what were likely squirrel insults his way.

"I don't think he's happy I kicked him out." Griffin pulled the screen door closed, making sure it was completely latched before turning to face Dianna. "How did the squirrel get in here?"

She sighed. "It's a long story." She pinched her lower lip between her teeth again, worrying it a second before meeting his gaze. "Did you really buy the house next door?"

He nodded, hating how disappointed he was at her dismay. "I did."

"So I guess we're neighbors then." Dianna glanced down the hall before adjusting the cutting board covering her front. "We should probably have a conversation." She took a step, keeping her front his direction as she backed away. "I'm going to go put a robe on. I'll be right back."

He wanted to tell her not to put a robe on for his

benefit, but he already guessed it wasn't for his benefit in the first place.

Or maybe it was since his cock was already a little too interested in the sight of Dianna's bare legs and the fullness of her ample tits. It was fucking ridiculous at this point how quickly he reacted to her. Ridiculous and frustrating.

Dianna was back less than a minute later, a flower printed, satiny robe wrapped around her tempting body, the cutting board and spatula gripped tight in her hands.

Griffin nodded at the kitchen utensils. "Those were your weapons of choice?"

"I wasn't trying to fight him." She went to the kitchen and dropped both items into the sink, turning to Griffin as he followed her into the small room at the back of the house. "I was hoping to use them as barriers and urge him back out the door."

Griffin pointed at the back door that still sat open. "This door?"

Dianna pursed her lips as she moved to slam the screen into place, hooking the lock through the eye. "I've spent months trying to make friends with that freaking squirrel. He just started taking peanuts out of my hand. I never expected he would think the next step in our relationship was to move in together."

"In my experience that's a pretty common progression for most relationships." It was probably also the reason every one of those relationships crashed and burned, frequently with the assistance of lighter fluid.

Dianna laughed, the sound surprisingly light. She

glanced at him as she pulled the coffee carafe off the maker, her laugh dying off. "Are you serious?"

Griffin gave her a single nod. "Unfortunately." Maybe confessing all his sins was the best option. Then Dianna would see all the reasons she had to keep pushing him away. Relying on her to keep him in line wasn't the most honorable of endeavors, but she seemed to be the only one of them who had any sort of wherewithal when it came to that.

Because if she peeled that robe off her body and asked him to fuck her right now, there's not a thing in this world that would stop him from making it happen.

Except her.

NINE

DIANNA

DIANNA HELD OUT the cup of coffee she'd poured simply to have something to occupy her hands. "I'm sorry I interrupted your morning."

She was still trying to wrap her head around the fact that Griffin was her new neighbor, but maybe that would make things easier. Now he could simply be Griffin, her neighbor, instead of Griffin, the gorgeous man with the sexy smile and the gravelly voice... who happened to have gone down on her and given her the most amazing orgasm of her life.

"You don't need to apologize to me for anything, Di." He took the cup, his rough fingers dragging across hers. "I should be the one apologizing to you."

She turned away, forcing herself to stay calm as she

poured out another cup of coffee. "You don't need to apologize to me for anything."

It was absolutely true. In fact, she would prefer he not apologize to her at all. It would make it seem like he thought what happened between them was a mistake. And while she might have claimed it was a mistake, it didn't actually fall into that category for her.

Not the way it should have.

She'd spent the last three weeks trying to work up some amount of regret over what happened. It should have been easy, since Griffin clearly shared her opinion that it was a mistake, since he'd walked away without looking back. By all accounts she should have had some sort of remorse over the whole interaction.

But that was not how she felt at all.

Once she got past the initial knee-jerk reaction of it, 'the bakery incident' as she called it left her feeling empowered. Desirable.

Like the fucking goddess she decided she was.

But that didn't mean it could happen again. Interactions like that could quickly muddy the clarity of the waters she was treading in, and she hadn't quite yet learned how to swim in this new pool.

"I do need to apologize." Griffin's voice was soft behind her. "I shouldn't have pushed you to—"

That sent her spinning to face him, the turn fast enough that her coffee sloshed, spilling down the front of her robe. "You didn't push me."

She'd been an active player in everything that

happened. To the point that if it had gone farther, she would have been one hundred percent on board.

"I took advantage of you at a time when you were vulnerable and—" Griffin continued on, like he fully believed what he was saying.

"You didn't take advantage of me." Dianna snorted out a little laugh. The thought was preposterous. "I'm almost forty. I'm a big girl. I know how to say no. And there were plenty of rolling pins within arm's reach. If I wanted to stop, we would've stopped." She almost couldn't believe how empowered she sounded. How confident and self-assured.

She'd been working so hard for so long to get over what other people put on her, and part of her was worried it might never happen. But while it wasn't simple to retrain the thoughts trying to control her, it was possible. And this moment was proof.

"I was an absolutely willing participant in what happened, Griffin." Her thighs pressed together at the memory. "So like I said, you have nothing to apologize for." Dianna quickly clamped her lips shut, sealing off an apology of her own.

The old Dianna would have followed Griffin's attempted apology with one of her own. She would've tried to carry the burden so he didn't have to. But there was no burden. Sure, she got off and he didn't, but she wasn't going to apologize for that.

Men certainly didn't apologize when they were on the receiving end of one-sided satisfaction, so why should she?

"Okay." Griffin's eyes met hers. "Then I'm not sorry for what happened."

He was simply agreeing with her, but it felt like more. Like maybe Griffin was admitting he didn't have regrets either.

"Good." Dianna automatically took a sip from the cup in her hand, not realizing she hadn't added cream until the hot liquid hit her tongue. It took everything she had not to cringe, but right now she was being Dianna the goddess, not Dianna the gagging apologizer.

Griffin's eyes moved down, dipping to the splash of liquid sinking into the fabric over her left breast. "You spilled some coffee on your pretty robe."

She tucked her chin to find she'd lost a little more from her cup than she'd initially realized. The rapidly cooling coffee covered a sizable section of her boob, including the nipple which was pulling tight as the fabric chilled against it.

"Well, shoot." She sat down her coffee and yanked on the tie, sliding her favorite satiny robe off her shoulders. It wasn't until she lifted her eyes to Griffin's face that she realized exactly what she'd done.

And it certainly wasn't anything that would help her current situation.

Griffin's blue eyes locked onto the wet spot that penetrated her nightshirt, making the thin fabric cling directly to her body. His presence in her house and Snickerdoodle's temporary invasion must have kept her brain from fully doing the math on the situation and realizing both layers would be in the same predicament.

Dianna glanced down at the wet spot, chewing her lower lip as she decided what to do next. The most logical action would be to excuse herself and go get dressed. Put on fresh clothes before finishing their conversation and sending Griffin back home.

But she couldn't make herself walk away from the hunger in his stare. It was as if he was starving and she was the only thing he wanted. For a girl only recently coming into her own power, Griffin's sultry gaze was a little like catnip.

And it made her want to rub herself all over him.

There was no fear of rejection. No worry he would think her body was lacking or unappealing. It was quite clear Griffin found her more than a little attractive.

And it fed a part of her that was a little starving too.

"Oops." Dianna managed a shaky breath as her heart started to race in anticipation. Anticipation, and maybe a little fear. Not fear of Griffin, but fear of the unknown. Fear of all the changes that were happening inside her. "I should probably take this off too."

Her fingers teased along the hem of her favorite pajama shirt, toying with the lacy edge.

Griffin's gaze locked onto her fingertips. He was completely still, to the point he might not even be breathing. "Do you need help?"

The air rushed out of her lungs at his offer, partly in relief, but partly because she needed a fresh lungful to feed her swimming mind. "You could help. If you want to." She nearly winced at the hint of insecurity that snuck through, but Rome wasn't built in a day.

And Griffin definitely didn't seem to notice because before she could blink his body was on hers, pushing her back until her butt bumped the cabinets as his rough and calloused hands dragged her nightgown up her body, sliding it over her head before tossing it to the floor and returning to her skin. He leaned in, claiming her mouth in a kiss that stole what little air she'd managed to reclaim, making her dizzy and lightheaded as his palms smoothed over her body to cup her breasts. He dragged his thumbs across her nipples before rolling them in tandem, the dueling sensations making her knees weak as his tongue teased hers.

Griffin was definitely way more skilled than she was when it came to this kind of thing, but it seemed like he might be a boob man—and she brought plenty of those to the table—so hopefully it made up for the imbalance.

He pulled his mouth from hers, tipping his head as he used his hand to lift one nipple to his mouth and pulled it deep into the hot wet warmth, his tongue flicking against the tip.

It was more sensation than she could handle and sent her knees buckling, forcing her to grip Griffin's shoulders if she wanted any hope of staying upright.

Ultimately, it didn't matter since a second later, Griffin turned, his arms tight around her as they went down to the linoleum in an uncoordinated, but careful tilt. The weight of his body came down over hers, his hips wedging between her thighs as one hand slid between them.

Griffin groaned as his fingers teased against her heated flesh. "Where are your panties, Di?"

She stifled a gasp as he found her clit. "I don't wear panties to bed."

Griffin worked her body, stroking at a steady pace. "So now I have to sit next door knowing you're over here with this pretty pussy out every night?"

His words sent a rush of heat through her, one that culminated in a release of wetness she could feel. How was he so sweet but yet so filthy? It was a perfect example of having your cake and getting to eat it too. The man version of a lady in the street but a freak in the sheets.

"Does it bother you when I say things like that?" Griffin's touch slid away from her clit, gliding back to sink into her body, the invasion sudden and unexpected, but not unwanted. He made an approving hum against her skin. "No. It doesn't seem like it does." He fucked her with his fingers, settling his thumb against her clit, each thrust making an obscenely wet noise. "Actually, it sounds like you love the things I say to you, don't you, Di?"

It was an embarrassing question to answer, but fear he might stop what he was doing dragged it free. "Yes."

Griffin made another approving hum as his mouth moved along her jawline. "That's what I thought." He continued to work her pussy with an expert touch, one that had her racing toward an orgasm almost immediately. "What else do you like, Di? What other things do you secretly want me to do to you?"

That was the million-dollar question. One she hadn't quite given herself permission to consider.

With one exception.

It wasn't anything freaky or what most people would consider outside of the box, but for her, it was a stretch. Asking for anything had always been out of the question. She'd spent her life taking what was offered and pretending it was enough to satisfy her, feeling like she didn't have the right to want more.

But she was a fucking goddess now and goddesses weren't afraid to ask for what they wanted.

So she opened her eyes, meeting Griffin's gaze. "I want you to fuck me."

The flash of surprise that crossed his face was worth every bit of terror she felt at making the request. But how many times in her life did a woman have an opportunity to have sex with a man like Griffin? Probably not many, so she was going to take full advantage.

Was it a terrible idea? Yes, probably. Was she going to regret it in the morning? No, unlikely.

Griffin's nostrils flared. "Say it again."

"I want you," the words came easier the second time, "to fuck me."

To her surprise, and also enjoyment, Griffin didn't make her ask a third time. Instead, he yanked at the waistband of his jeans, managing to get them open with one hand before shoving them just past his hips to reveal the most attractive cock she had ever seen. It was thick and long with a perfectly flared head that disappeared into

Griffin's fist as he worked it down his length in tight, steady strokes.

He leaned down to catch one nipple in his mouth as he dragged his delicious dick along her seam. Dianna lifted her hips, encouraging him to give her what she wanted.

And Griffin didn't disappoint.

In one swift thrust he sank deep, filling her completely in a move that stole her breath.

It had been so long since she'd been intimate with a man. Even longer since she'd wanted to be intimate with a man.

But she wanted this man. Desperately. So much so that she reached around, sinking her fingers into his ass to pull him closer, resisting the urge to acknowledge any of the shame trying to ruin this moment.

There was nothing to be ashamed of. She was a grown woman. He was a grown man. Everything that happened between them was consensual.

It was also proving to be way more than she bargained for.

Griffin gripped her behind one knee, lifting her leg to the side in a way that allowed him to sink deeper into her body. Deep enough that each thrust rubbed her in a spot that curled her toes and stole her breath.

"There." Griffin shifted above her, bracing on his knees as his free hand worked her nipples, teasing one before moving to the next. "That's the right spot, isn't it, Di?"

She could only whimper. Speaking at this point was completely beyond her capabilities. All she could do was lay there and try not to turn into a puddle of quivering goo.

"I want you to remember this. Every time you're in this kitchen I want you to think of this minute." Griffin leaned in, changing the angle of his body so it hit both that magical spot inside her and her clit with each body-bouncing thrust. "I want you to think of me fucking your pussy. I want you to remember how good it felt."

Griffin's hand wedged between them, fingers working against her clit as he started to move faster, each slap of his body into hers making her tits and thighs jiggle.

It was too much—more than she'd ever imagined sex could be—and it made it impossible to delay the inevitable, no matter how much she wanted to drag it out. Her climax hit hard and fast, possessing her body completely, overwhelming her to the point there was no controlling her movements or the sounds she made—most of which would probably make her blush when she thought back on this moment.

And she would think back on this moment.

Not just because of the reasons Griffin listed, though those were part of it. She would think back on this moment as the first time she had sex without worry. Without obsessing over what the man on top of her was thinking.

If he noticed the dimples in her thighs.

Or the stretch marks on her boobs.

If the softness of her stomach grossed him out.

For the first time in her life, she was in a place where she could accept that the man fucking her within an inch of her life was turned on by her dimpled thighs and her stretch marked boobs and her soft stomach.

As he should be. Because she was a fucking goddess.

And it turned out goddesses had really good sex. Sex where one orgasm accidentally led right into another.

The second climax took her completely by surprise, moving through her body like a lightning strike as Griffin yanked his cock free, pumping it with one hand while the other rubbed at her clit, dragging her pleasure out as he came across her stomach, the lines of his cum hot against her skin.

It was the most intense interaction of her life.

Immediately followed by the most awkward one.

Because what did a woman say to the man who just saved her from a squirrel and then fucked her brains out?

Apparently it was, "Do you want a coffee for the road?"

TEN

GRIFFIN

GRIFFIN RUBBED HIS forehead against the sleeve of his T-shirt, swiping at the drip of sweat trying to work its way into his eyes as he held a flame against the copper pipe that would soon feed the sink in the master bathroom.

He'd been hard at work on the house since taking possession. The first order of business was hiring a lead paint remediation company to assist in the process of pulling out destroyed lathe and plaster walls and removing all the peeling paint. It had taken almost three weeks to get any potential issues cleared away, packed up, and sent off to their appropriate disposal sites, but he was finally at a point where he could start actually accomplishing things.

And getting running water was at the top of that list.

The entire house had to be re-plumbed because the majority of the drains were corroded and clogged from years of use. Luckily, Brooks Pace shared the name of a plumber he knew who was skilled at renovating older homes, and he'd been able to pay the guy to come over and help him come up with a game plan. The contractor even stayed on to help with removing the old pipes and running the new ones, which was a nightmare of a job.

But it was done now and he was close to having a working sink he could use to brush his teeth and wash his face. It wasn't much, but after nearly a month without running water in the house, it felt like one hell of a luxury. He'd been using the only source of water, the backyard hose the contractor suggested they leave available when adding in a new shutoff valve, for everything from showering to washing dishes. And the weather was going to cool off soon, making those late-night cold showers a little more painful than they already were.

Living here during the renovation might not have been his brightest idea, but it was the only option he had. Troy and Amelie's feelings would've been hurt if he'd rented a hotel, and driving back and forth from Cross Creek every day would have eaten up too much time and dragged this project out longer than it already had.

Plus, the last thing his son and daughter-in-law needed was him crowding what little time they had left before Amelie had her baby.

His grandson.

The thought of it was still surreal. Less than a year

ago he didn't even know he was a father, and now here he was planning to be a papa.

The trickle of sweat started up again, sliding down his forehead as it headed straight for his eye. Griffin squinted as he worked the last of the solder into the seam, keeping the joint hot enough to pull it into the gap and create a water-tight seal. This house had seen enough water damage. It definitely didn't need to suffer more. And the last thing he wanted was for all his hard work to go to waste because he rushed a fitting.

When he was satisfied with the joint, Griffin shut off the flame and set the tank onto the floor before shimmying his way out of the custom cabinet he'd been working inside.

He stood, grabbing the hem of his dirty T-shirt and dragging it across his face, wiping away the sweaty grime clinging to his skin. Even with the windows open the house was hot, making him wish the cooler weather would hurry up. He'd brave a few cold showers if it meant he didn't have to spend each day sweating his balls off.

After giving his work a final look over, he glanced at the pile of boxed fixtures stacked in the corner, thinking maybe he would get started on the faucet. Knock another thing off his endless list. But before he could even snap the plastic bands securing the package, a jaw-cracking yawn snuck free. Suddenly he was fucking exhausted. There was no more ignoring the burning in his eyes and his body was starting to drag.

Griffin pulled out his cell and checked the time, feeling relieved that it was after midnight.

He'd been doing his best to avoid running into Dianna, and so far had been successful. She kept a pretty strict schedule, which made it easy to time his own.

With the exception of Sundays.

So he'd taken to driving out to spend the entire day with Troy and Amelie, helping out around the ranch and with the addition they were putting on the house.

But today was a weekday. Dianna would have gotten home just before eleven, and would now be in bed, just like the rest of his neighbors.

After collecting his tools, Griffin flipped off the portable work-light he'd been dragging from room to room. He made his way down the back stairs, managing it mostly by feel since the state of the electric was similar to the state of the plumbing, and only worked in a select area.

The cooler downstairs air was a welcome change and he peeled off his shirt as he made his way through the kitchen, happy to get the sticky fabric away from his sweaty skin. He grabbed the shower caddy he kept beside the back door and carried it out onto the cracked patio, setting it on the rusting table Nate's family left behind as he dropped down into the matching chair to work off his boots. Once they were off, he stood to chuck his filthy jeans, letting them drop to the cement before glancing around to make sure no one was looking.

Then he snapped down his last remaining article of clothing and stepped into the rigged up outdoor shower he'd crafted out of PVC pipe and an old shower curtain. It wasn't a perfect system, but it was functional, and right now all he needed was functional.

He made sure the fabric curtain was in place before gritting his teeth and turning on the faucet. It took a second for the water to hit, and when it did he nearly yelped as the freezing spray hit his heated skin, sending goosebumps racing over his arms and legs.

Every night he thought he was prepared for the shock that came out of the hose, and every night he was wrong.

Griffin reached out of the curtain, fumbling around the caddy for the gel style soap he preferred over a bar. It was better at breaking down the oil and grease he used to get all over him while working at the shops, but it was also turning out to do a heck of a job on the filth that came from remodeling a house.

He readjusted the curtain then squeezed a healthy dose into his hand and went to work scrubbing away the grime. Once his skin was clean he moved onto his hair, sucking in a deep breath before stepping fully into the frigid stream. He rushed through the process of rinsing the soap free, working fast to get all the residue out so he could warm back up. The second it was gone he shut off the water and stepped back.

Right onto the hem of the curtain providing him some semblance of privacy.

The structure of the makeshift shower wasn't the sturdiest since it was comprised entirely of plastic, so he jumped off the curtain before it applied too much pressure to the elbow joints keeping his dick from being publicly displayed. But in his haste to get one foot off the curtain, he managed to get another one onto it, and this time the placement was a little bit more problematic. Maybe it was the rocking of the entire contraption from one side to the other as he bounced around. Maybe it was simply flawed design. Whatever it was, the entire thing collapsed, dropping down to his ankles as the support bars fell out to the sides.

Someone gasped.

It wasn't him.

Griffin sucked in a breath, bracing himself as he turned to the fence line separating his property from Dianna's. He raised one hand. "Evening."

Dianna's full lips pressed tight together, but the pressure wasn't enough to stifle the sound of her laughter.

"Yeah, yeah." Griffin reached down to snag the curtain, yanking it loose from what remained of his shower before wrapping the hem around his waist. "Laugh it up."

Dianna pressed one hand to her lips, shaking her head. "I'm sorry. It was just unexpected."

"It was unexpected for me too." He stepped away from the mess, the plastic rings still clipped to the top of the curtain dragging across the concrete. "I didn't mean to wake you up."

Dianna's smile faltered. "You didn't wake me up." Her expression looked sad, but maybe that was just the shadows of the light filtering out of her kitchen window. "Why are you showering in your backyard?"

Griffin tried to keep his focus on her face, but his eyes

kept wandering down to the silky floral robe he was a little too familiar with. "The water inside the house is shut off while I redo the plumbing."

"I have a shower, Griffin. You're more than welcome to use it." Dianna almost sounded defeated.

It was an emotion he was spending hours every day working his ass off to avoid.

He wanted his relationship with Troy to be enough. It should be. And it said a lot about him as a person that it wasn't. That he couldn't stop thinking about Dianna.

"I don't think that's a good idea."

"Maybe not, but we can't keep going on the way we have been." She motioned to his makeshift sarong. "Why don't you go put some clothes on and come over." Her eyes met his. "So we can talk."

Talking probably wasn't a great idea either, but damned if the thought of getting to spend a little time with Dianna didn't make him weak enough to agree. Weak enough that he all but ran back into the house, dropping the shower curtain on his way to the back bedroom. He yanked on a pair of shorts and a T-shirt, slipping on a pair of shoes before picking his way through the never-ending mess and out the front door. When he got next door, Dianna's porch light was on and her front door was open, much like it was the last time he came here.

Griffin lightly rapped his knuckles against the wood of the screen door, shifting on his feet as the familiar scent of her home carried through the screen.

Dianna peeked at him from the kitchen doorway, lifting a brow at him. "You can come in."

"I didn't feel right just barging in." He stepped inside, this time slipping off his shoes before going any farther. "I didn't want to make assumptions. There's no squirrel threatening your life this time."

"That's not for lack of trying." Dianna carried in two mugs, heading straight for the sofa. "Ever since that day, Snickerdoodle waits outside the back door, looking for an opportunity to sneak back in." She sat down, tucking her feet under her body before lifting a cup his way, making it clear she wanted him to sit beside her.

"Thank you." Griffin took the coffee and eased down onto her couch. It was impossible not to relax back into the cushions. He'd been sitting on metal folding chairs and boxes of tile and flooring for weeks now. Being in a finished, comfortable home felt like fucking heaven.

"I don't want things to be awkward between us." Dianna set her cup on the coffee table without taking a drink. "I didn't mean to make you feel strange around me."

"I don't feel strange around you, Di." He wasn't usually one to talk about things like this, but there was no way he would let Dianna think she was the problem. "I've just been busy."

Her brows slowly lifted. "Oh." Her lips pressed into a frown. "Because it seems a lot like you've been avoiding me."

Griffin set his coffee next to hers, scrubbing one hand down his face. "There's just been a lot going on and I—"

"Accidentally haven't set foot outside your house when you thought you might run into me?" She kept pinning him down, trying to make him admit to something he didn't want to admit to.

Talking wasn't one of his strong suits and after putting his foot in his mouth more times than he could count, he'd realized it was just easier to keep it shut and let the chips fall where they may.

And usually where they may involved his shit being tossed out a window.

Or his car being keyed.

"Like I said, I've been busy." He stuck with the story least likely to dig this conversation any deeper.

Dianna studied him, her eyes narrowing. "I'm not looking for a relationship, if that's what you're worried about."

For some reason her comment chafed. He had no right to be bothered by it, but it still stung a little.

He knew he wasn't good enough for her. He should count himself lucky to have had as much as she offered. But part of him still wanted to think she felt the same way he did.

That Dianna still secretly wanted more too.

"I wasn't worried." Griffin picked up the coffee she made, forcing himself to swallow some of it down in the hope it might alleviate the sting in his gut. "It didn't seem like you were wanting more when you kicked me out of your kitchen."

Dianna's eyes barely widened, which was a great indication he'd already stepped over the invisible line that always stood between him and everyone else. It was one he was great at crossing, and did his very best to stay far away from. It was why he chose to keep his mouth shut whenever possible.

"I should go." He stood up, knowing that walking away was the best option available now that he'd said too much. "Thanks for the coffee."

"Uhh." Dianna scoffed. "We're not done here."

There was a sharpness to her tone he hadn't heard before and it stopped his retreat.

Made him turn.

"What?"

Surely he hadn't heard her right. Dianna was sweet and soft. Not the kind of woman to make demands. And maybe that was part of what appealed to him. She would never force him to fight like so many other women did. She wouldn't rage and throw things and make threats.

But maybe what she was doing was worse.

"We're neighbors, Griffin. We have to figure out a way to exist side by side." Dianna sat a little taller. "So we're not done talking yet."

ELEVEN

DIANNA

GRIFFIN CLEARLY WANTED to escape the conversation, but she couldn't let that happen.

No matter how difficult it was to speak up, she deserved to feel comfortable in her own house. And right now, she didn't.

Knowing Griffin was there next-door, doing everything in his power to make sure their paths didn't cross was driving her crazy. So, as hard as it was to force the discussion, she was going to make sure it happened.

"Sit back down." She wasn't trying to be bossy, but this sort of thing didn't come naturally. She'd always been the kind of woman who accepted only what was offered to her and nothing more. And she always did it without making a fuss.

But that was what landed her in an abusive marriage

that nearly broke her, so clearly something needed to change.

Griffin pressed his lips together, eyes darting between the sofa and the door. For a second she thought he might run, but eventually he sighed and came back to the couch, dropping to the cushions before leaning forward to catch his head in his hands. He dug his fingers through his damp hair, digging them into his scalp like she was putting him through actual physical pain.

Maybe she wasn't the only one who wasn't great at things like this. Somehow that possibility made it a little easier. She wouldn't be the only one flailing into uncharted territory.

"Before I came to Moss Creek, I was married." It was the easiest place to start. Not necessarily the beginning, but the beginning of the end. "I had a little bakery on the outskirts of LA and it wasn't doing well, so I decided to bring someone else in who had more experience running a business." It turned out to be the worst mistake she could have made—professionally and personally. Before she knew it, the man who was supposed to help her was running not just her business, but her whole life. Martin controlled everything, from their finances to their schedule. He always made it seem like he was doing her a favor. Like he did it all so she didn't have to.

But that's not what it was about. It was one of many layers of abuse and served as the foundation he could build the rest on.

"I ended up marrying him, but he wasn't great to me

and wasn't great for the business. I left LA divorced and bankrupt." It was a difficult admission to make, especially to someone like Griffin. He'd been so successful in his own career, and she didn't want him to see her as a failure.

She didn't want to be a failure.

"That explains why you're so hesitant to hire someone else to help you." Griffin's tone was gentle and filled with understanding, soothing a few of the sharp edges surrounding her past.

Dianna nodded. "It feels like the lesser of two evils. Yes, I'm working like crazy, but at least I'm not risking the well-being of my business." The Baking Rack's success had helped her in so many ways—financially and emotionally—if it failed now the loss would be devastating.

"But you know hiring someone else isn't an all or nothing deal, right?" Griffin seemed to relax a little as their conversation moved away from their relationship and toward business dealings. "An hourly employee is only there to work. They don't have any control over all the things that make your business what it is." He lifted one hand, holding it out to the side, palm up. "Hell, they don't even have to be there when the business is open. You could just hire someone to help you with all the prep work behind the scenes."

It was an interesting possibility, but not one that needed to be hashed out right now. "I appreciate the suggestion, but we're not here to talk about my business." She took a steadying breath before redirecting the conversation. "We're here to figure out how we can be neighbors."

Griffin stiffened up again almost immediately, confirming her suspicions that he struggled in situations like this just as much as she did. "We're already neighbors."

Dianna smiled softly at his attempt to avoid continuing. It's one she might have made herself not too long ago. "You know what I mean." She reached out to touch Griffin's shoulder, doing it without really thinking, but the second her fingers rested against him his eyes snapped to the point of contact.

Yeah, they definitely needed to have this conversation.

Dianna pulled her hand away, fisting it tight before letting it sit across her lap. "I'm not looking for a relationship right now, Griffin. That's why I said what happened in the bakery was a mistake and that's why I acted the way I did that day in the kitchen." She paused, giving him the opportunity to reply. When he didn't, she continued on. "My marriage broke me in ways I don't know how to fix. And until I figure that out, I have to focus on myself. I can't do that if I'm in a relationship."

She was already struggling to accomplish it not in a relationship.

Griffin's eyes held hers for a minute before drifting across the room. He sat quietly, but didn't seem as ready to run as he had a few minutes ago.

His jaw clenched, lips pressing tight. Finally he

sucked in a deep breath. "I don't have the best track record with relationships either."

His eyes came her way, lingering a minute before moving back across the room. "I'm sure you've heard what happened with Troy's mother."

Knowing about Griffin's past suddenly felt invasive, even though it wasn't meant to be. Amelie had explained how terrible Troy's mother was over lunch one day. Explaining to her, and the rest of the group, that up until two weeks before he showed up on Troy's doorstep, Griffin had no clue his son existed. Troy's mom didn't feel the need to share that with him until she decided she wanted retroactive child support.

Which thankfully, she wasn't entitled to.

"I'm sorry that happened. It was very selfish of her not to tell you she was pregnant." Technically she had, she just also told Griffin she had an abortion, choosing to keep his son from him as one last bit of revenge when he broke up with her.

"Part of me wishes I'd known about him sooner, but part of me wonders if maybe it's better I didn't." Griffin's gaze dropped to where his hands were clasped in front of him. "My personal life has always been a mess, and I'm not sure I would've been smart enough to shield him from seeing that."

Dianna swallowed hard, reacting to the pain and remorse Griffin was still clearly wrestling with. "I bet you would have." She reached for him again, unable to stop herself as she slid her fingers along his. "You're working hard to be a good dad. Everyone can see that."

He'd uprooted his entire life to move closer to the adult son he'd only recently learned about. Restructured his business to make that possible. There probably weren't many people who would go to that extent.

But Griffin had. It showed just how committed he was to being there for Troy. How important it was that he know his son.

Griffin chuckled, the sound bitter as he shook his head. "I'm not sure that's true." His eyes slowly found hers. "If it was, I'd have a much easier time staying away from you."

Guilt welled up, pressing against her lungs. "I don't want to steal your attention from Troy." She'd been so focused on her own reasons for needing to keep Griffin at arm's length it hadn't occurred to her he had reasons of his own. "I'm sorry. I didn't—"

Griffin clasped her hand in his, holding it tight as he turned toward her. "You don't have anything to be sorry for. I'm the problem." His free hand lifted, the tips of his fingers tracing along her cheek. "I've missed out on so much with Troy. I've got so much to make up for. It should be easy for me to concentrate on that." He barely shook his head as his touch skimmed across her lips. "But instead all I want to think about is you." His eyes dipped to her mouth. "That's why I've been staying away. I can't trust myself around you."

Dianna struggled to breathe as Griffin traced a line down the column of her neck. "But now you don't have to stay away from me since you know I'm not interested in being in the way."

"That's good to know." Griffin's eyes followed the path of his fingers as they moved across her skin, teasing along the neckline of her robe. "I don't want to get in your way either."

"Then it sounds like we've worked it out." She swallowed as he traced the upper swell of her breast. "We won't get in each other's way."

"Perfect." Griffin's touch skimmed lower, following the line of her cleavage. "Now we can stop avoiding each other."

Dianna nodded, struggling to breathe as his fingers inched toward her nipple. "Perfect."

Griffin's nostrils barely flared as he brushed across the already tightening peek. "Definitely perfect."

She sucked in a breath as he leaned closer, lips skating down her neck as his fingers teased her nipple to an aching point. "I'm glad we're on the same page."

"So am I." Griffin gripped the edge of her robe, peeling it back, snagging the low neckline of her nightgown as he went. With a flick of his wrist her breast was free, bared to the heat of his gaze. "I was going crazy staying away from you." His head dipped and a second later his mouth closed around her, hot and wet. As his tongue flicked against her skin, his hand traveled up the line where her thighs pressed together. When he reached her pussy he growled, the sound muffled by the substantial swell pressed against his face. He pulled his mouth free, sucking until the last possible second. "No fucking panties."

"I already told you I don't wear panties to bed." Her

whole body jerked as Griffin pressed deeper, his touch skating across her clit.

"Oh, I remember, but I've been working real fucking hard to forget." He braced one foot against her coffee table, shoving it back in a move that sloshed coffee onto the surface and sent it running dangerously close to the edge.

But she couldn't make herself care because Griffin immediately dropped to his knees, spreading her legs before burying his face between her thighs.

Her fingers dug into the cushions of the couch, clawing at the upholstery as he tongued her within an inch of her life.

It was an act she hadn't been afforded the opportunity to enjoy often since the men she'd allowed into her bed in the past were as selfish between the sheets as they were outside of them, so in this moment she made another promise to herself. Not only was she a fucking goddess, but she was also now a fucking goddess who didn't settle for men who couldn't get her off.

Or, in a more likely scenario, wouldn't get her off.

Luckily, Griffin was not one of those men. In what felt like less than a heartbeat, she was coming, grabbing a hold of anything within reach for stability as her body spun out of control.

Her limbs went limp as Griffin lifted his head, using one hand to wipe down his face, a smug smile settling on his lips as he reached the other up to tease the nipple he rescued from the confines of her nightgown earlier. "Don't look relaxed, Di. I'm not finished with you yet."

He moved his hand down her body, fingers teasing along her slit before spearing inside. "I want to feel your pretty little cunt squeeze me tight."

Every muscle in her lower half clenched at his words. Griffin's dirty mouth was starting to be less shocking than it was initially, which meant the only lingering reaction it caused was lust.

She knew Griffin found her attractive, but hearing just how much he wanted her lined up a few of the cracks she'd been struggling to repair. It made her feel stronger. Braver. Bolder. "Then why are you wasting time?"

The blue of his eyes darkened as his focus sharpened on her face. "It's a good thing I don't have to worry about you distracting me anymore, Dianna." He shoved down his shorts, freeing the rigid length of his dick before giving it a few pumps with his fist. "Because it would be real fucking easy for me to pay attention to only you." In one swift move, he lined his body to hers and sank deep. Filling her so fast and so completely it stole her breath. "And I'm pretty sure I would never get enough of you." He hooked his arms under her legs, gripping her thighs as he pulled her closer, scooting her ass off the end of the couch as he continued to fuck her with deep, consuming thrusts. "Or this perfect pussy."

Up until now she'd felt lucky if an orgasm accidentally snuck its way into her sexual encounters, but when Griffin settled his thumb on her clit she was racing toward a second climax, unable and unwilling to contain the pleasure he brought.

Because she fucking deserved it.

Griffin's free hand traveled up to slide across her face, two fingers pressing between her lips to thrust against her tongue as his hips bounced against the fullness of her ass. "Suck."

It was impossible to ignore his sharp command—not that she wanted to—and Dianna pursed her lips and sucked, licking against his skin.

"Just like that." Griffin's voice was raspy and tight as his thrusts became sharper. "Someday I'm going to let you suck my cock just like that." He leaned close, the scrape of his short beard rough against her cheek. "Would you like that? To get on your knees for me?"

Apparently words could cause orgasms because Griffin's questions sent one ripping right through her, making Dianna groan around his fingers as he slammed into her with unerring consistency. The clench of her pussy was barely calming when he pulled free, sliding his cock between them, thrusting against her belly twice before heat spilled over her skin, sinking into the fabric of the nightgown tangled around her body.

She struggled to catch her breath as Griffin carefully eased back, letting her slide the rest of the way off the couch and onto the floor, wedging them against the coffee table.

His eyes dragged down her body, lingering over where he'd made a mess of her front. He pushed to his knees, peeling off his shirt. He held it out. "Here. Change into this."

She eyed the offering, a little unsure, but the rapidly cooling stick plastering her robe to her body and the bonelessness of her legs made the decision easy. With only a tiny hesitation she lifted away her nightgown and robe, peeling them free. "You're going to run out of shirts if you keep giving them to me."

Griffin watched intently as she wiggled into the warm cotton. "I'll buy more."

TWELVE

GRIFFIN

"YOU DO KNOW it's too early to be working this hard, right?" Dianna peeked at him through the open front doorway, a plate balanced on each hand.

Griffin straightened, stepping away from the tiles he was sifting through after finding one of the boxes was completely shattered. "Hey." He glanced around the mess of his house, looking for a spot that seemed clean enough for her to be. "You probably shouldn't come in here. It's a mess."

Dianna shot him a grin, confidently stepping across the threshold. "I am too, so I'm pretty sure I'll be fine." She held out one of the plates. Based on all the take-out containers stacked in your garbage cans, I figured you don't have a functioning kitchen. So, I brought you breakfast."

Griffin glanced at his filthy hands, wiping them down his jeans before carefully taking the plate, making sure he didn't accidentally touch any of the food with his grimy fingers. "I've got a microwave, but I got tired as hell of frozen burritos."

Dianna rolled her eyes on a sigh as she held out a fork. "No one should eat frozen burritos all the time."

Griffin took the fork, his stomach growling at the prospect of a home-cooked meal. "It wasn't all the time." He stabbed a bite of sausage gravy covered biscuit. "Sometimes I ate noodle cups."

Dianna shook her head as she peeked around his shoulder. "You know they sell hot plates." She stepped around him, her eyes moving over the large entryway containing most of his tile and flooring.

"See, that would only be useful if I knew how to cook more than microwave burritos and noodle cups." He shoved in the bite and nearly groaned. "Damn this is good."

"Says the man who existed on noodles and frozen burritos." Dianna peeked into the large room to the left of the foyer. "Have you gotten a lot done since you moved in?"

His next bite stalled out, suspended right in front of his mouth. "You can't tell?"

He'd been busting his ass for over a month and had been making pretty good headway on the place.

At least he thought he had.

Dianna shrugged. "I've never been in here." She leaned deeper into the formal living room. "Vera was pretty protective of this place. She didn't let anyone inside."

"I think that was as much about protecting her independence as it was protecting the property. This place wasn't really habitable, let alone safe for an old woman." Griffin tipped his head toward the space Dianna seemed curious about. "You can go anywhere you want. I've already taken care of the collapsing floors."

Dianna's eyes widened. "Collapsing floors?"

"They weren't technically falling in yet, but they were on their way." He followed behind as she moved into the room. "I was able to save most of the hardwood and I think I can patch in the spots I had to replace, so hopefully no one will be able to tell what's original and what's not."

Dianna reached out to slide the tip of a finger along the top of the waist-high built-in lining one wall. "Vera would be so happy you're trying to preserve everything you can."

"I wish I could save more, but the bathrooms were pretty trashed." The tile was damaged and missing in spots and the walls and floors behind it had to be replaced. "But I'm going to do my best to make everything suit the house."

"I can't wait to see what you do with it." She moved to the back of the empty room, pointing across the small hall splitting this side of the house in half. "Is this one of the bathrooms?"

"That's the office." Griffin stepped in close, letting his body brush against hers in an act of self-indulgence. He pushed open the solid wood door to reveal the room he'd been living out of. "It was the best room in the house so it's where I've been staying."

Dianna walked inside, her steps muffled by the large area rug he spread across the floor to protect his bare feet in the morning. "I love the windows." She motioned at the floor-to-ceiling panes. "But I bet the light is tough to ignore in the mornings."

"I'm usually up before the sun is, so it doesn't bother me." Griffin crossed to the small fridge that held drinks, opening it to pull out a pop and offering it up.

Dianna sighed, taking the cola before sinking down to sit on the edge of his bed. "I don't even remember what it's like to sleep in anymore."

There weren't many people in this world who worked harder than he did, but after living next door to her for over a month it was clear Dianna was one of them.

And it drove him fucking nuts.

"You give any more thought to hiring someone to help out?" He snagged another drink and carried it over to sit beside her as she picked at her breakfast, positioning his body farther from hers than he wanted to.

He promised he wasn't going to be a distraction, and he'd done his best to stand by that promise.

Mostly.

Sure, he might have started taking his backyard showers right after she got home in the hopes Dianna would re-extend the offer to use hers. Showing up on her doorstep, expecting to use her facilities, didn't sit quite right. And sure, occasionally he would check on her in the mornings, hoping she might invite him to enjoy more than a cup of coffee.

But so far neither of those things had happened. They'd both been perfectly friendly and perfectly behaved.

Unfortunately.

"It's just scary." Dianna settled her plate onto her lap, looking surprisingly defeated. "But I feel like I'm starting to wear out, you know?"

"You've been working your ass off for almost a year and a half straight. Of course you're worn out." He reached out to smooth her dark hair behind one ear. "You could always hire someone and if it doesn't work out you can let them go." He struggled to pull his hand away, instead letting his fingers slide across her skin. "That's the nice part about being the boss."

Dianna smiled, perking up the tiniest bit. "You make it sound so simple."

Griffin shrugged, catching a strand of her hair between his fingers. "Business is simple."

It was everything else that was complicated.

Dianna sighed, refocusing on her breakfast and finally taking a bite. "I had someone I was considering, but that was weeks ago. She's probably found another job by now." She scooped up a bit of hash brown before collecting biscuit and gravy. "I wouldn't even know how to find someone else."

"You can always call her and start there. If she's busy then you can check with Mae and see if she knows anyone who's looking."

He wanted to help Dianna. Wanted her to have less stress. But not all of his reasons for pushing her to hire an employee were as selfless. If she was able to come home earlier at night, he could spend a little more time with her before she fell asleep on his shoulder and he was forced to come back to this big empty house.

Not because he was trying to be part of her life or because he was trying to make her part of his. It was just nice to have someone he could talk to about his day. Someone who didn't press him for more than he could give. Hopefully he provided her with the same.

"Maybe you're right." Dianna blew out another breath, her cheeks puffing with the exertion. "And I'm sure it will be fine. I'm not the same person I was and I don't think I would let someone walk all over me again like I did before."

Over the past week, Dianna had offered up bits and pieces of the life she had before coming to Moss Creek. He still didn't have a real clear picture of exactly what it was like, but he was starting to worry he could guess.

"I can't imagine anyone wanting to walk all over you." He wasn't sure what to say. How to reassure Dianna everything really would be fine. Even if he was the one who had to make sure it was fine.

There was no way he would ever let anyone take advantage of this woman. If he had to haul their asses out of town himself, Dianna would never have to worry about her business.

She lifted her eyes to his face, holding his gaze. "It makes me really happy to hear you say that. I've been working really hard to try to be," she paused, her brows pinching together, "different than I used to be."

Griffin returned her smile. "Me too."

It was the common ground that kept them both carefully navigating the situation. Each of them was working hard not to repeat the mistakes of their past, and in some way it felt like they were in it together.

Even if they technically had to stay apart.

Dianna aimed the tines of her fork at his plate. "You should eat that before it gets cold. Gravy gets a funny texture when it cools down."

Griffin took an obliging bite, carefully talking around the mouthful. "I would eat your gravy off the floor. Just so we're clear."

Dianna laughed, her head tipping back as the sound filled the room. The way it moved through the space was unexpected. The only noise he'd really heard in this place was the ear-splitting drone of power tools and his own curses when something didn't go the way he wanted it to. But Dianna's laugh sounded lighter here. Airier. Almost magical in a way. Which was a weird fucking thing to think her laughter sounded like.

But that's exactly how it was.

They easily fell into comfortable conversation as they ate, just like they did every morning when he stopped by to join her for coffee. Dianna asked questions about his plans for the house and offered up what she knew about its former owner.

"Vera loved to feed the birds." She smiled, the expression a little wistful. "I've heard she was kind of a crab to most people, but she was always a sweetheart to me. We would both sit out in the yard and watch the birds at the feeders, and when I was testing out recipes for The Baking Rack I would bring her all my overflow."

"So what I'm hearing is, it's going to be good to be your neighbor." Griffin set his empty plate aside, sliding it onto the box serving as a nightstand.

"Unfortunately for you, I've already worked the kinks out of most of my recipes, so it'll only be good to be my neighbor if I try to come up with something new to add to my rotation." Her mouth pressed into a contemplative line. "But I think if I try to take anything out there might be anarchy, so that might not happen for a while."

"Then I guess it's a good thing it's not just your baking skills I'm interested in." While he meant it as a tease, it was one that admittedly toed the line between them. But he was getting real fucking sick of that damn thing anyway. The moments he shared with Dianna were the best of his day. Ones he looked forward to from the time she left in the mornings until she came home at night.

Dianna's dark eyes met his, holding as the silence between them dragged out.

And then they were both moving, bodies meeting,

hands and arms tangling, as her empty plate slid to the floor.

It had been barely over a week since he'd kissed her, but it felt like fucking forever. Her lips were soft and sweet as they parted, her tongue carrying a hint of the gravy's richness as it slicked against his.

"Hello? Anybody home?" Troy's deep voice seemed to echo through the house, the surprise of it sending them both in opposite directions, putting as much distance between them as possible.

Dianna quickly collected the plates, stacking them on one hand and heading for the door just as Troy and Amelie peeked into the bedroom.

"Hey!" Dianna kept moving, turning sideways to get past them. "I just brought breakfast to bribe your dad to let me see the place." She didn't even glance his way as she flashed a warm smile at his son and daughter-in-law. "I'll leave you guys to your tour."

Before he could blink she was gone, walking out without so much as a wave in his direction.

Amelie watched her go, waiting until the front door closed to turn back. She thumbed over one shoulder in the direction Dianna left. "Does Dianna live around here?"

He resisted the urge to shift on his feet. "She does."

Amelie's eyes opened wide. "Lucky you." She rested one hand on her barely protruding belly. "She bring you the leftovers at the end of the day?"

Griffin struggled not to think of what he'd prefer to

get from Dianna at the end of the day. "I don't think she has much left over."

Amelie pushed out her lower lip. "Not surprising. Everything she makes is so damn good it always sells out."

Troy was quiet at his wife's side, watching him a little too closely. "I'm surprised you didn't tell us Dianna lived close."

Griffin shrugged. "I guess it didn't occur to me." He motioned to the hall. "Did you guys want to check the place out?"

Troy and Amelie came through right after he bought it, and it seemed like they both might have thought he was a little crazy to take on the project, so he was eager to show them how far he'd come. Hopefully it would make it easier for them to see the house like he did.

A little bit of a mess but one that would be worth the effort.

The place was one of the biggest in town, and definitely the most grand. Between the soaring ceilings, the extensive custom woodwork, and the multitude of fireplaces and stained glass, the house could be a showstopper. One he couldn't help but feel might be a little wasted on him.

Amelie rocked up onto her toes. "I'm excited to see what you've done." She hooked one arm through Troy's as they followed him down the hall. "That's why I dragged him down here this morning instead of making you come to us."

She didn't mean it the way it sounded, but he still had to clarify. "I don't mind coming to you."

He was the one who had missed out. The one who wasn't a part of his own son's life. The burden of effort in this situation fell squarely on his shoulders. Which was why he needed to be more careful about the time he spent with Dianna. Especially if Troy and Amelie were going to start dropping in.

"I know you don't mind." Amelie turned to grin at him over one shoulder. "But we don't mind coming to visit you either." She wiggled her brows. "Especially once this kid gets here. We might dump him on your porch and run away for a few hours."

The fact that he was about to be a papa still felt surreal, and honestly he wasn't remotely equipped for the position. He'd never changed a diaper. Never made a bottle. Hell, he'd never even held a baby.

"I might need a few lessons before that happens." Griffin scrubbed up the back of his neck, fighting through the sense of inadequacy always hovering a little too close. "Otherwise you might come home and find both of us crying."

THIRTEEN

DIANNA

"WELL LOOK AT you." Janie walked in through the back door of the bakery, hair pulled up on top of her head, dressed in the same leggings and T-shirt Dianna wore to work every day. "I like the change."

Dianna reached up, barely avoiding putting her fingers on the newest bit of her journey toward the woman she'd always wanted to be. "You really like it?"

Janie snagged one of the aprons from the hook inside the door, pulling it over her head and around her front. "I love it. It definitely suits your face."

Dianna smiled. She didn't want other people's opinions to affect her own, but it was nice to hear someone else felt the same way she did about the delicate gold ring laced through one nostril. "I love it too."

"That's all that matters anyway, isn't it?" Janie went straight to the fridge, pulling out the piles of dough they'd mixed up the night before and lining them down the stainless-steel counter.

The same stainless-steel counter she might have once been sprawled across.

Dianna forced her eyes away from the surface, wishing it was as easy to redirect her brain. Things had been different with Griffin since Troy and Amélie showed up at his house a week ago. He hadn't gone back to avoiding her like he did before, and she hadn't been avoiding him, but it was almost as if there was some unspoken agreement to put a little distance between them.

It was for the best, she knew that, but it was still disappointing in a way she couldn't entirely face.

"Tomorrow's going to be a really big day since it's Saturday, so I usually make extra of everything." She forced her brain to the task at hand, which was continuing to get Janie acquainted with the workings of the bakery.

After hurrying from Griffin's house Sunday, she immediately went home and dug around to find Janie's number, calling her up but never expecting she might still be available after all this time. Luckily, Janie had been helping her friend Mariah out at The Inn but was available to help Dianna as well since she only worked at The Inn in the morning, leaving her afternoons free.

"I figured as much when we put together all this dough last night." She pulled out the vat of blueberry pie filling they'd also cooked up, setting it beside the dough. "What do you want me to focus on?"

She and Janie had only worked together a handful of times, but already Dianna was kicking herself for not calling the woman sooner. It was very clear Janie understood she was only there to serve as an extra set of hands, and always made sure she was doing what Dianna wanted. Of course she did take initiative when she knew a process had to be started, like taking the chilled dough from the refrigerators, but she never overstepped and never pushed.

"If you could handle the cinnamon roll assembly, that would be amazing." Having someone else to handle that task was making a bigger difference than she ever imagined. It meant she was able to have cinnamon rolls available every day of the week instead of simply being part of the rotation, and she was already seeing how that could raise her income enough to more than pay for Janie's wages.

While Janie put together the rolls, Dianna focused on assembling the strudels, wrapping the first batch together before sliding them in the oven.

"I think these are going to sell like crazy." Janie carefully spread the blueberry glaze over a rectangle of dough before sprinkling on the cinnamon/brown sugar combination that went into all the rolls. "You might end up having to make a fruit variation every Saturday."

Dianna pressed her lips together, a little excited about the possibility. She hadn't had the opportunity to expand her offerings lately. It had taken everything she had just to handle her tried and true items. But she loved coming up with fresh ideas more than anything. It was what she'd done with her grandmother when she was a little girl, standing at the counter of the old farmhouse where she spent most of her summers, mixing up pies and pastries and cakes. Her grandmother showed love through food, and Dianna had clearly inherited that trait.

"I wonder how peaches would do?" She was already working through the recipe in her mind. "Maybe with almonds?"

"I'm willing to bet you can make just about anything taste amazing." Janie shot her a lopsided smile. "You're kind of making me regret dropping out of culinary school."

"You don't have to go to culinary school to be a good cook." Dianna worked through the next batch of strudel, piling up cherry filling before folding everything together. "I'm sure it probably helps you make connections, and gives you a certain amount of experience, but some of the best cooks I know never went to culinary school."

Janie positioned herself at the long end of the dough and started carefully rolling it into a log. "I'm guessing you didn't go to culinary school."

Dianna shook her head. "Everything I know I learned from my grandma. She was..." Dianna paused, thinking of her sweet Nana. The one she looked so much like. The one who was the only person in her past who tried to help her love the body type they shared. "She was a fucking goddess."

Putting those words on her grandmother felt almost as good as it did putting them on herself. She wasn't the only one whose body her mother voiced an opinion on. More than once, she'd been forced to listen to how disappointing her mother found her grandmother's shape to be, which was simple to take as a blanket statement that covered them both considering Dianna carried the same well curved shape.

"Then I guess that shit runs in the family." Janie finished sealing up the role of blueberry and cinnamon then went to work slicing it into evenly sized rolls. "My grandmother chain-smoked and watched soap operas."

"That would be my mother." She'd come home from school every day to find her mother stretched across the couch, eyes locked on the television. It usually took her a good hour to even notice Dianna was home, but once she did there was no escaping the nitpicking. Her mother had been a popular cheerleader and it was clearly the failure of her lifetime that she didn't produce her own skinny, outgoing daughter to parade around like a trophy.

Janie wrinkled her nose. "How is your mom now?"

Dianna shrugged, not having to fake disinterest. "She quit smoking, but I'm pretty sure she still watches daytime television." She sliced across the top of the strudel in front of her, revealing a hint of its contents before settling it onto a baking sheet. "I don't talk to her much, so other than that I'm not really sure."

She and her mother hadn't had a big falling out, they were just two completely different people. With so little in common, there was little to discuss, so any phone calls were short, simple check-ins. And that was probably for the best. She learned a long time ago she couldn't change her mother. All she could do was change the way she dealt with her.

"Then it sounds like you took after your grandma." Janie started lining the sliced rolls into one of the deep pans they baked in. "Which I'm going to say was lucky since she was a goddess."

Dianna smiled, sliding one hand over the curve of her hip, loving the lines of her body a little more easily since they directly connected her to the woman she loved so deeply. "It's definitely a win."

The room went quiet as she and Janie both focused on their tasks, quickly working through all the prep work that went into running a Saturday at The Baking Rack. By the time everything was done and ready to go, the sun was barely setting.

Janie finished wiping down the main counter before untying her apron and hooking it into place. "I think we shaved another half hour off our time." She grabbed her bag and looped it over her head, sliding the strap across her body. "And we put together about a third more than normal." She held out a fist. "We might be awesome."

Dianna bumped her knuckles against Janie's. Hiring her was definitely the right thing to do, not just for her business, but also for herself. Janie was turning out to be one hell of a hype girl. "You are awesome. I'm kicking myself for waiting so long to call."

Janie waved her off, pulling open the back door.

"Change is hard." She lifted her brows. "Trust me, I know." She held the door, waiting as Dianna collected her own belongings. "But sometimes change is the best thing that can happen. It definitely was for me."

Janie hadn't been super open about what brought her to Moss Creek, but it was starting to seem like she had a story of her own. Maybe one day she would feel comfortable enough to share it. Until then, Dianna would simply make sure Janie understood how grateful she was.

"Do you want to take home a little tray of cinnamon rolls?" They'd managed to fill up all the large trays and had two loaf pans that each had two rolls placed inside. Dianna opened the fridge and slid them out, holding one Janie's way. "These will be a pain in the ass to time in the big oven, so it only makes sense that we take them home with us."

"Well," Janie took the offered rolls, clutching them tight against her chest, "it does only make sense."

Dianna tucked her own rolls into one arm and grabbed her keys. "I'll see you Monday afternoon."

Janie paused. "Are you sure you don't need help tomorrow?"

Dianna shook her head. "I make sure Mondays are easy so I can have all day Sunday off. All I do Saturday afternoon is get everything organized so I can assemble it easily Monday morning."

She didn't hate a six-day workweek, but there was no way she would drag Janie into her insanity. She pulled the door closed and locked it behind them, giving her new employee a wave. "Enjoy your weekend."

Janie shot her a wink. "You too."

Dianna slid into her car, settling her bag and the rolls on the passenger seat, waiting to make sure Janie was on her way before driving down the alley and onto the main road.

It was impossible to ignore the way her heart rate picked up as she turned into the tiny neighborhood she called home. It was still relatively early and Griffin was probably still working at the house, which was good. She wasn't trying to get in the way of his plans, just like he wasn't trying to get in the way of hers. She could just bake up the rolls she had really quickly and drop them off so he could have a quick snack before getting back to work.

Dianna pulled into her little single-car garage, carefully easing her sedan into the cramped space before closing the door and jumping out. She may have been moving a little faster than she normally would as she quickly preheated the oven and rushed back to take a shower. Once she was scrubbed clean, the oven was hot, so she slipped the rolls inside and went back to dry her hair, using a boar bristle brush to smooth it into full, soft waves.

After a quick sift through her clothes, she settled on a fresh pair of leggings and a long-sleeved, tunic style T-shirt. The air was starting to get cool in the evenings, and as far as she knew, Griffin didn't have his ducts hooked up or the furnace running.

The oven timer went off just as she was stuffing her feet into a pair of sneakers. She mixed up a quick glaze as the rolls cooled, drizzling it over the top before grabbing a couple of forks and heading out, the warm pan wrapped in a towel so she wouldn't burn her fingers.

Griffin's front door was open, as always, but now it was blocked off by a beautifully carved screen door. The sight of it stopped her in her tracks halfway across the porch and she paused to admire the beautiful scrollwork covering the bottom and running up the sides.

"Everything okay?"

Her eyes centered on the screen to find Griffin standing on the opposite side. "I was just looking at your door." She reached out to run her fingers across the stained and varnished surface. "It's beautiful. I've never seen anything like it."

Griffin pushed it open, stepping back so she could pass him. "I had it custom-made. Nate had some old pictures of the house and I sent a copy of one to a door maker."

Dianna peeked at him under the lashes she might have added a couple coats of mascara to. "You're really going all out on this place, aren't you?"

Griffin's eyes held hers. "I don't do anything halfway, Di."

She knew that firsthand. Griffin was very... thorough. In all aspects of his life.

Not that she'd experienced those aspects recently, which was probably for the best. It would be very easy to get used to regular physical interactions with Griffin and that would be...

Well, probably not the worst thing that had ever happened to her.

"It looks like you brought me something." Griffin focused on the loaf pan in her hands. "Is this a new recipe?"

"It is." She lifted it up between them, giving him a better look at the blueberry streusel cinnamon rolls the people of Moss Creek would be enjoying tomorrow. "I told you living next door to me would have perks."

Griffin's blue gaze dipped down her front, hanging on her breasts for just a second. "It definitely has perks."

Her body reacted almost immediately and heat raced over her skin. She and Griffin had only been together a few of times, all of them sudden and somewhat spontaneous, resulting in frantic couplings in which neither of them had managed to get all of their clothes off. It was exciting and satisfying, but she still couldn't help but wonder what Griffin's naked body would feel like against hers.

But almost immediately, Griffin cleared his throat, stepping away to put a little more distance between them the way he had all week. He was respecting both of their boundaries. It was honorable and admirable...

And slightly disappointing.

"They're still warm." Dianna held up one of the forks she'd grabbed on her way out the door. "I thought maybe you could use a snack."

Griffin grinned as he took the utensil. "I am always

up for any snack that comes out of your kitchen." There was the hint of suggestion in his words, dragging her back to the day they ended up entangled on her kitchen floor.

He'd said he wanted her to think of that moment every time she entered the room. So far, he'd gotten his wish and then some, considering she also thought of that moment when she wasn't in that room.

Somehow little bits of Griffin had permeated just about every aspect of her life. He was at the counter of her bakery where they'd first met. He was in the back room where their mutual attraction first accidentally got the better of them. He was in her kitchen and her living room. Hell, she even thought about him when she was feeding Snickerdoodle every morning, being extra diligent to ensure the chubby squirrel didn't find his way into her house again.

Somehow, Griffin had become an integral part of her world. To the point that when she finished work a few hours early, his was the only face she wanted to see.

Which meant Griffin was still trying to hold up the boundaries they both set, but maybe she wasn't.

"Oh, no." Dianna shoved the pan of rolls at Griffin and backed away. "I forgot to do something at the shop." The excitement she felt over getting to see him twisted around, winding tighter until it became something else. Something that felt an awful lot like failure.

She was supposed to be focusing on fixing herself. Becoming whole and hale again.

Instead she was spending her days thinking about

Griffin and her nights wondering if he might show up on her doorstep.

"Di? What's wrong?" He stepped toward her. "Is it something I can help you with?"

She held up one hand. "No." The word came out too sharp but there was no fixing it now. "No, thank you. I just need to run." She pointed at the pan in his hands. "Let me know if you like those." She was halfway out of the house before she'd finished talking.

Somehow she'd fucked up.

Somehow she'd accidentally gotten attached to the man she promised not to want anything from. Accidentally incorporated him into her life.

Into her heart.

And now somehow she had to figure out how to get him back out.

FOURTEEN

GRIFFIN

"Something wrong?" Troy studied him across the engine of the side-by-side. "You're a little quiet today."

Griffin shook his head, straightening as he wiped oil from his hands. "I'm fine."

It tasted like a lie, but admitting that would only add to the list of problems he was facing.

"You sure?" Troy lowered the hood into place, letting it drop the last few inches. "You don't think maybe you might be working yourself too hard?"

"I'm okay. Promise." Too much work was never the problem. Up until now it had always been the answer.

Work was the only thing that never failed him. It was the only thing he never failed at. It offered him respite when he was struggling in his personal life.

At least it normally did. But recently, he hadn't quite been able to work himself to the point that nothing else really mattered.

The past two days were proof of that.

After Dianna rushed out Friday night, leaving him with a pan of warm cinnamon rolls and an ache in his gut, he'd done everything he could think of to keep himself busy, expecting it to take the edge off her abrupt retreat. All he'd ended up accomplishing was staying up most of the night and accidentally mislaying two rows of tile in his bathroom.

Griffin tipped his head toward the ATV they'd just finished working on. "How about you get that out of here so we can service the next one."

He'd been thrilled as hell when he showed up at Troy and Amelie's and discovered that his son was hoping they could give each of the ranch's work vehicles a run-through, making sure they were ready for the upcoming winter months. It meant he would have plenty to occupy his time and his mind. But even after two nights of barely sleeping and two days of working himself to death, he was still struggling to think of anything but Dianna.

Troy started up the engine and pulled out of the building, circling around to the carport that ran up one side where they parked all the side-by-sides. Griffin leaned against the wall, waiting for his son to return with the final one, wiping across his perpetually stained fingernails as he waited.

Was that why Dianna raced off like she did? Had she finally realized he wasn't worth spending time with? It had happened more times than he could count, and always came out of nowhere, a whole lot like Friday night did.

Except he and Dianna hadn't really been spending time together. They'd actually both gone to great lengths to make it clear they were nothing more than friends.

Friends who occasionally accidentally fucked.

He stepped out of the way as Troy backed the final UTV into their workspace. Once the engine was shut off and the hood was up, they got to work, spending the next hour changing out the oil and making sure everything was working in perfect order before lining it up with the rest of its cohorts.

When all their tools were cleaned and back in place, they made their way to the house where Amelie and her grandmother had just gotten back from spending the day in town. He helped them carry in groceries, doing his best to pretend everything was normal.

And maybe it would have been normal if Dianna had actually left her house after rushing from his. But her claims that she forgot to do something at The Baking Rack were clearly not true since she'd never actually left her house. That meant there was another reason she'd run out on him.

"I didn't realize how late it was." Amelie leaned back against the counter, blowing out a breath. "I haven't even thought of what to make for dinner."

"I don't need dinner." Griffin immediately seized the opportunity. He usually spent Sundays with Troy and Amelie, leaving after dinner and dessert, but right now he was itching to get home. Itching to find out why Dianna walked out like she did. "I should actually get back and finish tiling the shower so I can have that upstairs bathroom running this winter." It sounded like a reasonable excuse to cut out early.

But that's all it was. An excuse.

His reasons for leaving had nothing to do with tile or his bathroom, even though it probably should since he desperately needed to have a working shower. But he needed to know why Dianna left like she did more. He needed to know how to get back to their morning talks over coffee and their evenings on her back porch swing. Their time together was important to him. Their friendship—

The word grated. Peeled at his hide in a way that burned.

Because Dianna wasn't his friend. She was so much more than that.

And she'd walked out of his house like the time they spent together didn't matter to her at all.

"Well we wouldn't want you to have to keep showering in the backyard all winter." Amelie grinned at him, oblivious to the foul mood gripping him tight. "Do you need help? I'm sure Troy could—"

"No way. You guys stay here and enjoy your evening." He grabbed his jacket and his keys. "Let me know if there's anything I can do to help you out or if you have any more issues with any of those side-by-sides." He slapped Troy on the shoulder, giving Amelie and her grandmother a wave as he let himself out the back door. It took everything he had not to run to his truck. Now that he decided he was upset over Dianna walking out the way she did, he couldn't wait to find out why she'd left him.

Why she wasn't struggling with this the same way he was.

Even though he was pushing the speeds of the country roads way past their limit, the drive back to his house took forever. By the time he pulled into his driveway his teeth were grinding together in frustration. How could she be so detached? How could she be so completely unbothered by the fact that they couldn't explore what was between them?

And there was definitely something between them.

He shoved open the door to his truck, getting out of the cab and slamming the door. He was halfway across his front yard before he noticed the car sitting in Dianna's driveway.

It wasn't just any car. It was a cruiser for the local police department.

All the anger and turmoil bled from his body, replaced immediately with a level of fear he'd never experienced before.

Griffin immediately started to run, racing from his yard to Dianna's, taking the stairs to her porch in two giant leaps before yanking open the screen door and rushing inside. "Di?"

"Griffin?" Dianna's voice was close and filled with surprise. "Is everything okay?"

He turned to find her standing right beside him, looking healthy and whole.

Relief sagged his shoulders as he gripped the front of her shirt, using the hold to yank her body against his. He held her close, burying his face in her hair as he took a deep breath. "I saw the car in the driveway and I thought something happened. I thought you were hurt."

Dianna stiffened against him, her hands gently patting his back. "No, I'm fine." She wiggled loose, pressing one palm to his chest as she stepped out of his embrace, her eyes moving to the couch.

The couch where a strange man sat.

"Griffin, this is Cooper Staks. He's Nate's cousin. His grandmother was Vera, the woman who owned your house." She turned to the cop, giving him a smile that made Griffin's gut burn. "Cooper, this is Griffin Fraley. My new neighbor."

Cooper stood, looking him over before reaching one hand out. "Nice to meet you. Nate had a lot of good things to say about you."

Griffin shook Cooper's hand, squeezing it a little tighter than he probably should have. "I'm surprised I didn't meet you when everyone was over here helping move Vera's stuff out." It was a dig. One he might be ashamed of dishing out later. But not now. Not when Cooper had just been sitting so fucking close to Dianna, looking at her like she was the best thing he'd ever seen.

She probably was. But looking was all he was ever going to do to her.

"Yeah." Cooper hooked his thumbs into the

armholes of his vest. "I work nights, so I wasn't available to help as much as I wish I had been." He worked his jaw from side to side, continuing to hold Griffin's gaze. "That's a big place for one person. You planning on selling the house when you're done? Makin' some quick cash?"

Griffin crossed his arms, standing to his full height. "Nope." He lifted his chin. "I decided I like the neighborhood. Probably gonna live here until I die."

"I feel the same way about my place." Cooper lifted his own chin and rocked back on his heels. "I bought it because it was big enough to raise a family in."

The words seemed casual, but their meaning was clear. Cooper was reminding him he was old as fuck. That his days of creating a family had passed him by.

If he were a better man he'd take the reminder and back down. Leave Cooper and Dianna to whatever conversation they were having.

But he definitely wasn't a good man. Especially where Dianna was concerned.

"Must be tough. Can't imagine there's too many women lining up to make babies with a man who works nights." It was a low blow, especially considering Cooper worked a job that was dangerous and often thankless.

But this was war.

Cooper seemed unbothered by the jab. He shot Griffin a wide grin. "Not as tough as you might think." He turned to Dianna, putting all his focus on her in a way that made Griffin feel dangerously close to needing bail money. "I'm happy to hear you haven't had any problems." His voice lowered, as if it was just the two of them in the room. "You still have my card. Call me if you need anything." He shifted closer. "And I mean anything."

It was said in a casual enough way. One anyone else might have mistaken as a neighborly offer. But Griffin saw it for exactly what it was, and the offer Cooper was making Dianna was anything but neighborly.

Dianna smiled back at Cooper, the expression threatening to turn his back molars to dust as his jaw clenched tighter. "I will." She reached out to rest one hand on Cooper's arm. "Thank you for coming by. I really appreciate it."

It took everything he had not to relieve Officer Staks of the appendage Dianna was currently touching. He had no right to be so bothered by another man sitting in her house, but hell if he could change the reaction.

And hell if he wanted it to happen again.

Cooper turned to him, offering an easy smile as he slapped Griffin on the shoulder. "Nice to meet you. Might want to get a dog so that big house doesn't start to feel too lonely."

He'd come close to landing his ass in jail on more than one occasion, but never as close as he was in this moment.

"I'm sure I'll find someone to keep me company." He stayed in place as Dianna walked Cooper to the door, refusing to budge until the police officer was in his car and backing out of the driveway.

"Why was he here?"

Dianna closed the main door before turning to face him. One dark brow slowly lifted. "Because we're friends. I've lived next door to his grandmother for over a year. He would always check on me when he checked on her."

Griffin snorted. "I'm sure he did." He wanted to ask if she'd fucked the younger, more attractive cop. The question was on the tip of his tongue. But he wasn't here to hurt her, and that question would most definitely hurt. So he bit it back, dying a little inside at the thought of Cooper touching Dianna the way he had.

"It's his job to check on people and make sure they're doing okay." Dianna stared him down, her chin tipped at a defiant angle. "They pay him to do that."

"First of all, he hasn't clocked in yet if he works nights, so no one's paying him to do shit right now." Griffin moved closer, unable to stay away. "And second of all, he doesn't need to check on you. I'm right next door. I'm there to make sure you're okay."

He was the one she could call if she needed something. He was the one who could make sure she was safe. He was the one right beside her day in and day out.

Dianna's eyes narrowed, her gaze fixed on his face. "Why are you acting like this?"

"Because he doesn't need to come here." Griffin barely reined himself in. "He doesn't need to waste his time checking on someone who's already taken care of."

"So coming to see me was a waste of his time?" There was a slight edge to her voice. One that made it clear he was coming dangerously close to crossing the line. But at this point there were so many fucking lines he couldn't keep track of all of them.

"I'm saying it's a waste for him to come see you." He moved in more, needing to remind them both of all they'd shared. "He needs to go find some other woman to visit."

Dianna stared up at him, silent for a second. "He comes here because he wants me to go out to dinner with him."

"Of course he does. That's what every fucking single man in Moss Creek wants." Griffin shook his head. "That doesn't make him special enough to sit here on the couch with you."

He might be new to Moss Creek, but he'd been around long enough to know Dianna was on just about every available man's radar. Between her looks, her temperament, and her skills in the kitchen, she was exactly what most men were looking for.

But most men didn't deserve her.

They didn't realize how hard she worked to be strong. How difficult it was for her to stick up for herself. How she would get herself into messes because of the fearless way she tackled whatever life put in her path, whether it was asshole exes, leaking pipes, or friendly squirrels.

Only he knew all that.

Only he knew how to take care of her the way she needed.

The way she deserved.

FIFTEEN

DIANNA

THE SHOCK OF Griffin barging into her house was beginning to wear off, but only a little.

"I thought you were at Troy's."

He spent every Sunday from sunup to sundown out at Cross Creek with Troy. It was why she'd been outside puttering around in the flowerbeds when Cooper pulled up. She wasn't worried about having an awkward run-in with Griffin.

"I came home early." His eyes moved over her, like he was looking for something. "How long was Cooper here?"

She understood what was happening, but couldn't really wrap her head around the cause of it. "Not long." She took a steadying breath, digging down deep until she found the tiniest hint of the goddess she was working so hard to remember she was.

And goddesses didn't take shit from anybody. Including tall, gorgeous, jealous neighbors.

"And it doesn't matter how long he was here. This is my house. I'm allowed to have anyone I choose inside of it."

She'd been controlled before. Allowed a man to run her life, her business, and her brain. It broke her. Shattered her into so many pieces it was taking forever to put them all back together again. There was no way she would let it happen again.

"Fuck." Griffin raked one hand through his hair, squeezing his eyes shut as he stepped back. "I know I don't have any right to question you like this." His fingers gripped the silvery strands at the top of his head, pulling tight before falling away. "But—" His jaw clenched tight, lips pressing together as they sealed off whatever he was about to say.

But she wanted to know. No. Make that, *needed* to know.

"But, what?"

When she'd heard a vehicle slowing down while she was pulling weeds from around the mums blooming in the front bed, her heart skipped a beat and sent her straight to her feet, spinning to face the new arrival. When it was Cooper's cruiser instead of Griffin's pickup, the disappointment that hit her was swift and strong.

And telling.

Griffin shook his head, eyes dropping to the floor. "Nothing."

He went silent.

They were stuck. Caught at an impasse. Wedged against the goals they each had and the plans they used to shape their lives.

"No." Dianna stood a little taller, unwilling to let it go. "You came all the way over here, barged right into my house, the least you can do is tell me what you were going to say."

Her voice was a little shaky, but she still got the words out. Still fought to be the woman she so desperately wanted to become. A woman who didn't let anyone walk all over her. A woman who didn't brush things off or avoid important conversations just because they would be uncomfortable.

And this was an important conversation. Griffin didn't show up on her doorstep to be friendly. He wasn't standing in her living room because this was a casual drop-in. He was here because it bothered him that she was with Cooper.

And she was going to make him tell her why.

"But, what?"

Griffin's nostrils flared as he stretched one hand toward the door. "He doesn't even really know you, Di."

Her brows jumped up in surprise. "He's known me longer than you have. What do you mean he doesn't know me?"

"I mean he doesn't know you." Griffin dropped his arm to his side as he stalked back toward her. "He doesn't know you try to fix pipes instead of calling a plumber because you don't want to bother anybody. He doesn't know you spend hours on your back porch trying to make the squirrels and birds come to you." He kept coming, closing every bit of the gap between them in a few swift steps. "And I'm willing to bet he doesn't know the way you like your clit licked or the sounds you make when you come."

All the air rushed from her lungs, and it was suddenly impossible to replace it. That definitely escalated quickly.

But things usually did with Griffin. One minute they would be having a conversation, the next, part of her clothes would be missing.

But maybe that was by design. Maybe Griffin used sex to avoid difficult discussions.

"You are correct. He definitely doesn't know those last two things, but," Dianna fought to keep her focus, "you don't actually know me either."

Sure, he caught her at a few vulnerable moments then gleaned some information about who she was, but Griffin didn't really know who she was deep down. He didn't know about the insecurities she fought every day. The fear that she would never feel good enough. The desire to find a way to be fine again.

Griffin was silent, but his gaze was intense as it fixed on her face. "Then let me know you."

The request was soft and simple.

And completely and utterly terrifying.

"I don't know that I even know me."

It was a confession she hadn't made to anyone,

including the therapist who worked so hard to help her recover from the abuse Martin put her through. Somewhere in all that mess she'd lost herself. Bits and pieces of the woman she was were chipped away with every insult and every belittling word until there was so little left she couldn't make sense of it all.

But Griffin didn't seem to understand the gravity of the revelation. His lips curved into a little smile as he reached up to tease the tips of his fingers along her cheek. "Then shouldn't someone?"

It was a simple suggestion, and one that would do her absolutely no good. "How can I tell you who I am if I don't even know?"

Griffin's lips lifted a little more, like he wasn't seeing the flaw in his plan. "What's your favorite thing to bake?"

Dianna blinked, thrown off by the change in conversation. "What?"

"What's your favorite thing to bake?" Griffin repeated the question and it was just as confusing the second time.

"Are you trying to distract me?"

"No." Griffin caught a strand of hair that had fallen loose of the messy bun at the top of her head, twisting it around his fingers. "I'm getting to know you."

"And you want to know what my favorite thing to bake is? That doesn't seem very deep or like it would tell you much about me." His intent was sweet, but his system was flawed.

"I disagree." Griffin slowly inhaled, the action almost seeming to steady him. "My favorite thing you bake is the red velvet brownies with cream cheese frosting."

It was an interesting choice considering it was one of her least popular items. To the point that she didn't make them anymore. "Are you a big fan of red velvet?"

Griffin shook his head. "No. You had them the day I first came to Moss Creek and I ate one as I drove out to meet my son for the first time. Those brownies remind me of that day."

Oh.

Dianna took a shaky breath, trying to steady the emotion already attempting to tighten her throat. "My favorite thing to bake is angel food cake."

It was a somewhat difficult recipe, not conducive to mass production unless you coordinated it with a plan involving custard to use up all the egg yolks. But that wasn't the real reason she never made it at The Baking Rack.

The actual reason felt too personal. Too special to share. So she kept it for herself, holding it close.

But maybe hiding away all the best moments of her life made it easier for the bad ones to take up the space in her head.

"It was the first thing my grandmother taught me how to bake and I was the only person she ever shared her recipe with." Dianna swallowed hard, hoping to steady the waver in her voice before adding on the full scope of why she was so fiercely protective of anything her grandmother's memory touched. "She's the only one who's ever really loved me just the way I am."

The admission was painful, but entirely true. Everyone else in her life wanted her to be different. What they considered better. They all found her lacking and in need of improvement.

Everyone but her grandmother.

"Sounds like she was a smart woman."

Dianna's eyes jumped to meet Griffin's. She'd almost expected him to argue. To point out that certainly everyone thought she was fine just the way she was. But he hadn't.

And somehow that was better.

She smiled, a little of the weight pressing in on her lungs lifting. "I'd like to think so."

"I mean, she didn't get to see how your friendship with Snickerdoodle worked out. She might have changed her opinion if she had." Griffin gave her one of the lopsided smiles that always made her heart skip a beat. "But my guess is she would've thought that was fantastic too."

He wasn't far off.

Dianna pressed her lips together, another fond memory easily sliding into place. "She's the reason I feed the squirrels and the birds. She did the same thing."

Her grandmother had been one of the happiest people she'd ever known. Part of her thought if she just tried hard enough, she would find the same joy. But it turned out not to be so simple.

Griffin lifted his brows. "So it's her fault Snickerdoodle broke into your house."

Dianna laughed, unable to stop the sound. "Honestly, she would've probably found it hilarious."

"I think I would've liked this woman." Griffin's touch teased down the side of her neck. "Tell me more about her."

"Maybe later." Dianna grabbed the front of his shirt, giving him a little push. "If you get to know me better, I should get to know you better too."

Griffin scoffed. "I already told you what my favorite thing you bake is."

Dianna let her head tip back, eyes rolling to the ceiling. "Then it's your turn again."

"Fine." Griffin's expression sobered the tiniest bit. "Ask me a question."

There were so many possibilities. Enough that it should be difficult to narrow down to one.

But it wasn't.

"Have you ever been married?" It was hard to imagine Griffin as a husband, but also impossible to imagine it never happened. He was kind and funny and hard-working. And horribly attractive. The chances a woman hadn't found a way to legally bind herself to him seemed slim.

And for some reason that irritated the shit out of her. Possibly in the exact same way Cooper irritated the shit out of Griffin.

"No." Griffin's voice carried a hint of regret. "Never been married." He focused on where he touched her, eyes following the path of his fingers across her skin. "Never even got close."

She struggled not to find the same focus he did, but allowing herself to think about Griffin touching her was a slippery slope. One that had so far landed her half naked and completely satisfied. "Really?"

Griffin's blue eyes lifted to hers. "Is that surprising?"

"I mean," she fished around for an eloquent response that wouldn't show too much of what was bouncing around her brain, but couldn't come up with anything, "yeah. It is."

Griffin's gaze stayed on hers. "Why?"

"I just would have thought it would've happened." His touch slid lower, following the deep V cut of her T-shirt in a dangerously distracting way that sent her brain on autopilot. "You are exactly what most women are looking for."

"And what are most women looking for?" Griffin's fingers skimmed along the swell of her breast where it pushed up from the lace attempting to contain it.

"Someone kind and funny and hard-working." She rattled off three of the major points, managing to leave off the final one that focused on Griffin's less important attributes. Having a nice body was great and all, but nothing lasted forever, and a person's physical shape didn't actually say a whole lot about them outside of how easily they could reach things on a high shelf.

"So that's what you think of me?" He teased along her flesh with a whisper-light touch. "That I'm nice?"

"You are nice." She managed to inhale as Griffin's finger worked dangerously close to her nipple. "You hired that company to come help me clean up The Baking Rack when I broke the pipe."

"That wasn't me being nice, Di." His hand spread across her body, each point of contact driving her a little more toward the brink. "That was me trying to preserve my own sanity."

"It was still nice." She closed her eyes as his palm curved against her, the heat of his skin soaking through her shirt and bra. "And you helped me get Snickerdoodle out of my house."

"He was on my head. My options were limited." Griffin's thumb rubbed across her nipple, pinching at it through the layers between them. "I know you want to think I am, but I'm not a nice man, Di."

It made her a little sad that he didn't see it. Made her wonder if maybe his story was a lot like hers.

"Well I think you're a nice man." She tilted her head back, lifting her chin as she looked him in the eye. "And I'm allowed to think whatever I want."

She understood what happened when other people shaped how you saw yourself. How it affected you. How difficult it was to get past all their noise.

Griffin's eyes moved over her face. "I'm afraid you're going to be disappointed."

She wasn't backing down. Wasn't giving in to Griffin's demons any more than she would give in to her own. "That's my problem then, isn't it?"

Griffin's hand stilled before slowly sliding up to curve around her face. "You're something special, Di. I hope you know that."

She almost brushed the compliment off. Almost pushed it aside like she had so many others, choosing to keep the lies she carried instead. The lies had been there so long they were comfortable. They were known.

But they were heavy as hell and she was tired of carrying them.

So she smiled, letting his words sink deep enough that someday she might hear them first. "Thank you."

SIXTEEN

GRIFFIN

DIANNA WASN'T COMPLETELY wrong when she said he didn't know her. If he had to list her favorite food or where she was born he would fail miserably. But deep down he knew who she was. It was easy to see and impossible to forget.

Unfortunately, it didn't seem like she knew him in the same way. Somehow she'd decided he was nice. Kind.

He wanted to argue with her. Fight until she understood the truth. Spare her having to make that discovery on her own. But it was getting harder and harder to do the things he knew he should. Especially when those things would push Dianna away.

"Why is your shirt so dirty?" Dianna's fingers traced along a smudge of grease smeared across his chest.

"I helped Troy work on some engines at the ranch."

His eyes drifted to the hand he had on her face. His nails were rough and permanently tinted from spending years in oil and grime. They definitely weren't the kind of hands Dianna deserved to be touched with, but he couldn't make himself pull away.

"I'm a little dirty too." She glanced down at the T-shirt and shorts she wore. "I was out working in the yard when Cooper pulled in."

He wanted to ask how many times Cooper had tried to take her out. How often he showed up to make another request. Jealousy wasn't an emotion he had to fight with much in his life, and now that it decided to rear its ugly head he was understanding why it caused so many wars.

"I should probably take a shower." Dianna pulled from his hold. She took a couple of steps backward, sliding a loose bit of hair behind one ear as she went.

It wasn't how he wanted the night to end, but it was better than it ending with Cooper still sitting on her sofa. "I should go take one too."

Dianna reached out, snagging the front of his shirt. "You could take one with me."

He hadn't reminded her she'd offered to let him use her shower, even when the nights were freezing cold, because he knew exactly how that would end every single time. Part of him believed he'd be able to keep this thing between them under control if he stayed away.

Obviously that part of him was real wrong.

Griffin let her drag him along, offering up no resistance as Dianna pulled him down the hall of her little house. She led him into the first room on the right, flipping on the light to reveal a seafoam green bathroom. The original tile work would be attention grabbing under normal circumstances, but he barely even noticed it. The second the door was closed, Dianna reached down, grabbed the hem of her T-shirt and peeled it up over her head, immediately bringing all his focus to the heavy swell of her tits. He'd fucked his own hand to the memory of them more times than he could count, imagining what it would be like to shove his way between them, fucking the soft, creamy flesh while he teased her nipples to tight peaks.

That was part of the problem with Dianna. It wasn't just the way she looked that appealed to him, but also who she was, and the combination of it all made him weak as hell.

Dianna moved in close, grabbing his T-shirt the same way she had hers and lifting it up. "It was nice of you to help Troy today."

"I'm his dad. I'm supposed to help him."

"You say that, but there are plenty of dads who don't help their kids." She pushed his shirt higher, wrestling it until he had no choice but to lift both arms over his head. Once it was cleared and tossed to the floor she reached for the front of his jeans, continuing the conversation. "My parents don't help me." She flipped the button loose. "Actually, they barely talk to me at all."

Part of him had hoped Dianna had some support system he hadn't yet seen, and learning that she didn't even have her own parents to rely on sat uncomfortably in his gut. "Then they're fucking idiots."

The words were out of his mouth before he realized he shouldn't have said them. That was the way it always worked. He was always one to talk first and think later. That was why it was just easiest for him to not say anything.

But Dianna wasn't bothered by his tough words. She laughed, the sound too light for the conversation they were having. "Probably. That's why I'm not too upset over the fact we don't really talk to each other anymore." She raked down his zipper. "Being around my mother isn't great for me anyway, so it's for the best."

He held still as she shoved at his pants, caught in a weird situation where he didn't know what to say, but he wanted to know more. Wanted to know why Dianna wasn't upset over not having a relationship with her parents. "Was she not around when you were young?"

Dianna shoved his pants down to his ankles. "Oh no, she was definitely around."

He kicked away his boots and jeans, focused on what she was saying, not only because he wanted to know about her and her life, but also because of the insight it might provide him. "Then she just wasn't involved?"

"She was definitely involved." Dianna reached into the tub/shower combo to switch on the water. "She always had a lot to say." She slid the curtain back into place and faced him. "Very little of it was ever good."

He struggled to imagine anyone having a harsh word

to say about Dianna, let alone her own fucking mother. "Then she's definitely an idiot."

He didn't feel bad about saying it this time. He'd be hard-pressed to find anything about Dianna that wasn't perfect, and he was just some guy who lived next door. Discovering that her mother could not only find things, but also pointed them out, was unimaginable.

"So," Dianna moved in close again, her fingers toying with the waistband of his boxers, "now you see why I said helping Troy today was nice."

It was getting harder to argue with her reasoning. "He's my son. I don't want him to ever have a reason to not want me in his life."

Dianna's soft touch moved up his chest, sliding over his pecs to curve around his face. "So you're nice, funny, hard-working, and a good dad." She smiled, the expression brightening up the clouds hovering around him. "And anyone who doesn't see that is a fucking idiot too."

He grabbed her, pulling her body against his. "I'll be sure to tell them." Reaching behind her, he unhooked the clasp of her bra before skimming the straps down her arms to release the lush fullness of her tits. "Fuck, these things are magnificent."

Dianna laughed, the sound dying off in a squeak when he tipped his head to catch one tip in his mouth. Her nipples were dark and large, the skin of them smooth against his tongue for a split second before starting to pucker, tightening more with each pull of his mouth. It felt like he hadn't touched her in forever, but it had barely been two weeks. Two weeks of pretending he was fine being her friend. Two weeks of pumping his cock in bed at night to the memory of what it felt like to push into the wet heat of her body.

Two weeks of wondering if he'd ever get a moment like this again.

He grabbed the waistband of her shorts, gripping her panties along with them as he shoved everything down, getting Dianna fully naked for the first time. Clothing had been another thing he thought might keep him from losing his path. A barrier he hoped would keep him from losing sight of what was important.

He was wrong about that too, and at this point, there was no fighting it.

Dianna was already under his skin and digging deeper with every breath she took.

Griffin hauled her toward the shower, tangling in the curtain as he tried to get them into the damn thing.

Dianna held him tight, her head falling back on a laugh as he cursed his way under the spray, dragging her along with him. She continued to laugh as he wrestled the curtain back into place, fighting with the rings as they caught on the rod.

"You have more problems with showers than anyone I've ever met." She shivered as the overspray clung to her skin and hair.

"It's not the showers, it's the damn curtains." He wrapped one arm around her and braced the other against the wall as he turned, switching out their places so she was under the warmth of the water. "I'm putting in all glass screens next door."

She leaned into him, pressing those glorious tits against his chest. "Sounds pretty." She teased the tips of her fingers over his skin. "Will you take your underwear off when you use them?"

His head bobbed back in confusion, but a second later the wet cling of cotton registered.

He'd been struggling from the beginning when it came to her. It was why they'd never made it to a bed and why he had to fight to keep from coming the second she was tight around him.

Sex had always been simple. An easy way to offer the women in his life the connection they wanted. One that didn't require more than he was willing to give. He worked hard to be good at it. Good enough to make up for the things he wasn't as skilled at.

But never once in his life had he forgotten to take his underwear off in the shower.

"You fuck my head all up, Di." He stripped away the last barrier between them, wringing the shorts out in his fist before tossing them over the rod. "I don't know if I'm coming or going when you're around."

A sly smile twisted across her full lips. "So far it's usually been coming."

He laced both hands in her hair, using the hold to pull her close, the soft curve of her belly sliding against the length of his cock. "Was that a dirty joke?" He leaned in to trace his lips along the line of her neck. "Am I corrupting you?"

Dianna didn't seem to have a huge amount of experience when it came to sex, which was fine with him. He had no problem being the one to broaden her horizons. He loved it actually.

"Why didn't you come use my shower?" Dianna skimmed her hands up his arms.

Griffin moved in closer, fingers teasing against the junction of her thighs. "I'm asking myself that same question right now."

Dianna grabbed his wrist, gently pulling his hand away from her body. "That's not an answer."

He was a little thrown off.

Once a woman started to realize he'd rather fuck her within an inch of her life than talk, her reaction was usually one of anger. One that resulted in her hurling all kinds of insults at him. Calling him manipulative. Stunted. Selfish. When that didn't lead to him splitting himself open to offer the metaphorical bleeding they wanted, they started to hurl actual things. Things like plates and clothing. The first one at him, the second one out the window.

And while it seemed like Dianna might be figuring out one of his many, many flaws, her method of addressing it was much different. But it still didn't make him want to bleed. There was too much to even consider letting out. Too many regrets. Too many mistakes. Too much hurt and too much pain. It was like finding a suspicious Tupperware container at the back of your refrigerator, one you haven't seen in longer than you can remember. You don't pry open the lid and inspect the contents. You just chuck the whole thing in the trash and forget it ever existed. It was easier to go buy another container. To move on without digging through the mess and trying to clean it up.

"Don't you want me to touch you, Dianna?" Griffin let his lips brush against her ear. "It seems like maybe you forgot how good I can make you feel."

He tried to work his other hand in the direction of her chest, planning to find the tight pucker of a nipple to remind her of how good they were like this.

But again, Dianna snagged his wrist, holding it tight as she shook her head. "Not until you tell me why you didn't come here to shower."

He was stuck. She'd given him a boundary and never in his life would he touch a woman without her approval. That left him two options:

Give her what she wanted.

Or walk out in the hope that she would forget this whole night and tomorrow would go back to normal.

But even if she didn't fully believe it, he did know Dianna. And he knew she would bring this right back up the next time their paths crossed.

So he could either pull back the lid or accept that he'd never touch her again.

Griffin tipped his head, lifting his eyes to the ceiling. "I just want to be a good dad, Di." He leveled his eyes on hers. "I knew coming over here would be a slippery slope and I was trying to keep myself from sliding down it."

Dianna slowly released one of his hands. "But it was just a shower."

He shook his head. "It wouldn't have been just a shower. You know that." Their attraction was undeniable and encompassing. "We can't stay away from each other. We've tried."

Dianna's eyes held his as tiny streams of water slid along her cheeks and down her neck. "Then maybe we should stop trying."

Thinking it himself was one thing, but hearing her say it was another. He might've been able to stay the path if it had been just him wanting to take the trail, but now—

Griffin reached behind Dianna to shut off the water before yanking the shower curtain open. He grabbed her and dragged her along with him, moving out of the bathroom and into the hall.

Not once had he fucked her properly, and maybe that was on purpose. Another way he tricked himself into thinking this was a controllable situation. But it wasn't. Never had been. And accepting that made something inside him snap. Broke the levee he'd built and sent everything rushing through.

He wanted her too badly. Naked under him as he fucked her, over and over.

Thankfully the next door down was a bedroom. He pulled her in, going straight to the mattress and toppling their tangled bodies onto it.

His brain tried to feed him directions, reminding him of all the things he should do to distract Dianna from all the ways he was lacking, but it was impossible to focus. Impossible to think of anything but finding his way inside her.

He spread her soft thighs wide, running his dick

along the slickness of her folds before spearing into her wet heat with one rough thrust.

Dianna gasped, reaching up to grip the headboard with one hand as he set a brutal pace. Her free hand grabbed at the blanket under her back as he pressed his thumb to her clit. "You're going to come with me, Di, understand?"

She whimpered what sounded like an agreement. It wasn't good enough. If she was going to make him talk, he was going to return the favor.

"Say it." He rested one palm against her chest, pinning her in place as he drove into her over and over. "I want to hear the words come out of your mouth."

"I will." The words were followed by a gasp as he shifted, changing the angle of his thrusts.

"You will, what?" He needed to hear it. Needed to know she was still right there with him.

Dianna's back arched on a little cry as he found the spot inside her body he was seeking. "I'll come with you."

"That's right." He clenched his teeth, fighting the pull of his balls and the urge to chase his own climax. "I want to feel your pussy milk me dry."

A rush of air left Dianna's lungs as her plush thighs flexed against his hips and the sound of their joining bodies grew louder, wetter.

"You like that? You like hearing all the filthy things I want from you, Di?"

Her eyes met his. "Yes."

He held her gaze, unable to look away as her lips parted, back arching. "Griffin. I'm—"

It was the only warning he needed. He was so close to the edge, the squeeze of her body shoved him right over, cock jerking as he buried his face in her hair, thrusting long after he'd come because he couldn't seem to stop.

Which was par for the course when it came to Dianna.

SEVENTEEN

DIANNA

DIANNA CLOSED THE bathroom door, leaning back against it as she let out the breath she'd been holding. She'd finally wiggled her way from the tangle of Griffin's limbs and crept out of the bedroom, doing her absolute best not to wake him up. He probably wanted to sleep since they'd been up the majority of the night, giving her antique bed frame a run for its money.

She flipped on the light and twisted on the shower, cringing a little as the pipes in her aging house banged around. Dianna held her breath, listening for any sign the sound had woken up the man sleeping in the next room.

When everything continued to be quiet, she slipped off her pajamas and stepped under the spray. She scrubbed down, keeping her hair out of the way since the blow dryer would be loud and it was just going up on top of her head anyway. When she reached the spot between her legs, she winced at the dull ache lingering there.

She'd never had sex so many times in a row and her chafed, slightly swollen flesh was protesting. She gave it a careful wash before pulling the removable showerhead free and lowering the temperature, giving her nethers a cool rinse that soothed a little of the throb.

Marathon fucking sounded great in theory, but man was the fallout brutal.

Once she was clean and rinsed, Dianna put the shower head back in place and shut the water off, grabbing a towel as she stepped out. She had her morning routine down to a science since it came at such a ridiculously early hour. Start to finish, it took less than fifteen minutes to get lotioned up, dressed, her hair artfully piled at the top of her head, and the light makeup she preferred applied.

Once her used towel was looped over a hook and her counter was straightened up, she flipped off the light and cracked open the door, planning to creep her way back out.

But the scent of bacon had her pulling the door wide. She stepped out into the hall, peeking around the corner into her bedroom to find the bed empty, and the covers smoothed into place.

He'd made her bed?

Dianna turned toward the kitchen, moving quietly, the sound of sizzling meat getting louder as she moved. Her foot had barely hit the linoleum when the smoke alarm above her head started to scream, the wail sending her jumping back as her heart attempted to break free of her chest.

"Goddammit." Griffin fumbled around the counter, grabbing one of the large cookbooks she kept next to the stove and lifting it above his head. He'd just started to fan when his eyes landed on her.

"Good morning." She glanced at the smoking pan. "Everything okay?"

"I was trying to make you breakfast." He gave up fanning and reached to pop the battery free, leaving it to dangle from the wires holding it in place before turning to the stove. "Shit." Griffin grabbed the burning pan of bacon and carried it out the back door, chucking the charred meat over their shared fence and into his backyard. He set the pan on the cement patio before coming back in, pausing to glance back outside. "I figured you didn't want your house to smell like burnt bacon."

Dianna smiled, feeling relieved and happy and flattered all at the same time. "It wouldn't be the first time."

She expected this morning to be awkward. It was part of the reason she'd been working so hard to keep Griffin asleep. She'd also been a little worried he might go right back to his old habits and clam up, holding back anything he wanted to say. And that might still happen. But finding him standing in her kitchen wearing her well-worn apron around his hips, meant things had definitely changed. Maybe moved forward a little, as terrifying as that was.

Dianna went toward him, reaching out to finger the

ruffled edge of the fabric covering his front. "You look good in my grandma's apron."

Griffin went still. "I'm sorry. I didn't know this was hers." He reached behind him. "I can take it off."

"No." Dianna grabbed his forearms, sliding her hands over his skin. "It's fine. She would probably love that you're wearing it while you make me breakfast."

Her grandma hadn't lived long enough to see her get married, but she'd witnessed more than a few of Dianna's failed relationships and never hesitated to tell her she was settling.

And she had been.

But she couldn't help but believe her grandmother wouldn't have had as easy of a time finding fault with Griffin.

She glanced at the eggs and bread sitting on the counter. "I thought you didn't know how to cook."

Griffin lifted his brows. "I feel like it's pretty clear that I don't." He reached out to stroke her cheek. "But I wanted to try. You cook for everyone else. I thought it might be nice to have someone cook for you." His eyes moved over her face and hair. "You look pretty."

Yeah. Her grandmother definitely would've had a hard time finding fault with Griffin. "Thank you."

It was getting easier to accept compliments, maybe because she was so hopeful they could replace the negativity she'd allowed to collect. It seemed to be working though, so she wasn't going to complain.

"What were you trying to make me?"

Griffin pressed his lips together before sighing.

"Nothing impressive. Just a bacon egg and cheese sandwich." He lifted one shoulder, letting it drop. "It didn't seem too difficult when I googled it."

"You googled how to make a breakfast sandwich?" It shouldn't be as touching as it was, but the fact that Griffin not only tried to do something he didn't know how to do for her, but also researched it in the hope he could accomplish it well, warmed her insides.

And also proved just how low she'd allowed the bar to drop.

"I probably shouldn't have admitted that." Griffin's eyes went into the backyard once again. "Especially since I fucked it up so royally."

Dianna moved past him, snagging another skillet from the cabinet before settling it onto the burner. "Cooking is hard. It can take years of practice, so I wouldn't feel too bad that you didn't get it right on your first try." She peeled a few pieces of bacon free and lined them down the center of the pan, setting the burner to medium low. "And bacon is actually kind of tricky. Especially if you want it to be crispy."

Griffin watched her intently. "I'm guessing that means you like yours crispy?"

"Definitely." Dianna washed her hands off in the sink, peeking at him over one shoulder. "What about you? How do you like your bacon?"

Griffin shrugged. "I eat it however it comes." He shot her a little grin. "You don't really have the right to be picky when you're not the one doing the cooking."

She dried off her hands, mulling over exactly how

deep she wanted to dig. Normally, she would've stopped there. Decided the only thing that mattered was that Griffin was nice enough to try to make her breakfast and that made him wonderful. But she had a habit of not looking deep enough. Or, maybe looking over things she shouldn't.

"If you don't cook, how have you been eating all these years?"

Griffin kept his eyes on the bacon, staring a little too hard at the meat as it began to sizzle. "Take out."

"All you've ever eaten your whole life is take out?" She wasn't going to believe that. Especially since Griffin seemed to like to skirt around conversations that might be uncomfortable. "I'm sure you've had more than a few women cook you breakfast."

Her rational mind recognized the fact shouldn't bother her. Griffin was grown. He'd lived a full life before moving to Moss Creek. Of course there were women in his past. But the thought of another woman making him breakfast still made her want to smack someone with a spatula.

He tipped his head to one side. "I've lived with a few women over the years. They usually cooked since I worked such long hours." He continued to stare at the bacon, brows pinching together. "I always figured if they were nice enough to cook for me, I should be nice enough to eat it without complaining."

His point of view would've been a revelation to her not long ago. After spending a lifetime around people who loved to pick her and everything she did apart, meeting someone who kept his mouth shut in appreciation would have been impossible for her to comprehend. Or, honestly, believe.

But Griffin did seem to be pretty skilled at keeping his mouth shut. Sometimes to a fault.

"That was probably the right decision." Dianna moved to the nonstick pan Griffin hadn't yet used. She turned the heat on, setting it and letting it warm up as she pulled out her toaster.

"Maybe." Griffin finally pulled his eyes away from the bacon, focusing on hers as he moved in close. "Can I help?" He rested one hand on her lower back. "I don't expect you to cook for me, Di."

"I know that." And she actually did. But like so many other things, it was difficult to break away from the behaviors she'd carried for so long.

Like sneaking out of the bedroom so the man in her bed could sleep.

Like jumping to cook for him.

She slid the carton of eggs his way, determined not to keep making the same mistakes she always did. "How are you at cracking eggs?"

Griffin frowned at the carton. "I'm going to give you one guess."

Dianna laughed, her mood lightening almost immediately. "Then you're on toast duty for now." She snagged the loaf of multigrain bread she'd baked up at work one day during the afternoon lull, sliding it in front of Griffin before going to the fridge. "How do you feel about avocado?"

Griffin gave her a wicked smile. "I feel like I've made it clear I will eat anything that's put in front of me." His hand slid down the curve of her ass. "You're more than welcome to make me prove it though."

Dianna snagged the half left over from yesterday's lunch and passed it off, ignoring his blatant innuendo. "Smash that up with a fork."

Griffin's eyes twinkled as he took the avocado, clearly undaunted. "Yes, ma'am."

They spent the next ten minutes cooking, assembling, and laughing.

Griffin really wasn't exaggerating when he said he couldn't cook. She had to coach him through removing the pit from the avocado and cupping it in his hand while he mashed the tender flesh, using the tough skin as a bowl of sorts.

But Griffin was a good sport about it. He was completely unbothered by the fact that she knew how to do something he didn't. Yet another way he was completely different from any man she'd spent time with before.

By the time they settled onto the swing hanging on her back porch, she was relaxed and looking forward to the day.

Because the voices in her head were finally shutting the fuck up.

Griffin kept one foot on the ground, using it to ease the swing back and forth as they ate, listening to the birds as the sun started to lighten the sky.

"How late do you work tonight?" He passed over her

coffee, waiting for her to take a sip before sliding it back onto the table beside him.

"My best guess is eight." She swallowed down the mouthful of bacony goodness. "The girl I hired has really made a huge difference." She peeked at him from the corner of her eye. "Thank you for pushing me to hire someone."

"I just know what it's like to work yourself to death because you think that's how it has to be." Griffin relaxed back, stretching one arm along the top rail of the swing, his fingers curving to tease against the skin of her neck. "Plus, I was tired of waiting until after midnight to hose myself off in the backyard."

Dianna tipped her head back, resting against his forearm as she laughed. "I can't believe you kept doing that when there was a perfectly functional, heated shower right next door."

"A heated shower that was dangerously close to a woman I have proven I can't resist." Griffin was quiet for a minute, staring across the porch as he continued to swing them.

"I won't get in the way of you being a dad, Griffin." She understood what it was like to feel your focus couldn't be split. "Troy's the most important thing in your life. That's part of why I like you." She wanted to ease his fears. Help Griffin understand she knew what it was like to be afraid of putting too much effort into the wrong place.

Griffin turned to her, and for a second she thought

he might open up a little. Give her a peek under that layer he held so close.

Instead, his eyes dipped down to her plate. "You better finish eating. If you're late and those Cowboys don't get their cinnamon rolls there will be mayhem in the streets of Moss Creek."

"WELL AREN'T YOU chipper today." Janie strode through the door, grinning as she wiggled her brows. "I don't think I have ever walked in here to find you whistling."

Dianna looked up from the batch of cookies she was scooping out onto a tray. For a second she considered denying Janie's accusation, but there was no hiding her good mood. "I've just had a really good day."

Janie hung her purse beside the door and snagged an apron. "What I'm hearing you say is you got laid last night."

Once again, Dianna considered being coy. Holding her secrets close.

But she'd held so many secrets close when it came to men and relationships, none of them good. For once she wanted to be able to be open about what was happening, and she felt like Janie might be her friend—or was at least on the road to becoming one.

"I did get laid last night." She dropped a wad of

dough onto the baking sheet with a thunk, lifting her eyes to where Janie was tying her apron in place. "A few times."

Janie's mouth opened in a surprised smile as she slowly nodded. "*Yes*. Good for you." She blew out a loud sigh. "I was hoping I'd be able to catch myself a dick considering how many cowboys there are around here, but I'm finding out this isn't a great season to be shopping for them."

Dianna dropped another cookie onto the sheet. "I'm not sure any season is good to try to shop for a cowboy. They all seem to work as much as I do." She'd noticed that the men who worked on the ranches surrounding Moss Creek seemed to swarm the city at specific times of the day, and on specific days of the week. "Maybe one day I'll have you come in and help me run the register in the morning." She wiggled her brows. "You'll definitely get to meet plenty of cowboys then."

Janie wrinkled her nose. "I didn't say I wanted to get out of bed early to find one." She went to the large cooler and pulled out the flat of eggs, preparing to mix up the dough for tomorrow's cinnamon rolls. "I kinda just want one to show up in my bedroom occasionally on an as-needed basis."

Dianna laughed again. "Not looking for anything serious?"

Janie blanched. "No. Definitely not." She went to the large mixer in the corner and started measuring in flour. "If I wanted something that refused to communicate with me I'd get a pet rock." She squinted toward the ceiling, thinking for a second. "Actually, a pet rock might emotionally connect with me more than my last boyfriend."

Dianna pressed her lips together, focusing a little more on Janie as she continued laying out cookies. "He wasn't one to open up?"

Janie scoffed as she added in yeast. "That's putting it lightly."

Dianna finished lining up the dough and grabbed the sheet, carrying it toward one of the ovens in the back room. "Why was he so closed off?"

"Because he was an asshole?" Janie shrugged. "Who knows."

Dianna slid the cookies into place and closed the door. "You didn't ask him?"

"Sure I did, but—shocker—he didn't want to talk about it." She snagged the milk from the fridge. "And at a certain point I didn't give a shit anymore."

Is that what would happen with Griffin? He'd given her glimpses of what he thought and how he felt, but that was it. The possibility put a damper on her good mood. She'd settled more times in her life than she could count and wasn't going to do it again.

Breakfast attempts and endless orgasms were nice and all, but if she was going to dip her toe back into the relationship pool it would be with someone who could swim as well as she could.

Because there was no fucking way she was going under the water again.

EIGHTEEN

GRIFFIN

GRIFFIN RUSHED TO the front of his house, glancing out one of the large windows before turning to race back into the single room he'd been living out of for over a month. The microwave beeped just as he reached the doorway, signaling the end of its cook cycle. He crouched down, popping open the door to reach in and stir around the contents, spreading everything out so it would cook evenly before closing the door and resetting the timer.

Not long after Dianna left for the day it started to sink in just how little had been expected of him in his past relationships. He didn't cook. He didn't clean. All he did was pay the bills and provide a physical service just about every man worth his salt was willing to offer.

Sure, he sent flowers and bought gifts, offering up

what amounted to bribery any time a woman asked him for more.

More conversation. More connection. More intimacy.

That's all any of them had ever really wanted from him, and he'd done everything in his power to avoid it.

He'd worked hard to prove he was more than the poor kid with alcoholic parents. More than the man who wasn't smart enough to be in real school and spent his days as part of a co-op program instead. Confessing how all of that still affected him would shine a spotlight on every flaw. Every crack. Every blemish.

Once they saw all that, they'd do the smart thing and walk away.

And he wouldn't have blamed them.

The microwave beeped again, dragging his focus back to the task at hand. He couldn't cook, this morning proved that. Even if he had the means, he didn't have the skill set, but he could make shit work. It was one of the few skills he possessed, so he decided to put it to good use today.

He opened the appliance and checked on its contents, testing to make sure everything was heated through before rotating in the second dish. While it was cooking he raced back through the house, cutting through the dining room on his way to the front windows. He cupped his hands against the glass, peering out into the dusky evening, looking for any hint of headlights. When he didn't find any, he turned and rushed back, repeating the process two more times before finally finishing his task.

Once everything was hot, he set both plates on the makeshift table he'd cobbled together from a pair of sawhorses and a spare piece of wood, using a stick lighter to light the candle he picked up while he was out running errands. Once everything was situated, he hurried back to the front of the house, pulling the door open and stepping onto the porch.

Dianna said she would be home around eight, and it was nearly a quarter after, so hopefully her estimate wasn't far off.

Barely two minutes later a set of headlights cut down the unlined street, easing closer as he strained to make out the vehicle they belonged to. He stood on his darkened porch, waiting as they came closer. He had one foot on the top step when he realized it wasn't Dianna's car, but a police cruiser slowly creeping down the road.

"Fucking Cooper." Griffin leaned against the thick pole bracketing the steps leading from his porch and crossed his arms. Cooper looked straight at him, holding his gaze as he coasted past.

No doubt the younger man was hoping to catch Dianna. Do his best to convince her to give him a shot.

Well he was too fucking late. Someone else already beat him to it. Someone else who was about to do something he'd never done before just for her.

He was about to initiate a conversation—one Dianna would hopefully enjoy, and he would suffer through—

over Mae Pace's reheated meatloaf and mashed potato dinner.

Less than a minute after Cooper's car disappeared, another set of headlights streaked through the darkness. This time the car was moving a little faster. Almost like the driver was in a hurry.

And this time when Griffin's foot hit the top step, he didn't slow down. Not until he reached Dianna's open garage door.

She climbed out of her car, lips twisting into a little smile that made it seem like she was happy to see him. "Fancy seeing you here."

"You haven't seen fancy yet." He tipped his head toward his house. "Come on. I've got dinner for us."

Dianna's chin tucked as she tipped her head to one side. "Are you sure? I don't hear any smoke alarms going off."

Her jab caught him by complete surprise, and he couldn't stop the bark of laughter that sprang free.

He was starting to realize that Dianna's sweet, soft ways weren't the full extent of who she really was. There was so much more to her than what she showed the world. It made it hard to regret what happened last night. Hard to convince himself he was doing the wrong thing by making room for her in his life.

"I'm technically not responsible for the bulk of the preparation." He stepped closer, itchy to get his hands on her after being away from her the whole day. "All I did was reheat Mae's cooking."

Dianna's eyes widened as she shimmied along the side

of her car and squeezed out the tiny gap between the bumper and the frame of the door. "You got us food from The Wooden Spoon?"

"Well I wasn't going to try to cook unsupervised." He snagged her as soon as she cleared the door, pulling her close and brushing his lips across hers. "I'm trying to learn from my mistakes."

Dianna smiled against his mouth. "That makes two of us."

This was the perfect moment to ask about her mistakes. Share some of his own. But he couldn't bring himself to do it.

Especially when the alternative was nipping at her lower lip and slicking his tongue against hers. She tasted just as sweet as she smelled, as if the sugar she worked in every day had become part of her. Plus, he was hoping Officer Cooper might decide to make another pass and get an eyeful of Dianna's body pressed against his.

But as much as he wanted the younger, better-looking man to know he'd missed his chance, he'd been in Moss Creek long enough to know gossip spread around town like wildfire, and the last thing he wanted was for Troy to catch wind that he'd been attempting to devour Dianna in her front yard.

Griffin leaned back, gently sucking Dianna's bottom lip between his teeth as he pulled away. "Come on. Let's go have dinner."

Dianna seemed a little surprised that he was hitting the brakes on their physical interaction, and honestly so was he. It wasn't like him at all. Physical connection was so much easier to manage than the rest of the parts that went into a relationship. That's why he relied on it so heavily, hoping to make up for all the ways he lacked when it came to everything else. But the thought of Dianna looking at him the way so many women had before made him feel sick. He didn't want to disappoint her. He didn't want her to see how incapable he really was.

It left him walking a very fine line, one that put him in danger of exposing all his faults.

"What are we having for dinner?" Dianna's hand was soft in his as he led her across their front lawns and up the steps to his house.

"Tonight we are having a delectable ground sirloin slice, along with a root vegetable mash, topped with a savory beef reduction."

Dianna grinned. "Meatloaf and mashed potatoes with gravy?"

"It sounds like you already knew what the daily special was." He opened the screen door Dianna had admired, pulling her into the front room and toward the dining room, which he was using for its intended purpose for the first time.

"It's Monday, and Monday is for meatloaf." Dianna's eyes sparkled in the dim light. "It's also one of my favorites."

"Mine too." Griffin backed into the dining room, watching her face as she came in behind him.

Dianna's free hand came to her chest, resting there as her eyes moved over the set up he'd put a surprising amount of effort into. She sucked in a breath, the hand on her chest moving to her mouth. "You didn't say it was meatloaf by candlelight."

Griffin pulled one of the drywall compound benches he'd crafted away from the table, giving Dianna room to settle onto the slab of wood he stretched between two 5-gallon buckets. "Since most of my light fixtures haven't been delivered yet, a lot of what happens around here is by candlelight." He adjusted the tabletop to make sure Dianna could reach her meal before taking his own makeshift bench seat across from her.

Dianna looked over the table, dark eyes moving from the food to the candle to the flower arrangement he picked up from the local florist. "I can't believe you went to all this trouble."

Griffin swallowed hard, a little surprised at how quickly the most important part of the evening was presenting itself. Now was when he would normally blow her comment off. Spew something about how it was no trouble, or it wasn't a big deal.

But tonight was a big deal, and it had nothing to do with the food or the flowers or the candle.

"Why not?" It was only two words, but it was a step he'd never taken before. One that left the conversation following it in Dianna's hands.

She pressed her lips together, continuing to study the table before finally lifting her eyes to meet his. "No one's ever done something like this for me before."

Griffin resisted the urge to fidget. The need to touch

her in a way that would refocus Dianna's attention. But he was starting to realize how unfair that was.

"I'm sorry." He had to offer something, and that was really the best he could come up with.

Dianna's lips pulled into a small smile. Maybe he wasn't stumbling as bad as he thought. "Thank you." She picked up her plastic fork, moving around the potatoes. "But, honestly it's my own fault. I allowed myself to stay with men I shouldn't have."

He was bothered by her comment. The amount of responsibility she carried for other people's actions. He'd been in plenty of relationships he should've left, everyone had. But life was complicated and things were never clear-cut or easy, even when you knew they were wrong.

"I think you're blaming yourself a little too much, Di." His fingers itched with the desire to pull her close and kiss her until this conversation was over. "When you're with someone it's not always easy to walk away, even when there are plenty of reasons you should." It was advice he could probably turn back on himself, but that was something he would have to deal with on a different day.

Right now this was about Dianna. About helping her see that holding onto the pain of your past would only taint your future.

Even more advice he could probably stand to throw in his own face, but taking on her demons was turning out to be easier than dealing with his own.

"My ex-husband was..." Dianna took a shaky breath,

her eyes lifting to the ceiling. "This is really hard to admit."

He finally gave up trying to keep his hands off her and reached across the table, lacing his fingers between hers. Walking the line between offering comfort and getting caught up in their physical connection was yet another thing he didn't know how to accomplish. But he would have to figure it out, because there was no way he wasn't touching her right now.

"It's so embarrassing." She shook her head. "Admitting I allowed myself to be in a situation like that is humiliating."

"We've all stayed with people we shouldn't have, Dianna. People we knew weren't right for us." He was trying to soothe her. To let her know she wasn't alone. That he would never judge her.

Dianna's eyes dropped, meeting his across the table. "This wasn't just him not being right for me." She swallowed, her throat working. "He was abusive. Angry and condescending and violent."

There was no stopping the tightening of his hand around hers. "He hurt you?"

Dianna's nod was almost imperceptible. "Physically. Mentally. Emotionally." She blinked, sniffing softly. "I allowed him to hurt me in just about every way possible."

"That's not how abuse works, Di. You don't *allow* it." He'd had a front row seat to an abusive relationship at one point in his life. One that was evenly matched and jointly dysfunctional. But there is no way that's what this was.

His mother was just as angry and violent as his father, instigating their physical bouts equally often.

But that wasn't Dianna.

It wasn't a lot of women.

"Come here." He used his hold on her hand to heft her up, shoving his makeshift bench back enough that he could drag her down into his lap. "Don't take responsibility for someone else being a piece of shit. That's on them. Not on you."

Dianna sniffed, tucking her face into the crook of his neck as she curled against him. "I understand what you're saying, but taking responsibility for where I've been in my life makes me feel like I have the power to keep from ending up there again."

He held her in silence, completely at a loss for what to say next.

He'd spent his whole life making sure he never ended up in a relationship like his parents had. Stuffing down any upset or frustrations he felt to avoid creating a conflict that would escalate. But he'd also ended up missing out on experience handling moments like this, and right now that left him feeling completely inept. Completely unworthy of the woman he held close.

And, unless he focused her attention somewhere else, she'd figure it out sooner rather than later.

But intentionally distracting her in this moment felt wrong. Manipulative in a way he didn't recognize before.

Dianna lifted her head, his stomach sinking as she

focused on his face. He waited for whatever question he would have to answer. Whatever layer she wanted to peel away so she could get a look at all he tried to hide.

But to his surprise, Dianna smiled, the expression soft enough to soothe the upset in his gut. Her lower lip pinched between her teeth as she glanced back at the table. "You didn't happen to also get pie, did you?"

NINETEEN

DIANNA

GRIFFIN HAD CLEARLY put a lot of effort into dinner, but it was something else he was working hard at that made her change the topic of conversation. He wasn't a big talker, not when it came to anything involving vulnerability, but tonight he was trying to give her that. Even though it was clearly difficult and uncomfortable for him.

And, after working so hard to make the evening special, she didn't want him to feel either of those.

Dianna traced the lettering across his shirt with one finger. "I'm actually kind of worn out. Maybe we could just relax and eat pie.

Griffin glanced around the empty space, blue eyes drifting over the buckets of paint and collection of tools lining the walls. "I'm not sure I have anywhere we can relax." His eyes dropped to her mouth. "The only other furniture I have is my bed."

She could definitely come up with worse places to be than Griffin's bed, so Dianna stood up, struggling a little with the dismount as she slid free of his embrace. "Pie in bed sounds like heaven to me."

Griffin snagged her hand, giving her a smirk that made it clear he was feeling less out of his element now that the bedroom had been mentioned. "You in my bed sounds like a good idea."

She agreed, but probably not for the same reason.

Griffin was a very focused man, especially when clothing started to come. But in all the times they'd messed around, she'd barely done more than look at his dick. Maybe tonight that needed to change. Maybe tonight she would be the one doing the distracting. The one with a singular focus.

Dianna helped Griffin collect their food, carrying it into the room he'd been living out of since moving into the house. She peeked into the kitchen as they passed, immediately becoming distracted by what was inside, proving she wasn't going to be great at the singular focus thing.

"Oh my gosh." Dianna immediately made a detour, walking into the large, open space. She'd never been in Vera's house when the older woman owned it, so it was impossible to really grasp how much work Griffin had done, but based on the amount of exposed wires and pipes she saw, hopefully it had been a lot. "I didn't realize there was a full line of windows looking out over the backyard in this room too." She moved to the backmost wall, peering out into the darkness. "These are fantastic."

She loved her little kitchen. Loved the quaintness of the small layout and the antique finishings. But it was barely a quarter of the size of Griffin's kitchen, and it was impossible not to imagine how gorgeous a space like this could be.

"During the day they let a lot of natural light in, just like the ones in the office." Griffin came to stand behind her, his eyes meeting hers in the reflection on the glass. "But they take away a whole wall's worth of storage."

Dianna gave the space another look, sizing up the few remaining cabinets collected in one corner. "You could put a bank of just lower cupboards here." She motioned down the long wall. "That would be a huge amount of storage." She could fit everything she owned in that many cabinets. "Plus, there would be a huge counter space where you could look outside while you worked." It was easy to imagine standing at the counter, kneading bread dough or scooping cookies as the warm summer air filtered in through the windows.

"I thought we established that I don't do much working in the kitchen." Griffin tipped his head to the plates in his hands. "Unless you count turning on the microwave. I'm decent at that."

Dianna turned away from the line of windows, shoving the image they'd inspired to one side. "There's always time to learn." She moved out of the kitchen and into the small hall that ran between it and the large room

Griffin used as his bedroom. She paused to peek inside the door spaced between them.

"That's a half-bath." Griffin was close behind her, following but not rushing. "My best guess is that it was originally a butler's pantry someone repurposed."

"A butler's pantry sounds amazing, but I can understand the desire to have a bathroom on the main level." She knew Vera's house wasn't in the best condition, but it was somewhat surprising to discover it was updated more recently than her little cottage. "It's a shame all the cabinets are gone though."

"I'm just glad most of the hardwood was intact and a few of the original kitchen cabinets were left." Griffin moved into the bedroom, setting both plates onto the foot of the bed. "I've tried to salvage anything I can, but over the years this place has seen a lot of changes."

Dianna sat down with a sigh. "Haven't we all." She wasn't exactly trying to circle back to the kind of conversations Griffin struggled to have, but she also didn't want to build something superficial and purely based on physical attraction.

Because good sex simply wasn't enough for her.

She'd made herself a promise, and if Griffin wanted to be around her, which it seemed like he did, he would have to be a part of that promise. It wouldn't be easy since she was still new at voicing her opinions and recognizing her value, but it was the only way this could happen.

Whatever this was.

Griffin slowly lowered to the bed beside her, feet on

the floor, hands loosely clasped between his knees as he leaned forward, taking a deep breath. "How have you changed?"

Dianna swallowed hard, emotion clogging her throat. Emotion brought on by memories of what she'd overcome, but also by how far Griffin was pushing himself. How hard he was trying to prove she wasn't the only one who'd changed in their life.

"For most of my life I've let other people's opinions dictate how I felt about myself." It was a simple way to sum up the drastic extent of what she'd allowed others to hold over her. The power she'd let them possess. "I'm doing my best not to let that happen anymore."

"If anyone can do it, it's you." It was easy to hear Griffin fully believed what he was saying, and maybe a year ago she might have believed him too.

"I'm starting to think maybe it's not something I'll ever be done with." She'd been through therapy. Journaled and meditated and changed her own mindset. It helped, but it didn't fix it. It didn't take all those words she'd heard away. It didn't heal all the cracks left from putting herself back together. They were all still there and some days all it took was one wrong hit for them to open up.

For those old, painful words to seep back out.

"I think some things just can never truly be fixed. I think sometimes no matter how hard you've worked to get rid of them, those old ways will still sneak back and try to take over. They're a part of you forever whether you like it or not." It was strange to have such a profound epiphany sitting on Griffin's bed in clothes that still smelled like cinnamon and sugar instead of a therapist's office.

But that was the way this whole thing had sort of panned out for her. Therapy was a huge part of it, for sure. It gave her the tools she needed, but the work came down to her. It was slow and painful and happened at the oddest times. It happened in the shower. Sitting in her car talking to the neighbor's grandson. Feeding the birds and bribing the squirrels.

And apparently, when she was sitting next to Griffin, trying not to make things weird.

"That's kind of a depressing thought." Griffin tipped his head, eyes meeting hers. "I was really hoping I could move here and move on. Say 'fuck the past' and only worry about what was in front of me."

Dianna nodded. "Me too." She sighed, understanding why Griffin preferred to avoid moments like this. They were exhausting. "But it seems like the past is kind of a stalker and she will find you no matter where you go."

Griffin gave her a little smile. "Then I won't update my mailing address. If she wants to find me, I'm going to make her work for it."

Dianna smiled back, the weight of the conversation easing the tiniest bit. "That's smart thinking. I wish I'd thought of it."

Griffin reached out to curl a loose bit of her hair behind one ear. "I guess it's a shame I didn't move here sooner then. We could have gone into hiding together."

Dianna leaned into his touch. It was an easy thing to get used to, which was a little terrifying. She'd been scared of men in many ways before, but there wasn't a doubt in her mind that Griffin would never purposefully hurt her. "There are worse people I can think of to be stuck with."

"Yeah?" He sounded skeptical. Like he didn't quite believe her claim.

"Oh, for sure." She leaned a little closer, fighting through the twist of nerves in her belly pushing the sadness and lingering pain even farther from her mind. "Can you imagine hiding out with Maryann Pace? She would run everyone ragged."

Griffin's head tipped back on a loud laugh. "I lived at the bed and breakfast she runs for almost a month straight, so I think I've been about as close to being stranded with Maryann Pace as it gets." He grabbed her around the waist, pulling Dianna across his lap until she straddled his thighs. "And I will say that when Maryann Pace tells you to jump, the only thing you can do is ask her how high."

Dianna wrapped her arms around his shoulders, settling against his body. Fighting that tiny voice trying to tell her she was too heavy to be in this position. "I promise I won't ever tell you how high you have to jump."

Griffin's smile slipped the tiniest bit but his focus stayed on her face. "You probably should. I'm not a big jumper."

It reminded her of an earlier plan she'd been concocting. One to reward Griffin for tonight and for opening up.

And also maybe to turn the tables on him a little bit.

She pressed against his chest, urging him backward toward the mattress. "Unfortunately, I started to realize that being bossy might not be in my nature, so you'll have to be the captain of your own jumping."

Griffin went down to the mattress easily, his hands roaming up her thighs and ass as she landed on him, breasts smashed against his chest. "If I can learn to jump then you can learn to be bossy." His fingers gripped her ass, kneading her flesh. "Maybe you can start practicing tonight. You can tell me where I need to put my mouth first." One hand slid up to curve around the fullness of her breast, the tips of his fingers teasing against the nipple through her shirt and bra. "Here?" His hand slid down to cup between her thighs. "Or here."

Dianna pretended to think, looking off to one side in mock ponder. She smirked and brought her eyes back to his. "How about neither."

It was hard to tell if the look on Griffin's face was confusion or disappointment. It didn't really matter, she wasn't going to leave him confused and disappointed for long.

Dianna eased down his body, working her way over the edge of the bed.

Griffin sat up immediately. "Where are you going?"

Her knees hit the floor between his feet as her hands worked the buckle of his belt. "Not far."

She lifted her eyes to meet his and what she saw there stole her breath.

Griffin stared down at her, expression full of hunger and longing. His nostrils barely flared as she flipped the button of his jeans free and raked down the zipper. "What are you doing, Di?"

Was she brave enough to answer that? Brave enough to use the same blunt words he did? The ones that sent desire shooting straight to her pussy and always had her nipples pulling tight.

Maybe not, but she was going to attempt it anyway.

"I'm getting ready to wrap my lips around your cock." She spread open his unfastened jeans and hooked her fingers into the waistband of his underwear, just beside where the tip of his rigid dick pressed against the soft fabric, a spot of wetness collecting in the cotton.

The sight made her bolder. Braver.

"Do you want that?" She pulled at the elastic, stretching it away from his body as she reached for him, sliding her fingers along his hot skin. "For me to suck you off?"

Griffin groaned as she gripped him, pulling the hard line of his cock from the confines of his pants. The sound was rough and ragged. Like he had no power to stop it from breaking free.

It was an appealing thought. One that made her feel wicked and seductive in a way she'd never felt before. Seductive enough that she kept her eyes on his face as she parted her lips and guided him between them.

"Christ." Griffin's rough hands curved against her

head but didn't pull at her as he watched her swallow him down inch by inch. "You look real fucking good sucking my cock, Di."

She took in as much of him as she could manage, pausing a second before pulling back, sucking just a little, fighting the urge to smile as Griffin groaned again.

It was becoming clear she didn't really understand all sex could offer a woman. Up until Griffin showed up she didn't believe it offered much of anything at all. But then he proved her wrong, offering up more orgasms than another person had ever given her.

And that was great. Fantastic even.

But this...

This was giving that a run for its money.

Dianna pursed her lips, squeezing him tight as she pushed over him again, gliding her tongue against the underside of his cock as she gripped his base with one hand and the opening of his jeans with the other.

"Just like that." Griffin's hold on her head barely tightened. "Show me how much you can take."

His words made the ache between her thighs deeper, stronger. Almost unbearable.

She pressed one hand against it, trying to ease the need as she rocked over him, her mouth making wet sounds as she moved faster.

Griffin's eyes darkened as they shifted to where her hand was wedged between her thighs. "Play with your pussy for me."

His ragged demand was a relief. She was feeling

braver in the bedroom, but not quite brave enough to do something like that on her own.

No matter how desperately she wanted to.

Dianna immediately shoved one hand into the waistband of her pants, the thought of touching herself while sucking Griffin's cock making her thighs clench in anticipation.

"No." Griffin's voice was sharp. "Pull them down. I want to see it."

She paused, keeping her mouth on him as she shoved the stretchy fabric down her thighs, hesitating just a second before reaching for her slick flesh.

TWENTY

GRIFFIN

*H*E WAS GOING to die and it would be all her fault. This woman was sending every bit of the blood in his body rushing from his brain to his dick, leaving him with nothing to function on.

It might be worth it.

Dianna was definitely a little on the inexperienced side when they met, but she sure as shit wasn't letting that hold her back now, proving just how dangerous she could be. How easily she could steal every bit of power he pretended to have and leave him fighting for his life.

Because it wasn't just his brain suffering right now. His jaw was twitching from being clenched so tight. His arms were aching with the restraint it took to keep from dragging her mouth closer. His eyes were on fire since he hadn't blinked in what felt like forever.

But he didn't want to miss a second of this. He wanted to burn the sight of Dianna like this into his memory, making sure it stayed there forever.

Hopefully he lived long enough to make that happen since right now Dianna's searching hand was teasing along her cunt, barely making contact as she doubled down on her efforts to ruin him completely.

It was almost too much. The wet heat of her mouth pulling his balls tighter with each stroke. The way her eyes stayed locked onto his, as if she wanted to bear witness to his destruction.

He had to do something to stop this. To take back a little of the power she wielded so beautifully.

"Are you going to touch yourself the right way or do I need to drag you up here and do it myself?" He was fighting for focus. Fighting for control in a situation he would normally rule.

Part of him desperately hoped she'd take him up on the offer. That Dianna would stop what she was doing and let things go back to normal. But that part of him was shrinking more every time her lips shuttled over his skin.

Griffin watched, unable to look away and fighting the need to come, as Dianna's fingers pressed deeper between her flushed folds. Rubbed harder. Stroked against her clit as she whimpered around him. The soft vibration of the sound nearly sent him over the edge. Only sheer will kept him from spilling in her mouth.

That and the desire to drag this moment out as long as possible.

"Good girl. Show me how you touch yourself." He barely bit the words out as her hips started to rock, searching for more. It was the sexiest thing he'd ever seen in his life and more than he could physically take.

He gripped her head, intending to pull her away. "Di, I'm—"

Dianna moaned, bucking against her teasing fingers as the hand gripping his cock squeezed tight. Her wicked mouth sucked him hard, the added pressure sending him right over the edge.

There was no stopping it. No holding back. No sparing her the full wrath of his climax as his cock jerked against her tongue, pulsing hot spurts of cum into her throat while she sucked him impossibly deep, taking everything he had.

Right down to his soul.

Her lips slid free, swollen, pink and parted as she sucked in sharp breaths, her glassy eyes still resting on his face.

"Come here." Griffin snagged her by the arms, pulling her up onto the bed. He held her close as they fell back against the mattress, limbs and clothes tangled.

He tucked her head against his neck, breathing in the sweet, fresh scent of her skin as he tried to come to terms with finding himself in a spot he'd never been before. He'd given Dianna nothing just now. Barely even touched her. He'd offered no value. No initiative for her to be here with him.

And yet her body was draped over his, relaxed and

showing no inclination to walk away. To leave him and all his shortcomings behind.

It should have scared him shitless. Should have him shutting down and closing off. But he couldn't make himself do it.

Because if she was brave enough to be here after all she'd been through, he could be too.

"Griffin?" Dianna's voice was soft and sleepy.

"Yeah?"

She shifted around a little and he instinctively held her tighter. Just in case he'd been wrong and she did think leaving him was a good idea. He'd never stopped a woman from walking away before, but he would try to stop her. Do whatever Dianna wanted to keep her here with him.

Bargain, beg, and bleed.

Dianna fumbled around, wiggling in his hold before letting out a sharp sigh. "Can you let me go? My ass is still out."

THE SOUND OF birds woke him up before the alarm on his phone did.

He'd gotten used to sleeping alone with nothing but the ceiling fan to keep him cool. The added warmth of Dianna's body draped across his, fantastic as it was, turned his bed into a furnace, so he'd opened the window during the night, letting in the cool air—and probably a few bugs considering it didn't have a screen. But it was worth it to keep Dianna pressed against him.

At least it was until he opened his eyes and nearly shit his pants.

Snickerdoodle sat in the center of his chest, staring down at him with beady little eyes.

"Di?" Griffin kept his voice as calm as he could given the circumstances. "I need you to wake up." He'd had one run-in with the animal and wasn't excited at the opportunity to have another.

Dianna barely shifted on the bed next to him, sucking in a deep breath. "Hmm?"

"We've got a visitor." He went still as Snickerdoodle's head dipped and his nose twitched. There were only a few inches separating him from a set of teeth he didn't care to become acquainted with.

Dianna inhaled again as she tried to roll away, but Griffin held her tight, doing his best to make sure nothing startled the feral rodent. When she couldn't move, Dianna made a little grunt of protest, opening her eyes.

They immediately locked on where Snickerdoodle sat. "Oh shit."

"Any idea how we get him out of here?" He was starting to feel cornered and it was making him antsy.

Dianna pulled one hand loose and waved it in the squirrel's general direction. "Shoo. Go back outside."

Snickerdoodle took a few steps back, moving down to his stomach, but then sat back down, watching them both as he licked his paws and smoothed them down his fur.

Griffin scoffed, not really believing what he was seeing. "Is he taking a bath?"

"*Snickerdoodle.*" Dianna sat up, pushing back the sheet covering her body. "Go outside." She shooed at him again, and this time the squirrel jumped off his body, dropping to the floor before bouncing to the corner.

Then he sat down and went back to grooming himself.

"What the fuck is happening?" Griffin tossed back the covers, dropping his feet to the floor as he grabbed a pillow in each hand and stalked toward the rodent. "You live outside." He held the pillows out in front of him, using them as both a shield and a barrier as he closed in on the squirrel.

But Snickerdoodle acted completely oblivious to his advance, continuing to lick at his paws and his fur.

"Is he moving?" Dianna went up to her knees on the mattress, stretching to get a better look at the situation.

"Not at all." Griffin bumped the squirrel with one of the pillows. Snickerdoodle barely flinched, shifting around before going back to his bath. "He's fucking ignoring me."

Dianna snorted.

He turned to give her a serious look.

She pressed one hand to her lips. "Sorry. It's not funny."

It might be a little funny. But it wouldn't be once the

squirrel started shitting all over the place. "How do we get him out of here?"

Dianna shifted around, sliding off the bed. "Maybe leave the window open and close him in. I bet he finds his own way out." She moved toward the door. "I usually feed him around this time so he'll probably come to my house for his peanuts if I'm over there."

It made sense. Not only where the squirrel was concerned, but also because Dianna needed to get ready for work. He still wasn't ready for her to go. For her to leave him.

Dianna paused at the door, turning to face him and lifting a brow. "Are you coming?"

She didn't have to ask him twice.

"Yup." Griffin shoved on his boots while Dianna yanked on her sneakers. He rested one hand against her back, directing her out the door before closing it behind him, leaving Snickerdoodle to do as he may.

"You really think he's going to go out the window?" Griffin led Dianna down the little hall, taking her past the half bath and out into the foyer.

"He's kind of a whore for peanuts, so yeah." She opened the front door and stepped out onto the porch, shivering a little in the chilly morning air. "He doesn't miss the opportunity to stuff himself." She glanced out at the dew-covered grass. "Especially with winter coming."

Griffin closed the front door and followed Dianna across their joined yards, waiting while she unlocked the deadbolt. He kicked off his shoes as soon as they were inside, carefully lining them up on the square of linoleum beside the door before turning to face her.

Dianna thumbed over one shoulder, pointing in the direction of the bathroom. "I'm going to go get ready." She motioned around the living room. "Make yourself comfortable."

Griffin snagged her by the front of the shirt, leaning down to press a kiss against her lips. "How about I make us some coffee instead."

It was yet another mistake he wasn't going to make with Dianna.

And maybe mistake was the wrong word. The women he'd been with before seemed perfectly content with the cooking and cleaning part of their relationships. It was him not sharing anything outside of his money with them that they had a problem with.

But that was when he worked eighty hours a week. Now he had free time. The ability to carry more of the load. So that was exactly what he intended to do.

As soon as he figured out how in the hell to do it.

Griffin watched Dianna disappear into the bathroom, taking in the full curve of her ass until it was completely out of sight before ducking into the kitchen and staring down her coffee maker. Luckily it was a pretty basic model, so he easily managed to fill it with grounds and water, setting it to run with no problem.

Coffee, done.

Next, he turned to the refrigerator, pulling it open to stare down the contents. There were plenty of options to choose from. There was still bacon left from their breakfast yesterday. A pack of sausage. Plenty of eggs, and a whole stack of butter. Surely he should be able to accomplish something with all that.

Griffin grabbed the sausage, skipping over the bacon in the hopes the ground pork would be less temperamental. He slid the sausage onto the counter, adding the eggs and a couple slices of American cheese before turning to the collection. A sausage, egg, and cheese sandwich couldn't be that difficult to manage. Especially since he'd seen Dianna make most of the parts yesterday.

He fished around the cabinet, finally finding a pan that looked familiar. He set it on top of the stove and went to work patting out two thin slabs of sausage. He laid them across one side of the large pan before washing his hands and moving on to the bread. He sliced off four thick pieces as the meat started to sizzle, taking a break between each cut to make sure nothing was starting to burn. Luckily, his hunch was right, and sausage was more forgiving than its sliced counterpart.

He had the bread in the toaster and was cracking eggs into the pan when Dianna walked in, looking fucking beautiful and maybe a little impressed.

"You don't give up easily, do you?" She moved closer but didn't make any attempt to correct what he was doing.

"I like figuring shit out." Griffin didn't take his eyes off the eggs and sausage. "And I'm pretty sure I can figure out how to make a breakfast sandwich."

Dianna smiled at him. "Considering everything I've

seen you're capable of, I'm positive you can handle a breakfast sandwich."

She hadn't said a whole lot about all the work he'd done on his house—probably because she didn't actually realize how much went into plumbing and electrical work. But the fact that she did understood he'd been working his ass off made his chest puff up a little bit. "I'm not against any advice you have, though."

Dianna beamed at him. "Good, because if you put a lid on that you won't have to mess with flipping those eggs over at all."

Griffin studied the delicate whites as they started to firm up. "I was wondering how in the hell I was going to manage that."

Dianna laughed as she reached into the cabinet and pulled out a lid, settling it on the skillet. "What do you have planned for the day?"

Griffin grabbed a cup, pouring in some coffee before adding the cream and sugar he knew Dianna liked, and held it out to her. "I need to work on finishing the upstairs bathroom. I'd like to have it fully-functioning before winter."

He'd been making do with a water hose and the toilet in the half bath on the main floor, but he needed a real bathroom. Especially if Dianna was going to spend more nights in his bed.

Which he hoped she was.

Dianna sipped her coffee, relaxing against the counter like this was a normal way for them to spend the morning. "Are you close to being done?"

"Close enough that if I buckle down I should have it finished by the end of the week." Griffin poured out some coffee of his own, drinking down a mouthful as he peeked at their sausage and eggs. "What about you? Anything exciting on your schedule?"

"I do pretty much the same thing every single day." Dianna grabbed one of the packaged cheese product slices from the counter and went to work unwrapping it. "But, now that I have Janie to help in the afternoons, I have extra time in the evenings." She lifted the lid to slide the cheese onto one of the eggs. "So maybe I can help you with your bathroom when I get home."

The offer was what should have captured his full attention, but Griffin was still tripping over something else she said. "Janie?"

Dianna nodded, going to work on the next slice of cheese. "She's the girl I hired. She's awesome and so freaking sweet." She added the cheese to the other egg. "One of the most genuinely nice people I've ever met."

The clench in his stomach relaxed a little. "That's good. I'm glad to hear she's working out and you two are getting along so well." He studied her a second longer. "I don't see you doing well with someone who's high strung and demanding."

Dianna shook her head. "Definitely not, so I am thrilled I found Janie."

Griffin fought not to wince as she said the name yet again. "Me too."

The story of a Janie he once knew sat on the tip of his tongue, heavy and hard. But it was the kind of story that would make Dianna see him differently. See just how lacking he really was. So he kept it to himself. Focusing instead on showing her he could be better.

Showing himself he could be better.

He lifted the lid off the pan and carefully slid a sausage patty onto two of the toast slices, topping each with an egg before stacking on the final piece of toast. He turned to Dianna, holding out the proof that he could learn. Proof that he could be worthy. "I didn't even set the smoke alarm off this time."

TWENTY-ONE

DIANNA

DIANNA GLANCED UP as Janie came in through The Baking Rack's back door. "Hey."

She found herself looking forward to Janie's daily arrival a surprising amount. After over a year of working in silence, it was nice to have someone to chat with while she prepped for the next day.

No. It was better than nice. It was great. Especially since Janie felt more like a friend than just an employee.

And today her friend looked surprisingly salty.

Dianna paused what she was doing and focused on Janie as she dumped her purse by the door and yanked an apron free. "Everything okay?"

Janie groaned, letting her head drop back. "I was just really hoping there were fewer assholes here." She yanked the neck loop over her head and aggressively tied the strings around her waist. "But I should have realized asshole is a universal language."

Dianna dropped a cookie onto the baking sheet in front of her as Janie opened the fridge. "What happened?"

Janie slid a vat of cinnamon roll dough onto the counter. "So I'm on my way here," she turned to grab another container of dough, "and the tire light thing comes on in my car, so I pull over." She slammed the second container down. "I make sure I'm all the way off the road and get out to walk around so I can see which of my tires is being a dick." She leaned against the counter, working her jaw from side to side. "And the next thing I know, some cop is pulling up behind me with his lights on."

Dianna scooped another cookie, nodding as if she understood why Janie was so perturbed. "Did he get out and talk to you?"

Janie scoffed. "No. The asshole got out and lectured me." She tipped one of the containers, dropping the dough inside onto the stainless-steel surface before grabbing a bench scraper. "Went on and on about car maintenance and how I needed to check the tread on my tires regularly." She hacked off a chunk of dough and chucked it to one side. "Then he went on and on about how I should have someone I can call to come help me in an emergency situation like this." She sliced off and slammed down another hunk of dough, dropping it in line with the first. "Like I'm incapable of changing my own fucking tire." She held both arms out, swinging around the bench scraper still gripped in one hand. "Do I look like a damsel in distress?"

Dianna almost laughed. Janie looked about as un-helpless as it got. She had wild dark hair and colorful tattoos covering her left arm. She was tall and thin, but definitely not in a way that made her seem delicate or fragile. But it was mostly her attitude that put Janie squarely in the obviously self-sufficient category.

Dianna shook her head. "No. You seem pretty capable of handling yourself."

Janie lifted her brows. "Right?" She snorted out an indignant sound as she went back to cutting off hunks of dough. "So I told him he needed to worry about himself. I had my shit handled."

Dianna blinked, surprised, but also not. "How did that go over?"

Janie dropped both hands to the counter, hitting it surprisingly hard as she leaned toward Dianna. "The prick threatened to arrest me."

Dianna pursed her lips, doing a quick run-through of all the information she'd been given. "He threatened to arrest you because you told him you could take care of yourself?"

Janie squinted, tipping her head from side to side. "More or less."

Dianna pressed her lips together, doing her best to suppress the laugh threatening to come out. She was absolutely positive it was not *less* that led to the threat of arrest. "Which police officer was it?" She was pretty familiar with the majority of the force, so she might be able to offer Janie some pointers in the event she had another run-in with the Moss Creek PD.

Janie rolled her eyes so far into her head only the white showed. "Officer Peters." She stabbed at the dough with the bench scraper. "Dick."

Dianna chewed her lower lip, knowing what she was about to say next was probably not what Janie wanted to hear. "He's had a rough few years." She hesitated, but couldn't let Janie continue thinking Devin Peters was an awful person. For his sake, and for hers. "His wife died of cancer and now he's taking care of three teenage daughters all by himself."

Janie dropped her back toward the ceiling with a loud, dramatic sigh. "Don't make me feel bad for him." Her eyes leveled on Dianna's as she pointed the bench scraper her way. "I'm not one of his fucking daughters. He can't talk down to me like that."

"Was he really talking down to you, or was he offering advice?" Dianna dropped another cookie into place, hoping she wasn't pushing the conversation too far. But Janie was her friend and she hoped if their situations were reversed, Janie would offer up any advice she had to share.

"I don't want to think about it. I just want to be mad for a little bit." Janie sucked in a breath and blew it back out, having at the dough again as she focused on Dianna. "Let's talk about you. How are you doing?"

She understood Janie's interest in changing the subject, and for once, didn't hate the opportunity to discuss her own life. It was nice having a life she actually wanted to talk about. Especially with a friend.

"I'm fantastic." She finished filling the cookie sheet and carried it to the oven. "Things are wonderful."

"And by things, you mean your boyfriend's penis, right?" Janie smirked as she worked through measuring out the balls of dough, ensuring they were all uniform.

"I mean, definitely that, but there's more to Griffin than just his fantastic penis." Dianna slipped the cookie sheet into the preheated oven and set the timer, spinning to face Janie.

Janie stared at her, an odd look on her face. "What else about *Griffin* is fantastic?"

Dianna tried not to be bothered by the odd way she said it. "Well, for starters he's a hard worker."

Janie lifted an eyebrow, looking entirely unimpressed. "So am I, but you don't see men lining up to tell me how fantastic I am." Janie was back to slamming around the dough. "And being a hard worker doesn't mean shit if that's all he brings to the table."

Janie definitely wasn't exaggerating when she said she was just in the mood to be mad. "He's not just a hard worker. He's also funny and smart and thoughtful."

"Thoughtful." Janie slapped another wad of dough against the counter. "Please don't tell me you're considering flowers and gifts thoughtful." She slapped another hunk of dough. "Because anyone can buy you shit."

For a second, Dianna was a little irked at her friend's reaction, but then she got sad.

Sad because Janie obviously understood where to set

the bar when it came to relationships. She was clearly the kind of woman who made men prove they were worthy of her time and would probably be appalled to know everything Dianna allowed to happen in her life. Everything she accepted.

"No, he's actually never bought me anything." She lifted one shoulder as she went to work filling the next cookie sheet. "Unless you count dinner." She tipped her head to one side, thinking back a little farther. "And he did always grossly overpay when he came in here."

"So what I'm hearing is he's fantastic because he does the bare minimum." Janie slammed her hands against the counter again, eyes fixing on Dianna's face. "Are you sure you're not just blinded by good dick?"

"Blinded by good dick?" Dianna shook her head. "I don't even know what that means."

"It means he's so good in bed you don't notice how shitty he is everywhere else." Janie slammed another wad of dough down. "At least not right away."

Dianna thought about it for a second. Griffin was definitely good in bed. But was he good enough to make her overlook things the same way she had in the past?

No. That would probably be impossible.

"Listen." Janie's tone gentled as she rounded the counter and came to stand in front of Dianna, resting both hands on her shoulders. "I'm not trying to be a jerk. I just think you should be with a man who deserves to be with you." Her expression hardened the tiniest bit. "And it doesn't sound like *Griffin* is deserving of all the amazingness that you are."

Janie gave Griffin's name a little added inflection again. Like she was just as mad at him as she was at Devin Peters. Honestly, she might be. It seemed like Janie was letting her interaction on the way in bleed over to taint the entirety of the male species.

Yet another thing Dianna understood completely. She'd felt a similar sort of way after splitting up with Martin. It was simply easier to expect every man to be bad than it was to face the daunting task of deciding which ones were and which ones weren't.

"I promise I will never be with a man who doesn't deserve me." She leaned in, softening her tone just the tiniest bit. "As long as you promise not to give Officer Peters too hard of a time the next time you see him."

"Now that's just mean." Janie sighed, eyes rolling up to the ceiling. "Fine. I won't be mean to Officer Peters the next time I see him."

Dianna smiled. "Good."

Janie's eyes met hers. "Unless he's mean to me first."

Dianna tipped her head to one side, giving Janie a stern look. "You're going to need that emergency contact he told you to get." She bit back a smile. "But not to help you change a tire. You're going to need it for bail money."

Janie waved her off, looking unconcerned. "I've already got a bail money bitch." She went back to her spot at the workstation, being a little kinder to the cinnamon roll dough as she worked. "It's one of the most important things a girl can have."

Dianna chuckled, going back to her cookies. "I don't think I've ever had one of those."

Janie gave her a bright smile. "Well you do now. I would be honored to be your bail money bitch."

It was an oddly touching statement. One that made her take Janie's earlier comments a little more to heart. Clearly, Janie was more discerning when it came to the men she allowed in her life, so she should at least give her friend's fears a tiny bit of consideration.

Even though she didn't really need to.

Griffin was working really hard to open up. Little by little he was sharing more and more of how he thought and felt with her. But maybe she could expect a tiny bit more. Maybe a little insight into what his life was like before coming to Moss Creek. How he felt when he found out he had a son.

Hell, she didn't even know if he had brothers or sisters.

The realization was sobering.

And disappointing.

It made her think maybe Janie had more of a point then she'd realized.

GRIFFIN WAS OUT on his porch waiting when Dianna got home. By the time she got out of her car he was standing at the open garage door, greeting her with a kiss that eased a little of the turmoil winding up her insides.

"Hey." He held her close, filling his hands with her ample backside as he ran his nose up the side of hers. "How was your day?"

"Busy." She leaned back, meeting his gaze, relaxing a little more at the warmth in his blue eyes. "How was yours?"

"Long." Griffin stepped back, lacing his fingers with hers as he pulled her across the yard. "And fucking frustrating."

She lifted her brows. "That's not good."

She'd driven home filled with dread. Worried Janie was right and she really was turning a blind eye to problems she should be focused on.

Again.

But Griffin was ready to talk about his day right out of the gate, and it eased her worry and shoved away the sick feeling she'd been fighting. "Tell me all about it." She was ready to soak up every little tidbit he offered. To let Griffin fill in all the empty spots Janie liked to point out.

He led her up the stairs of his house, taking her in through the front door. "The main issue is that I ended up having company all day long." He pulled her inside, down the width of the main hall, and into the smaller one leading to his bedroom.

Her heart sank a little. Was Janie actually going to be right? Was she really blinded by good dick?

Dianna slowed her steps, putting up a little resistance. "I thought you were working in the bathroom?"

She motioned in the direction of the front stairs. "We can go look at it."

She knew exactly what would happen if they walked into Griffin's bedroom. It was the same thing that would happen if they walked into her kitchen. Or her living room. Or hell, the back room of her bakery.

"I didn't get shit done in the bathroom today." Griffin grabbed the knob and twisted it open, shoving the door to his bedroom wide. "Because of this."

Dianna peeked around the frame, attempting to keep her distance from the danger lurking on the other side.

The room looked exactly the same as it did when she left it this morning. Neat and tidy, but also a jumble of tools and building materials. "I have no idea what you're talking about."

Griffin pointed at his bed. "You don't see that?"

She'd actually been avoiding looking at the bed. The bed made her think of problematic things. Things like being on her knees in front of Griffin, sucking his cock while she got herself off.

"No?" Dianna scanned the blankets she'd slept under the night before, eyes skimming the line of pillows fluffed against the headboard. One of them did seem a little furrier than she remembered.

Dianna stepped into the doorway to get a better look. "Is that Snickerdoodle?"

The fat squirrel was curled into a tight ball right in the center of one white pillowcase, sound asleep.

"He won't fucking leave." Griffin pointed toward the back yard. "I stood out there with peanuts and carrots and apples and anything else I thought might get the little pecker to climb out the window." He gestured at the bed. "The bastard just curled up and went to sleep."

It wasn't funny.

It was NOT funny.

Dianna choked a little as the laugh she tried to swallow got caught in her throat.

"What am I supposed to do with a squirrel, Di?" Griffin widened his eyes at her. "He can't just stay here. He's not a house pet."

Dianna pressed her lips together, giving him the most serious look she could manage. "Are you familiar with TikTok?"

TWENTY-TWO

GRIFFIN

DIANNA CUDDLED on the porch swing, tucking the blanket draped across their laps a little tighter against the chill of the morning. "I'm really going to miss this when it's too cold to sit out here."

He used the arm he had draped around Dianna's shoulders to tuck her body tighter to his, doing his best to give her all the warmth he had to offer as she took another bite of the French toast she'd coached him through making. "If we upgrade to an electric blanket we might be able to stretch it out a few more weeks."

They'd spent every morning for the past two weeks rocking in her swing while they ate breakfast and talked. It had quickly become one of his favorite parts of the day, coming in right behind how they spent their nights.

"That's a good idea." Dianna pointed her fork his direction. "You're pretty smart."

Griffin took a deep breath, the way he always did when she offered an opening like this, bracing for whatever might come next. "You're probably the first person to ever accuse me of being smart."

Dianna tipped her head to one side, giving him a disbelieving stare. "No way."

He shrugged, doing his best to act unbothered. "I didn't even go to real high school, Di. I was in a work program because I struggled so much in the regular classes."

It was something he'd only ever admitted to one other person, and that was Troy. Even then, he'd only done it because he didn't want his son to feel like he was alone in his struggles. He wanted to carry a little of the responsibility Troy felt over an issue he'd clearly passed on to him.

"That doesn't mean you're not smart." Dianna used her fork to cut off another chunk of custardy bread. "Book smart isn't the only kind of smart that exists." She shoved the bite into her mouth before poking her fork toward his house next door. "I've only seen part of what you know how to do and it's really impressive. You have to be pretty damn smart to understand how all that renovation stuff works."

He wanted to argue, but disagreeing would only show her the full depth of how bothered he still was by all the things adults said about him when he was a kid. Not that his parents were a part of that. They couldn't be bothered to say anything about him at all. But teachers. Counselors. Student advisers. They all had plenty of opinions about his potential, and none of them were good.

"As long as you think I'm smart, that's all that matters to me." He leaned in and pressed a kiss to her temple, willing his words to be true. Dianna was brilliant and sweet and kind. Her opinion should carry more weight than people who were probably long dead now.

That was part of the reason he preferred not to revisit old feelings. Because, as much as he hated to admit it, they still tried to matter even though they shouldn't.

"I'm positive I'm not the only one who thinks you're smart." She cut off another bite and held it out for him. "I'm willing to bet Troy also thinks you're smart since you were able to help him renovate not only Amelie's grandmother's house, but also help him with the addition he's putting on the back of his."

Griffin took the offered bite, using it as an opportunity to avoid answering. But deep down he hoped she was right. He wanted his son to think he was a decent human. One who was good enough to be his dad.

"What are you going to do today?" He eased the conversation back into more comfortable waters, needing a little break from the past he worked hard to keep where it belonged. "Lots of rest and relaxation?"

Dianna laughed softly. "If that's what you call laundry and cleaning the house, then yes. I will be doing plenty of relaxing."

"I can help when I get back." He was stuck in an odd

place. One that didn't sit well. He normally looked forward to his Sundays out at Cross Creek. Couldn't wait to head out to visit Troy and Amelie and spend the day with them. But today he was torn. Caught between his desire to see his son and his desire to stay here with Dianna.

"I'm sure that would be a ridiculously fun way for you to spend your evening." She rocked her head toward him, resting her temple against his shoulder. "Cleaning someone else's house."

"It wouldn't be cleaning someone else's house. It would be cleaning your house." He reached out to slide his hands along the length of her thick dark hair, enjoying the feel of the soft strands. "And I fully expect you to return the favor when my house is finished."

Dianna's bark of laughter was immediate. "Don't make your decision to buy the biggest house in Moss Creek my problem." Her smile was wide as she jabbed at him with one finger. "You should probably start looking for a housekeeper now, because I'm not sure anyone's going to have enough time in their schedule for that place."

She was teasing him. He knew that. But she also wasn't wrong.

He'd been so excited to finally find a project that would occupy his time, he didn't fully think through the enormity of it. Not just the project itself, but the house in general.

Griffin swallowed hard. "I thought about seeing if Troy and Amelie would want to trade me." He focused on the weave of the blanket, instead of the difficulty of the conversation. "It's the house for a family, not a house for an old guy living alone."

Dianna wrinkled her nose. "First of all, you're not old." She inched closer, her focus on his face. "And you have a family. You have a son and daughter-in-law and soon you're going to have a grandson."

Griffin lifted his eyes to hers. "They might come over on the weekends, but a house like that should have kids running through it all the time."

It was one of many parts of his past he chose not to dwell on. Purposefully focused hard on not allowing to come up. At one point, when he was young and stupid, he thought he'd have the chance to prove he could be a better parent than the ones fate dealt him. That he might not have been given the family he wanted, but he'd have the chance to create it instead. But as the years went by, it started to become clear that wasn't in the cards either, so he threw himself even more into his job, making it his entire focus.

Then he found out about Troy and those old hopes tried to creep back in.

But this time they carried the knowledge that he could have had it. It had been there all along. Someone just took it away. Ripped the rug out from under him before he realized he was standing on it.

Dianna watched him for a second longer before turning to stare across the yard. "I wanted to be a mom." Her next breath was shaky, but she kept talking. "I tried to get pregnant when I was married, but it never happened." She slid her plate onto the little table beside the swing. "Turns out I have something they call polycystic ovary syndrome and it makes it hard to get pregnant." She lifted one shoulder and let it drop. "I know it was for the best. I can only imagine how much more horrible everything would have been if there'd been a child in the mix." Her gaze came to his, emotion filling her eyes. "And I'm happy with my life now, but some days I still wish that could have happened for me."

She made it seem so easy, to open up, to share the most painful parts of her life. It made him ashamed it wasn't as simple for him, but also made him want to push through. Made him force something out no matter how difficult it was. "I will never not regret missing out on Troy's life. I know it wasn't my fault, but I still feel that way, does that make sense?"

Dianna nodded, her hand sliding into his. "Complete sense."

Griffin fought to keep going. To give her more of what she wanted. What she deserved. "I think that's part of the reason I'm so excited about the baby. I know he's not mine, but it feels like Troy and I will get to experience fatherhood for the first time together."

Finding out he was going to be a grandfather gave him hope he never had. Hope that he would get to be a part of helping raise a kid. Hope that he would finally get all those things he believed would never be his.

But it was also terrifying. What if he was no better than his parents? What if Troy's mom had actually spared him—spared them both—the pain of discovering he was destined to carry on the history of selfishness and neglect that made him who he was?

It was too much to think about. More than he could handle.

"I should probably get going." Griffin carefully eased away from Dianna, doing his best not to disturb the blanket keeping her warm. "I'll be back after dinner."

Dianna immediately jumped up, grabbing the blanket as she steadied the swing. "Do you want to take that cake with you?" She followed him into the kitchen, going to the box containing the chocolate mousse cake one of her customers hadn't been able to pick up yesterday. "I'm certainly not going to eat it, so unless you want to be the one to eat it—"

Griffin snagged the box from the counter. "I'll take it." He gave her a smile, fighting to tamp down all those old memories and feelings their conversation dredged up. "I've heard Amelie mention this specific cake more than once, so I'm guessing she will be happy as hell to see me walk in with it."

It might also be a way to ease into telling his son and daughter-in-law that he and Dianna were spending time together. He didn't want to keep any part of his life from Troy, but hadn't quite come up with a good way to explain the situation. To make sure Troy knew he would always come first. That Dianna understood he wouldn't let anything get in the way of their relationship.

Dianna beamed at him, her bright smile helping to push a little more of the darkness away. "Thank God. I was really scared I was going to be left alone in this house with that cake all day, and I wasn't sure how that was going to work out."

He gave her a quick kiss, needing just a little bit more of her before he left. "You want me to bring you back a piece?"

He initially assumed owning a bakery meant unlimited treats, but that wasn't how it worked out. At least not Dianna's bakery, because she was either one hell of an efficient businesswoman, or the people of Moss Creek were determined to buy everything they could get their hands on every single day.

Honestly, it was probably a little bit of both.

Dianna shook her head. "No way." She leaned in, lowering her voice like she was telling him a secret. "Tomorrow I'm making triple berry tarts and I actually kind of have my heart set on one of those."

He lifted his brows. "Triple berry tarts you say?"

Dianna dropped the blanket onto the couch as they moved to the door. "Should I maybe set two aside instead of just one?"

"I wouldn't be upset if you accidentally had one left at the end of the day you needed to get rid of." Griffin snagged her, bringing her in for another kiss, brushing his lips over hers one more time. "Maybe make that two."

"I'M SO EXCITED about this damn cake." Amelie slid Dianna's gift from the box and carried it to the center of the table. "I've been craving one of these for weeks, but I'm trying to be good and feed the baby more fruits and vegetables instead of just the pancakes and peanut butter toast I lived on the first twelve weeks."

"Considering his genetics, you should probably eat as much sugar as possible. See if you can make him a little sweeter." Troy sliced into the layers, shooting Griffin a grin before his eyes focused on his wife.

Amelie stacked the dessert plates beside him, leaning in close. "You're sweet."

Troy dropped a slice of cake onto the top plate and passed it to her. "I wasn't talking about me."

Amelie scoffed, jaw dropping open in mock outrage. "Are you really giving your pregnant wife a hard time—" Her brows pinched together and one hand went to her belly.

Troy went still, watching her closely. "Everything okay?"

Amelie blinked a few times, her lips pressing down at the corners. "I'm okay." She set her plate on the table and backed away. "I think I just have to go to the bathroom." She rushed from the room, moving a little faster than normal.

Griffin glanced at the remnants of their taco dinner. "Do you think the food upset her stomach?"

Troy shook his head. "I wouldn't think so." He set down the knife he was using to cut the cake and turned toward the hall just as Amelie screamed his name.

Troy took off running with Griffin following close behind him. He shoved open the bathroom door and they both stopped in their tracks.

Amelie sat on the toilet, pants around her ankles, streaks of red blood covering her thighs.

"*I shouldn't be bleeding.*" Her voice was filled with panic as she grabbed a wad of toilet paper and wiped at her skin. "*Why am I bleeding?*"

"We need to go to the hospital." Troy grabbed Amelie and lifted her off the toilet, dragging her pants up her legs. "Now."

"I can take you." Griffin bit back the fear trying to make his voice rise. He didn't know anything about pregnancy, but even he recognized something was seriously wrong. "Get her in the backseat of my truck. Keep her feet propped up."

He followed Troy and Amelie out, helping get her loaded up before taking off toward town. Troy sat in the back seat, holding his wife close as she called the doctor and cried into his chest. Each tear that fell down her cheek pushed his foot closer to the floor.

It felt like it took forever to reach the hospital. When they finally arrived, he pulled right up to the doors Amelie's doctor directed them to, threw the truck into park and jumped out, helping Troy get Amelie unloaded and into the waiting wheelchair.

"I'll park the truck and be right in." He turned, ready to get through the process as fast as possible.

"You go home." Troy glanced at his wife as a nurse wheeled her inside. "I'll call you when we know something." Then he was gone, rushing into the hospital, leaving Griffin standing alone.

Alone with an amount of pain he had no right to feel and no idea how to handle.

It wasn't old and aged enough to offer the distance he needed to shove it away like he had so many others. It wasn't one he could turn away from or ignore. It was consuming. Terrifying.

Overwhelming.

And it left him desperate to see the only face that could help him survive this.

TWENTY-THREE

DIANNA

*D*IANNA DROPPED DOWN onto the couch, setting the last basket of laundry at her feet as the rain outside picked up, pelting her roof and her windows. Normally, this would be a perfectly cozy way to spend her Sunday evening, sipping a cup of tea, watching one of the many shows she didn't have time to keep up with while folding socks.

But the storm outside was starting to worry her. Not because she was concerned about the power going out, or flooding, or how it might affect her in general. She was worried because right about now Griffin should be driving home from Cross Creek, navigating narrow country roads in the downpour.

She checked the time again, glancing out the front window before forcing her butt back to the couch. She'd spent the day rotating clothes and sheets through the washer and dryer while vacuuming, dusting, and scrubbing toilets. It wasn't glamorous or fun, but it was necessary. And they were things she would rather not have to do when she could be spending time with Griffin instead, so she was taking full advantage of the time he spent with Troy.

But that was usually finished by now, and the fact that Griffin wasn't home was starting to make her antsy.

She did her best to focus on the television, sorting through her whites as drama unfolded between the characters of Bridgerton and the smell of the pot roast she had in the oven started wafting in.

Griffin had probably already eaten, but it would be perfectly good reheated tomorrow after work, and great to make sandwiches with later in the week. She'd also gone to the grocery store and was set up with simple meals for the rest of the weekdays so Griffin could have a good dinner each night since she was pretty sure he didn't eat much during the day.

Was she going back to old ways by taking care of him?

Probably. And a few weeks ago she might have shamed herself for it. Might have tried to tell herself it was the wrong thing to do. That she was ushering the past in so it could repeat itself.

But this was who she was. Food was how she showed she cared, just like it was how her grandmother did. And, like the body type they shared, labeling it as wrong just because someone else used it against her wasn't okay.

Liking to cook for the people she cared about wasn't bad, just like her thick thighs and soft belly weren't bad.

They were just her. Who she was and who she would always be.

The realization was liberating, releasing another layer of guilt and self-deprecation, freeing her up to focus on more important things. Things like the storm that seemed to amp up a little more with each passing second.

Dianna tossed the final pair of socks into the basket and stood up, glaring out at the downpour. No doubt it was responsible for Griffin being later than normal. She snagged the basket from the floor and carried it back to her bedroom, putting everything away before setting the empty basket on top of the washer in the hall laundry closet. Then she went to check on her pot roast, lifting the lid and breathing the scent of roasting meat deep into her lungs. She'd just replaced the lid and slid the pot back into place when a flash of lightning made her jump. The lights flickered as a huge crack of thunder shook the house.

Dianna glared up at the fixture over her head. "You better not go out. If this roast is ruined I will—"

A solid metal *thunk* dragged her attention to the front of the house. It sounded an awful lot like a heavy car door slamming and had her rushing through the living room. She yanked open the door, hoping it would help provide Griffin a speedy entry and spare him from being soaked.

But Griffin didn't seem to be concerned about the torrents falling from the sky. His steps were slow, almost like his feet were too heavy to lift, as he crossed their yards. By the time he reached the base of her steps, his hair was plastered flat to his head and his clothes clung to his skin.

But she barely noticed any of it, because the look on his face had her stomach twisting in knots. "Griffin?" She rushed out onto the porch, her bare feet moving across the damp planks as she hurried toward him. "What's wrong?"

His eyes suddenly found focus and snapped to her face, expression full of devastation as he started to move, taking the steps two at a time before wrapping her in his arms and pulling her tight against him. He buried his face in her hair, breathing in deep, heaving gulps.

She held him close, the twisting in her stomach winding so tight she almost felt sick.

Griffin's arms squeezed tighter, to the point it was hard to breathe. "Amelie started to bleed." The words were broken and soft. Like it took all he had to push them free. "It was everywhere." He sucked in a ragged breath. "I didn't know what to do." His hand came to cradle the back of her head, fingers digging into her hair like he couldn't hold her close enough. "She can't lose him, Di."

She wanted to tell him it would all be fine. That the baby he so wanted would be born happy and healthy. But that would just be something to pacify him. Something to help placate and push down all the fears and feelings he was struggling to navigate.

Dianna leaned back, barely managing to get enough

space between them so she could press her forehead to his as she offered up the only truth she knew. "This might not go the way you want it to, but I promise we will get through it."

Griffin's blue eyes held hers as the rain clinging to his hair dripped down his face. "What if I can't? What if I can't be what they need me to be?"

The fear in his voice broke her heart almost as much as the understanding that she wasn't the only one who carried voices from the past.

The ones that tell you you're not enough. That you will always be lacking.

But while she faced them, dug them from all the places they hid and replanted words of her own, Griffin tried to bury his deeper. Tried to pretend they were gone forever.

But that just gave them room to grow roots.

"What they need you to be is what you've always been." Dianna brought her hands to his face, forcing his eyes to stay on hers.

Because if he wouldn't dig those fuckers up then she would.

"You have shown up for them since day one. You've been there." She stood a little taller, spoke a little louder, as if she could shove the truth into his brain with sheer volume. "You sold your house. You restructured your business. You moved your whole life. You wanted to be there for them and you figured out how to make it happen. You will figure this out too." She softened her voice just a little. "You figure shit out, remember?"

Griffin's eyes moved over her face as the wind whipped around them, carrying a wave of chilly mist that was mostly blocked by his big body. "You make it sound easy."

Dianna shook her head. "Oh, it won't be." She smoothed away some of the rain on his skin. "But you take it one step at a time." She focused on where her fingers brushed over the salt and peppery hairs peeking out along his jawline. "And sometimes you accidentally go back instead of forward, but all that matters is you keep trying."

She'd gone backward more times than she could count. Had moments where she laid on the bathroom floor and cried, wrapped up in regret and remorse. Longing for what might have been. But those moments needed to happen. She had to grieve to go on. And if all this went the worst possible way, Griffin would need that too.

He closed his eyes, taking a deep breath before opening them again. "I don't think I deserve you, Di."

The admission was unexpected, but maybe not as shocking as it might have been ten minutes ago. Before today it never occurred to her that someone like Griffin would carry the same kind of demons she did. That he would feel lacking or deficient in any way.

But it explained a lot.

"I thought this was my second chance. I thought—" Griffin's voice cracked.

"It can't be your second chance if you never had a first chance, Griffin." She understood what he was trying to say, but it wasn't the reality of the situation. "You weren't responsible for not being in Troy's life." Her eyes searched his, looking for some sign that he understood. "That's someone else's burden to bear. Let them fucking carry it."

It'd been one of the first realizations she'd come to after her divorce. She was trying to take full responsibility for what happened. Trying to feel like she had some power over all of it. But she didn't. Someone else took it from her and then left her smothered under the weight of failure. Failure that wasn't hers. Failure she now refused to own.

Hopefully one day Griffin would do the same.

Griffin's clinging fingers relaxed the tiniest bit, his hold on her gentling. "You're fucking amazing, Di."

The initial reaction to blow his complement off was still there, but it was weak and short-lived. "Thank you." She gave him a little smile, tracing the path of a waterdrop as it slid down his temple. "You're pretty fantastic yourself."

Griffin opened his mouth then stopped. He tucked his chin, taking just a second before responding. "Thank you."

Her smile widened with pride and a little relief. She didn't want to settle again. And being with someone she could talk to—someone who would talk to her—wasn't anything she was willing to do without.

Another gust of wind cut across the porch, but this one came from a different direction and slapped her body with a heavy pelt of cold rain that immediately sank into the T-shirt and joggers she was wearing. A full body shiver seized her muscles as her skin and nipples pulled so tight they almost hurt.

Griffin frowned. "Apparently I'm not fantastic enough to get you in out of the cold and the rain." He pulled her body against his, hauling her across the porch and through the door, releasing her only long enough to kick off his boots. Then he grabbed her again, hands coming to her face as his mouth found hers, hungry, needy, and a little desperate.

She understood completely. What just happened made her feel closer to him. More connected. It also made her want to soothe the upset he was still certainly fighting. Offer a distraction she knew he desperately needed. And maybe a little bit of a reward for being so vulnerable. She didn't want him to associate this moment with only suffering.

Dianna fisted her hands in the front of his wet shirt, using the hold to drag him through her tiny house as Griffin's mouth bumped against hers in hot, claiming kisses that bordered on being a little messy as they rushed down the hall. The second he was in her room she raked the clinging cotton up his chest, fighting the distraction of his warm skin until the thing was falling toward the floor. She flattened her palms against the solid width of his chest, sliding them down his front, eyes rolling closed as his lips skimmed the sensitive skin of her neck.

"You are so fucking perfect." Griffin grabbed at her clothes, managing to remove them much more efficiently than she did his, and before she realized it, her body was bare and his touch was everywhere. "So fucking soft and sweet." He wrapped one arm around her waist, pinning her body to his, the damp fabric of his jeans rubbing the fronts of her thighs as he pushed her toward the bed. Griffin gave her body a little shove with his, sending her falling back to the blankets she'd spent the day washing. His eyes skimmed down her frame, filled with reverence.

But her first reaction was still to hide. To cover the body so many people had judged and found lacking. It took all the control she had to stay still. To let his gaze slide over the way the weight of her breasts slid to the side. The way the full curve of her belly indented at her middle. The selection of dimples clustered along her thighs.

She'd been ashamed of it for so long. Punished it for not living up to the expectations of small-minded men and judgmental women.

Griffin reached out to slide the tips of his fingers up one of the thighs that carried her through life, offering support and strength. "Fucking perfect."

Dianna stared at his face, taking in the unshuttered look of awe and lust there. In that moment, it was easy to agree with him. Easy to see what he did.

Griffin dropped to his knees, hands gripping her thighs and spreading them wide. She gasped as the heat of his mouth connected with her flesh, teasing her toward an orgasm that hit so fast she didn't have time to prepare, only to react. She gripped his hair, holding him in place as her body convulsed, possessed by the man offering so much more than adoration and acceptance.

There was barely breath back in her lungs when he pushed to his feet, working his pants off as he moved before bracing her thighs against his chest, and sank into her, the fill of his body dragging a ragged moan through her lips.

Griffin leaned into her legs, angling his body closer to hers as one hand spread the lips of her pussy, baring her clit to the friction of his body with each thrust.

Her back arched off the bed at the new sensation as she struggled to regain the oxygen she would need to survive long enough to see this night through.

And she absolutely wanted to see it through.

Especially when Griffin's free hand caught the weight of one breast, fingers stretching to tease her nipple with a pinching roll that walked along the edge of pain.

It was too much sensation at once. More than any reasonable woman could stand.

But she'd never been particularly reasonable.

A second climax ripped through her, the sound of a voice similar to her own filling the room as Griffin grunted and pushed deeper, pinning her with hard, punctuating thrusts that raked against her exposed clit and dragged out the pleasure contorting her limbs.

Griffin stiffened, rocking against her as his cock twitched and swelled, the heat of his release making her clench around him.

Dianna blinked, her lids moving slower than normal as she went limp, unable to do anything as Griffin rolled her body to the center of the bed and climbed in behind her, curling his warm body against her back.

She wanted to sleep. To give in to the pull of exhaustion and bliss trying to close her eyes.

But she couldn't. So to continue with her awkward tradition of saying the wrong thing immediately after sex, she rolled to face him, giving Griffin a little smile. "I need to go check on my meat."

TWENTY-FOUR

GRIFFIN

*D*IANNA WATCHED, GAZE unwavering as he paced around her small living room, cell phone pressed tight to his ear so he didn't miss a word his son said.

"Why are they sending her home if it could happen again?" It didn't make sense to him. If Amelie and the baby were still at risk she needed to stay in the fucking hospital.

"Because there's nothing anyone can do at this point to keep it from happening again." Troy's voice was raspy and rough from lack of sleep and probably a dozen other things. "It will either happen again or it won't. Apparently they can't predict things like this."

The news was better than he had anticipated, but still

not enough to ease his fears. "When do you need me to come get you?"

Troy murmured what sounded like a question, waiting for Amelie's response before coming back to the line. "They're expecting to send her home sometime this morning, so just head this way whenever you're ready."

Griffin nodded, even though his son couldn't see it. "I'll get over there as soon as I can."

He felt a little better now that he knew everything was currently okay. He'd tossed and turned all night, struggling to sleep even though Dianna was beside him. And, based on the slightly pale color of her face and the tired tilt of her eyes, his struggle became her struggle, which fueled the guilt he seemed to always carry.

Dianna sat up a little straighter, expression hopeful as he disconnected the line. "What did he say?"

"Their best guess is that the placenta grew too close to her cervix." He carefully recited Troy's explanation, being sure to use the same terms. "They said sometimes it will separate and move away on its own, trying to correct the problem, but when that happens there can be a lot of bleeding." He swallowed hard, struggling with the last bit. "It can also lead to the loss of the pregnancy if the placenta doesn't reattach properly."

Dianna's lips flattened into a grim line. "Did it reattach properly?"

Griffin quickly nodded, not wanting her to worry. "This time it did. But they said her placenta is still pretty close to her cervix and there's the chance it could happen again." He took a steadying breath. "And the risks are the same if it happens again."

Dianna's shoulders lifted and fell in a deep breath. "So what do they do to make sure it doesn't happen again?"

This was the part he was struggling with the most. He was a do-er. He figured shit out and found a way to fix it. But apparently that wasn't possible in a situation like this. "There's nothing they can do." Griffin clenched both fists at his sides, fighting the anger and frustration building on top of the helplessness they used like a platform. "They're sending her home because there's nothing anyone can do but wait and see."

Dianna's jaw dropped, her mouth hanging open. "Wait and see?" She jumped to her feet, voice rising. "Wait and see? What kind of fucking medical opinion is that?"

"They said there's only so much that can be done." He reached for her, pulling her close, convincing himself he was offering comfort instead of taking it.

"Well that's fucking stupid." Dianna leaned into him, her arms wrapping around his waist.

If he had it in him to smile right now he would. Her reaction made him feel a little bit less like he was overreacting. The emotions still weren't comfortable, but at least they were warranted.

Griffin stroked one hand up and down her back, stealing a few final moments with Dianna before she had to go to work and he had to face down a situation he was ill-equipped to tackle. "Troy said they'll be discharging her sometime this morning, so I told him I'd head over there as soon as I could."

Dianna nodded, pulling away from his hold a little too soon. "Of course." She went to the kitchen, her steps hurried. "Do you want to take breakfast with you?"

He'd planned to grab something on the way, but the temptation to eke out just a few more minutes with her was too great. "That sounds like a good idea." He stepped in beside her at the counter, easily falling into the comfortable routine they'd established in such a short period of time.

"A breakfast sandwich would probably travel the best." Dianna started grabbing items from the fridge and sliding them onto the counter. Just as the eggs were in place, her eyes snapped to his face. "Do you want to take something for Troy and Amelie too? I can't imagine hospital food is that great." Her lips pressed into a frown as she scanned the line-up. "But I'm also not sure how warm everything will stay on the trip." She chewed her lower lip, eyes narrowing the tiniest bit. "I could pack it in an insulated lunch box." Her eyes jumped back to his. "If you think they would be hungry."

He understood what she was asking. It was the same question she'd been asking when she sent the cake yesterday, and it had nothing to do with how hungry Troy and Amelie might be. They were getting to the point where he was going to have to tell his son what was going on between them. He would have to confess his lack of self-control and focus.

He'd considered it a number of times but putting it

into words had been impossible so far. So maybe he didn't have to put it into words. "I bet they're starving."

Dianna's lips curved into a soft smile before pressing together. She nodded. "Okay."

They started to work, assembling his favorite sausage, egg, and cheese sandwich together, him in charge of making the patties and the toast, and Dianna monitoring the actual cooking. In under fifteen minutes everything was packed and ready to go, including a large travel mug filled with coffee.

Dianna ushered him out onto the porch, giving him a final kiss before sending him on his way with the promise she would see him later that night.

Griffin packed everything into the truck and backed out, giving her a wave as he pulled away, watching her watch him in the rearview mirror.

Part of him wished he could stay behind with her. That everything was still right in the world and he could sit with Dianna on her porch swing, wrapped up in the electric blanket he'd ordered to extend their mornings on the porch.

But his son needed him, and this was where he could prove that no matter what, Troy would always come first.

THE DRIVE TO the hospital felt dramatically faster than it had the night before—probably because he wasn't consumed by panic and fear—and before long Griffin was pulling into a spot in the garage and heading for the main entrance. He collected an identification badge at the desk, gaining permission to enter the maternity ward, before making his way to the third floor.

Amelie looked surprisingly well when he walked in, sitting cross-legged on the hospital bed, wearing a set of pajamas that looked soft and expensive.

"I don't remember hospital wear looking quite that comfortable." He greeted Troy with a hug before leaning in to kiss Amelie on the top of her head.

Amelie glanced down, smoothing the soft looking top across her pregnant belly. "These are definitely not hospital issue." Her hands stayed against her stomach, cradling it close. "Evelyn brought these over for me last night because I was uncomfortable in what they gave me and the clothes I had on were ruined."

His stomach clenched, the guilt he felt earlier over keeping Dianna up all night compounding immediately. "I could've brought you something."

He hated that Amelie and Troy didn't think they could count on him. That he wasn't someone they considered reliable enough to reach out to when they needed help.

Amelie relaxed back against the upright portion of the bed. "We didn't want to bother you. Especially after you had to drive us all the way out here." She smiled, like she was trying to reassure him. "Plus, I'm sure you had other things to do."

He opened his mouth to argue, but it would've been a lie. He did have other things occupying his night.

And maybe that was a bigger problem than he'd wanted to admit.

"What you got there?" Troy motioned toward the insulated bag still gripped in his hand.

Griffin stared down at it, the opportunity he thought it presented suddenly feeling all wrong. "I made up some breakfast sandwiches in case you guys were hungry." It felt wrong to cut Dianna's involvement out, but bringing her in didn't seem right either. Not when it would confirm Amelie's suspicion that he wasn't a person they could always rely on.

"I'm fucking starving." Troy settled into the chair beside Amelie's bed. "The food here fucking sucks."

Griffin set the bag onto the rolling table, his gut churning as he opened it up and passed out the wax paper wrapped sandwiches Dianna had taken so much care to assemble.

Troy immediately tore into his and took a huge bite, groaning a little as he chewed. "This is amazing." His brows pinched together as he swallowed, eyes going to the stack of homemade bread and perfectly cooked sausage. "You made this?"

The opportunity to claim Dianna was being served up to him on a silver platter. The chance to come clean. To confess all his sins. To tell them how much she meant to him. How much he hoped he meant to her.

But, like they so often did, the words stuck together, clogging into a mess that wouldn't come out.

Griffin nodded. "I googled it."

It wasn't an outright lie, but it omitted a hell of a lot of truth.

And the truth was he'd done exactly what he wasn't going to do. He'd allowed himself to be distracted. Allowed himself to lose focus on the thing that mattered to him most.

And it hadn't gone unnoticed. When Amelie and Troy needed something, they didn't call him. They assumed he had more important things to do and because he was an asshole who couldn't seem to learn from his mistakes, they weren't entirely wrong.

Griffin sat down in the remaining chair, forcing himself to eat. Amelie and Troy were quiet as they ate, watching television and drinking shitty hospital coffee until a nurse finally came to wheel Amelie outside.

The conversation on the way home flowed, but he struggled to pay attention. Struggled to be present. Yet another way he was failing his son right when he needed him most.

As soon as Troy and Amelie were home, his son sent him on his way. The dismissal further proof he wasn't reliable enough to be needed.

Griffin went home, trying to focus on all he had to accomplish at his house instead of how he'd fucking failed again, but his mind was caught up in a vicious cycle. One he couldn't escape.

Almost right out of the gate he'd gone and done exactly what he knew he shouldn't, proving how incapable he was of creating any sort of healthy relationship.

And it wasn't just his relationship with Troy he was going to fuck up. Sooner or later he would fail Dianna. She would see him exactly as every woman had before.

Unless he ended it before that happened. Then they could go back to being just neighbors.

Just friends.

The thought sat heavy in his gut as he tried to work on his bathroom, adding a fresh layer of misery to all that was stacking up.

Griffin finally gave up trying to accomplish anything worthwhile and spent the day sitting on his back patio, tossing scraps of bread to the birds and sharing peanuts with Snickerdoodle. The fluffy rodent sat on the arm of the rusty metal chair Nate and his family left behind, chewing through nut after nut as Griffin stared out at nothing in particular.

Maybe he should do what Cooper suggested and turn the house for a profit. Take the money and go back to his initial plan of building a place on Grizzly Peak. But that option sat just as heavy and miserable in his gut as the thought of leaving Dianna did.

He was still on the back porch, stewing in his own misery, when he heard Dianna's garage door open and the low hum of her car's engine as she pulled inside.

He should march over there now. Explain that he simply didn't have the capabilities of being Troy's dad and her—

Hers.

But it was starting to become clear that walking away from Dianna might not change that fact. Yes, it might mean she was no longer his, but he wasn't confident it would mean he wasn't hers. Because deep down, he'd been hers for a long fucking time. And he couldn't imagine that would change anytime soon. No matter where he lived.

Griffin pushed up from his chair, going back through the house he was once so excited to call his own. The house that was supposed to solve all his problems but only ended up creating more. Suddenly it no longer felt like a home. Not when he thought about the possibility that Dianna wouldn't be in it anymore.

Griffin forced his feet out the front door and down the steps, going to where he knew she would be waiting for him.

Dianna's focus snapped to him when he reached the open door of her garage. Her brows pinched together immediately. "Is everything okay with Amelie and the baby?"

He nodded, relieved when she didn't immediately sense the real issue he was struggling with. "As right as it can be." He stayed in place as she worked her way out of the tiny garage. "She's home now resting. I'm going to go out tomorrow and check on her."

Sure, he could call, but he'd already clearly proven to them he was lacking, so it was important that he show up. Change their minds. Prove he could be what they both needed him to be.

Dianna nodded, expression full of understanding. "I'm sure she'll appreciate that." Her eyes moved over his face. "How are you doing?"

"Fine." The response sounded shorter and more clipped than he intended, but right now he was holding on by a thread. Caught between what he should do and what he wanted to do.

And what he wanted to do was pull Dianna close and pretend he was the kind of man she deserved.

So that's what he did. He snagged her by the front of her sweatshirt and dragged her body against his, holding her tight.

Because no matter how hard he tried to be a good man—one deserving of both his son and the woman he couldn't make himself stay away from—that's just not who he was.

He was, and always would be, exactly what so many women called him.

A selfish asshole.

TWENTY-FIVE

DIANNA

GRIFFIN WAS QUIET beside her on the swing, saying little to nothing as they ate their breakfast.

But that had been par for the course the past week. He was still clearly struggling with the scare Amelie had, but instead of continuing to open up to her about it like he had the first night, Griffin seemed to be shutting down.

Which was a problem. Not just for his sake, but for hers.

Of course she didn't want him bottling up how he felt, but she didn't want to have to do it either. Especially on a day like today.

"Do you have anything planned for today?" Dianna

made an attempt at starting up a conversation, hoping he would latch onto it the way he used to.

Griffin tipped his head in a small nod. "I'll probably work a little on the house and then go check on Amelie."

She held her breath, waiting. Hoping he might elaborate on something. Offer up a few words she didn't have to pry out of him. But like he had so many times over the past few days, Griffin fell silent again.

"I'm sure Amelie appreciates you coming out to check on her while Troy has to work."

She understood Griffin's desire to make sure Amelie was well taken care of. She was like a daughter to him. He'd been devastated by the thought that not only might something happen to the baby, but that Amelie would suffer as well. He was so open about it initially. Spilling out all his fears easily. Holding her so tight she could barely breathe. Desperately in need of reassurance and comfort.

Which made her worry. What if Griffin was capable of sharing his feelings, but only on his own terms. Only when his own needs outweighed the discomfort that came with opening up.

The possibility was devastating.

"What about you?" He glanced her way. "Anything special on your agenda?"

Dianna swallowed hard, nearly choking on the lump that immediately formed in her throat as she set down her barely touched plate. "I just want to get through the day." She blinked a few times, working away the line of tears threatening to spring free. "It's the anniversary of my grandmother's death, so today's always a tough day."

Griffin's expression immediately softened and he pulled her close, tucking her head under his chin as he cradled her face with one hand. "I'm sorry."

Dianna relaxed, sniffing a little but feeling better at his display. Maybe she'd been wrong. Maybe she was just overreacting and emotional because this dreaded day had been hanging over her head.

Maybe Griffin wasn't the issue at all. Maybe it was all her. Creating problems that didn't exist. Overreacting. Expecting to be let down like she had so many times before.

He pressed a lingering kiss to her forehead, breathing deep as his lips rested against her skin. Then he stood up, carefully extricating himself from the blanket as he collected his plate and hers, just like he did every morning.

Normally she was grateful. Normally she appreciated that he took the plates inside and washed them without being asked. But this morning, everything felt colder than normal and it had nothing to do with the weather.

When Griffin showed up on her doorstep a week ago, broken and battered, filled with fear and uncertainty, she'd dropped everything to be there for him. To make sure he knew he wasn't alone. And while she understood he needed to put Amelie and Troy first, only getting a forehead kiss and a few words of apology on a day like today didn't sit right.

Dianna worked her way up from the swing, folding

up the electric blanket Griffin bought and carrying it inside with her as he finished up the dishes, stacking them into the rack before drying off his hands and turning her way. "I need to go pick up the tile I ordered so I can get started on the floor of the bathroom." He lingered in the doorway, his uncertainty encouraging her to push him for more.

But she couldn't do it. Not today.

"Okay." Dianna smiled, ignoring the ache in her chest that seemed to be compounding by the minute. "I can't wait to see it when you're all done."

Griffin almost looked sad, the flash of it squeezing her heart as it moved across his handsome features before being replaced by a hint of the wolfish smile she used to see so often. "You might decide you're the one who needs to shower at my place once you get a peek at it."

The glimpse of what they had such a short time ago was like a breadcrumb, tempting her to keep following along even though it wasn't nearly enough to sustain her.

Griffin came close, his large frame taking up all the space and stealing all the air as his hands slid over her hips to cup her ass. "It's plenty big enough for two people and comes with a free overnight stay in my bed if you need any extra motivation." The press of his hard body was solid and warm as he pulled her closer, leaning down to brush his mouth along the line of her neck. "I also installed grip bars just in case you need a little stability while you're getting all soaped up."

She smiled against his lips as they brushed hers. "You're just tired of fighting with my shower curtain."

Griffin laughed, the deep sound of it making her heart skip a little beat. "I'm not going to argue that." He caught her lips again in a consuming kiss that left her head spinning and her lungs fighting for air. "I wish I could stay longer, but you've got to get to work and I need to pick up that tile before they try to unload it themselves and break half of what I ordered." He kissed her again, his teeth gently raking across her lower lip as he pulled away. "I'll see you later?"

Dianna nodded, easily smiling as he traced her lips with his thumb. "You know where to find me."

Griffin's eyes followed the path of his thumb, lingering on her mouth. "I'll miss you."

A little more of the upset she'd been struggling to make sense of eased at his hushed confession. "Good."

Griffin's hand slid from her face and he backed toward the door, giving her a wink as he slipped out.

Maybe everything was fine. Maybe he was still just struggling with all that happened.

She needed to relax. Give him a break. Stop being so demand—

The thought stopped her in her tracks. Sent her back to the moment those words were first put on her. But they weren't true then.

And they probably weren't true now.

Her bad mood returned in a flash, bringing along a healthy dose of self-loathing that followed her all the way to work.

By the time she walked in through the back door of

The Baking Rack she was sick to her stomach and filled with disappointment.

"Hey." Janie's greeting sent Dianna stumbling back as she walked through the door, one hand pressed to her chest as her heart raced.

"What are you doing here?" She sucked in a breath, leaning against the wall for balance. "You scared the shit out of me."

Janie winced. "Sorry. I wasn't trying to scare you."

Dianna blew out a breath as she hooked her purse into place and wiggled out of the jacket she pulled on over her sweatshirt, lining it onto the same hook. "I think I'm just wound up today."

Maybe wound up wasn't the right word. Maybe she was too many things to list and wound up was just an easy way to summarize.

"That's part of the reason I'm here." Janie picked up the plate sitting on the counter in front of her, holding it out between them. "I knew today would be tough for you so I figured I would bring you a present and come in and help." She shook her head. "No charge. Not as an employee, just as your friend."

Dianna turned, her eyes landing on the item balanced in Janie's grip. She pressed one hand to her mouth, fighting the sudden flood of tears trying to leak free. "You made me an angel food cake."

Janie tipped her head to one side. "Technically, Mariah made you an angel food cake since I had no clue how in the hell to do it." She smiled a little bit. "And also because I wanted it to actually be good enough to commemorate your grandma's memory."

Dianna rushed at her, wrapping Janie in a tight hug as her friend struggled to get the plate back to the safety of the counter. "I think this is the nicest thing anyone has ever done for me." A sob escaped, one only half due to Janie's kind gesture.

"Oh, honey." Janie squeezed her tight. "I know it's hard when you lose someone you love." She rubbed a circle along Dianna's back. "And it doesn't get any better, which fucking sucks a bag of dicks."

A twisted combination of a laugh and a cry sent a little snot leaking out of her nose, forcing Dianna to use the sleeve of her sweatshirt to wipe it away. "It's not just that." She leaned back, dabbing at the corners of her eyes as she took a jumpy breath. "I'm also a little worried you might have been right."

Janie's brows pinched together. "That doesn't sound right. I'm pretty sure no one has ever said that about me before, so you're probably wrong."

"I think I might be a little blinded by good dick." Dianna managed another watery smile. "Maybe my expectations are just too high."

Janie's expression immediately sharpened and she pointed one finger at Dianna's face. "You are not the problem. You are never the problem." She lifted her brows. "You're a fucking goddess, remember?"

Dianna sniffed again, doing her best to rein in the onslaught of emotion. It wasn't like her. She normally kept everything under control. She had years of practice keeping her reactions as tame as possible after being called dramatic and crazy more times than she could count. "Then you were definitely right and I was just blinded by good dick."

She'd almost been willing to overlook everything when Griffin pulled her close this morning. Kissed her and reminded her of how good they were together. And she might have managed it if Janie hadn't been standing here with an angel food cake and an offer of emotional and physical support, making Griffin's forehead kiss and 'I'm sorry' seem lame in comparison.

"I don't expect him to make me a cake, but he could at least ask me if I'm okay." The sadness she'd been struggling with started to turn, souring into something slightly easier to manage. "I told him today was the anniversary of my grandma's death and he just said he was sorry and kissed me on the head and then basically left to go on about his day." Her summary left out the part where Griffin had done her dishes and made out with her a little, but both of those things seemed completely insignificant now.

Janie leaned in, reaching up to wipe at the tears still sliding down Dianna's cheeks. "That's because he's a fucking piece of shit with no emotional capacity." She rested both hands on Dianna's shoulders. "And you deserve better. You've been through so much. Don't settle again."

Was that what she was doing? Settling?

"It seemed like he was really trying though. He told me how he felt like being a grandpa would give him another chance at enjoying fatherhood. He talked about how guilty he felt over not being a part of his son's life." She shook her head, disappointed all over again. "One night he literally poured his heart out to me and I thought—"

She thought they'd turned a corner. And maybe they did.

Just not the one she wanted.

"I think maybe he only opens up to me when it fills his needs." Saying it out loud was like a knife to her already upset gut, twisting until the urge to throw up was almost unbearable.

Janie smoothed back Dianna's hair, the gesture similar to a mother comforting a child. "I've been there, and sometimes you just have to walk away before they make you think you're losing your mind."

The timer on one of the ovens dinged, signaling it was finished preheating. Dianna glanced toward the appliance. "Did you already start the ovens?"

"Of course I did. I told you I came to help." Janie gave her a wry smile. "If you need me to help move a body later I'm available for that as well."

Dianna smiled, rolling her eyes a little. "I would never ask you to do that for me."

Janie moved toward the refrigerator, pulling out the first tray of cinnamon rolls and setting them on the counter to finish rising. "You know what they say. Friends help you move but real friends help you move bodies."

Dianna snorted out a hiccupy laugh, falling in

beside her 'real' friend as they prepped for the day together. Monday mornings were usually light anyway, but with an added set of hands the process was smooth as butter. By the time the doors opened, everything was organized and ready, keeping Dianna's stress level as low as it could be, all things considered. The rest of the morning flew by with Janie helping her at the register, filling orders, making coffees, and passing out cake orders. By the time the afternoon lull arrived she was feeling a little better. Maybe not great, but at least not overwhelmed.

"I'm going to go get started on prepping for tomorrow." Janie pointed at the register. "You got this?"

Her tone carried more than a hint of sarcasm.

Dianna took a bite of the angel food cake they'd been snacking on all day, leaning against the counter. "I think I can handle it."

Janie shot her a grin. "I never doubted you for a second." She bumped her way through the swinging door and into the back room, leaving Dianna on her own behind the counter.

She scanned the contents of the cases, reorganizing the bits and pieces remaining into one single display before clearing away the stray crumbs and swipes of frosting in the other. She was crouched behind the counter, working on the bottom shelf when the bell on the door dinged, bringing her to her feet.

And face-to-face with Griffin.

Griffin and the biggest, most beautiful bouquet of flowers she'd ever seen.

He moved to the counter, setting down the collection of roses and lilies. "How's it going?"

Dianna struggled to look away from the flowers, but managed to bring her eyes to his. "Okay."

"Not too sad?" He reached out to slide a loose bit of hair behind one ear, his fingers trailing down her neck.

Dianna leaned into his touch, an immeasurable amount of relief sagging her shoulders. "I'm a little sad." She smiled. "But it's getting better."

"Better enough that you don't want this?" He pulled a small box from his pocket and slid it across the counter. She glanced down at it, her heart squeezing.

"What's this?" She picked it up and lifted the lid to reveal a necklace with a tiny bird charm dangling from the delicate chain.

"I wanted a squirrel, but they didn't have any so I had to settle for a bird." He reached out to take it, slipping the necklace free before unlatching the chain. "I'm sure Snickerdoodle will understand." He leaned across the counter, securing it around her neck.

Dianna rested her fingertips on the charm, swallowing at the lump that was back in her throat. Maybe Griffin wasn't ever going to be completely open with his feelings, but that was okay. As long as he kept trying, that would be enough. As long as they talked when things really mattered and he showed up for her, she could be patient.

Everything could be fi—

"Are we doing cherry something tomorrow?" Janie pushed in from the kitchen, looking down at the list in her hand. "Because there's a whole lotta cherry pie filling—" She froze as her eyes landed on Griffin, her jaw going slack.

Griffin stared back at her and tension twisted the air. He tipped his head in greeting. "Janie."

Janie crossed her arms, lip curling as she shook her head. "I knew it was going to be you."

Dianna looked between them, eyes bouncing from Griffin to Janie. "You two know each other?" It was a stupid question to ask. Obviously they'd met.

But it was also obvious they'd done more than simply meet, and a few pieces slowly started falling into place.

She swallowed hard, eyes on Janie. "No." She shook her head, struggling to believe exactly what was going on. "You would have told me if you thought—" She rested one hand against her head as her stomach rolled, fighting against the angel food cake she'd been so happy to receive from the woman she thought was a 'real' friend.

But would a 'real' friend be suspicious that you were dating their ex and say nothing? An ex they clearly despised and thought so little of?

No. A real friend wouldn't do that.

Dianna turned to Griffin, bringing her accusations along with her. "Why didn't *you* say something?"

Griffin shifted on his feet, his focus leaving Janie to fix on her. "There's more than one Janie in the world, Di. I didn't think—"

"You didn't think the woman who was working for me who was a little bit older than me, had a whole sleeve of arm tattoos, and dropped out of culinary school was the same Janie?" Her words were fast and rambling but so were her thoughts. She'd mentioned so many things to him. Things that were irrelevant at the time, but suddenly added up to a level of deception she struggled to stomach.

But it wasn't just Griffin holding back on her this time.

She turned to Janie. "You knew it was him." All their conversations came flooding back. The anger Janie still carried. The way she seemed to know exactly what was happening. Exactly what Griffin was doing wrong.

Because he'd done it to her.

She thought Griffin holding back his feelings was the issue they would have to work through, but that was before she realized he was keeping more than feelings from her.

And for someone who pushed her to dump a man who didn't treat her right, Janie sure seemed fine with letting her make a fool of herself talking about the man they'd both shared a bed with.

"I want you to go." Dianna pointed to the door, closing her eyes because she couldn't stand to see anything else. "Both of you."

They might not have lied to her face, but guilt by omission was a very real thing and it hurt just as bad.

Dianna waited, holding her breath, terrified one of them would argue with her. Try to convince her to change her mind.

But they didn't.

A minute later the door opened and closed and the only sound in the store was her own choppy breaths.

She rushed to lock the deadbolt, flipping the sign just as the tears started to fall.

Heartbreak she'd kind of been expecting.

But betrayal she had not.

TWENTY-SIX

GRIFFIN

"YOU REALLY DON'T have to sit here and wait on me all day." Amelie pulled the blanket covering her legs and belly a little higher, relaxing back against the pillow propping her upright on the couch. "I'm perfectly capable of laying here and doing nothing all by myself."

"But then you would have to get up and make your own lunch." Griffin carried over the grilled cheese and tomato soup he'd managed to create, carefully setting the plate onto the tray positioned over Amelie's lap. "And then do the dishes."

Using his daughter-in-law's condition as an excuse, he'd moved back to Troy and Amelie's house almost a week ago, packing up only what he absolutely needed and reclaiming the bedroom upstairs.

"Both things I can do because staying off my feet isn't technically going to make a difference." She gave him a weak smile. "I just feel like it can't hurt and it makes me feel like I'm doing *something*."

Griffin gave her a little nod. "I understand." And he did. More than she probably realized.

So much of his life was out of his control right now, and being here with Amelie, making her lunch and doing the dishes so she could rest, made him feel like he hadn't lost everything.

Only almost all of it.

Amelie picked up half the grilled cheese and took a bite, giving him a smile around the mouthful. "You're getting better at this." She held it out so he could see. "The cheese is all the way melted this time."

Like everything else he'd attempted to tackle recently, cooking was proving to be more difficult than he'd anticipated. "I think I might just need to learn to have a little more patience and stop trying to cook everything as fast as possible."

Amelie's smile slipped a little. "It can be really hard to have patience sometimes." Her free hand went to rest on her belly, fingers splayed across the curve of it. "Especially when you're worried about how things are going to turn out."

Unfortunately, he knew how things typically turned out for him, and it wasn't good.

Griffin sat down in the chair across from her, taking a bite of his own grilled cheese—the one he rushed, burning the outside without fully melting the cheese. "Are you feeling okay today?"

Amelie shrugged. "I feel just as fine as I have every other day." She sighed. "That's part of what's so scary. I didn't even feel bad. I just started to bleed."

"Sometimes things sideswipe you out of nowhere." Griffin dropped the remnants of his sandwich onto the plate, his appetite disappearing. Because he honestly hadn't been sideswiped. Dianna was right when she accused him of knowing who Janie was. He'd narrowed down the possibility almost immediately.

But, like he did with so many other things, he ignored the very real possibility, the likelihood even, that the Janie she worked with was probably the same Janie he once knew. The same Janie who chucked his clothes out of the window when he refused to admit how he felt about her, their relationship, or life in general.

Should he have questioned Dianna about her new employee? Explained they might have a connection? Probably. But he should have done a dozen other things too, and every one of them haunted him, keeping him up at night and torturing him during the day.

"So, are we ever going to find out what happened?" Amelie didn't look at him as she dunked one corner of her sandwich into the bowl of soup.

Griffin forced his thoughts from Dianna and the aching pain losing her left him with. "What happened to what?"

Amelie lifted a brow as she bit off the soup-soaked

bread. "What happened with you and Dianna." She eyed him from where she sat. "You guys were dating, right?"

"I—" Griffin ran both hands down the front of his jeans, wiping away the slick of sweat suddenly collecting on his palms. "I'm not trying to have a relationship. I just want to focus on you and Troy. I want to be here when you guys need me."

Amelie's brows pinched together as she stared at him, silent and frowning. She stayed quiet long enough that he continued talking, needing to explain so she understood she and Troy were his top priority.

"I just want to be available when you guys need me. I don't like that you feel like you can't count on me. You two matter to me more than anything."

Amelie's head slowly cocked as she continued to stare at him. "I don't think I understand what you're saying." She shook her head a little. "Like, at all."

"I came to Moss Creek to be around you and Troy. That's it." This was why he didn't try to open up. It was too hard to let anything out without risking all of it flooding free.

He couldn't dig into what really happened with Dianna. Why her face no longer greeted him every morning. Why her soft body no longer pressed tight to his while he slept. Why she didn't share his cologne in the mornings and fill her body with his at night.

Amelie focused on his face, abandoning her lunch. "You know you're allowed to have a life of your own, right? We didn't expect you to move here and give up everything."

Griffin swallowed hard, fighting the urge to clam up. But that was a big part of what landed him where he was now—miserable with no real idea of how to find his way out of the mess he'd made. "I didn't have anything to give up. My life was just about work. That's it. That's all I had." He fought in a breath. "Finding Troy gave me a second chance and I don't want to waste it."

Amelie watched him, expression full of something uncomfortably close to pity. "Can I ask you a question?"

"Of course. You can ask me anything." He loved her like a daughter. Wanted her to see how much she mattered to him. And it was finally becoming clear that opening up was one of the most important ways to do that.

"Do you expect Troy to ignore me after I have the baby?"

Griffin's chin tucked, the surprise of her question throwing him off a little. "No."

"You don't think he would be a better father if he focused only on our baby?" Amelie's follow-up question homed in on the point she was trying to make.

It was a point he was happy to argue. "Troy's a better man than I am. He's already proven he's capable of being a good husband, so being a good father too isn't that far of a stretch for him."

"You've already proven you're capable of being a good father. It's not a stretch to assume you would be capable of being a good partner in a relationship too." Amelie threw his words back in his face, twisting them just enough to suit her need.

"But I haven't proven I'm a good father. You had to call Evelyn to bring clothes to the hospital because you thought I was too busy to bring them to you." Not being there when they needed him still grated. "If I was that good of a dad you would've called me first."

Amelie crossed her arms, resting them on the swell of her belly as she stared at him like he was the biggest fucking idiot she'd ever seen. "You've helped us more than anyone." She lifted one hand, raising a finger in the air. "You helped fix up my grandma's house." She lifted another finger. "You've helped around Cross Creek every Sunday you've come over." She lifted a third finger. "You've helped with the addition, you've taken my grandmother to doctors' appointments, and you've been here every day for almost a freaking week waiting on me hand and foot." She lifted her last two fingers at once. "Do you want me to keep going?"

Griffin stared at her, frowning and frustrated because Amelie clearly wasn't looking at things the right way. "Those are just things a dad should do."

Amelie's lips slowly lifted at the corners, her expression turning victorious. "Do you see my dad doing any of those things?"

If she was a marksman that would've been a kill shot. One that took down every argument he was trying to make. But it still didn't make him believe he was a good dad, which meant maybe nothing would. Maybe he was destined to always feel like a fucking failure in everything he did. Maybe there was no escaping something you'd carried for so long.

"So now that we've established you can be more than just Troy's dad," Amelie's expression softened, "what happened with Dianna?"

He wanted to keep it in. To hold back the truth. To hide yet another of his failings from Amelie in the hopes that her delusions of his fatherhood skills would continue.

But he was fucking miserable. The most miserable he'd ever been in his life.

"I fucked up." Griffin raked one hand through his hair, leaning forward, elbows on his knees as he hung his head. "I ruined it all the same way I always do."

And then he did what he should have done before. He flayed himself open and bled, pouring it all out.

She sat quietly, listening to every word he said, no sign of judgment or disappointment on her face. When he was done, she took a deep breath, blowing it back out again. "That sucks."

That's all she had to say? He was dumbfounded. After hearing all he confessed, how was Amelie not glaring at him, questioning how she could have ever considered him decent? "That's it?"

Amelie shrugged. "What did you expect me to say? That you're an awful person for fucking up?" She shook her head. "I'm not going to because we've all done it. Me included." She rested both hands on her belly, relaxing a little deeper into the sofa. "So how are you going to fix it?"

"Fix it?" He snorted. "I can't fix it."

"Well, maybe not alone." She held his gaze. "You weren't the only one who fucked up."

Griffin pressed his lips together. She couldn't be suggesting—

"If I were you, I'd start by talking to the other person who fucked Dianna over. Maybe apologize for whatever made her hate you so much." Amelie paused, eyes staying on his. "She might even give you some insight that might come in handy in the future."

GRIFFIN STARED AT the front porch of The Inn at Red Cedar Ranch, still uncertain Amelie's plan was a good one. But for the first time since leaving The Baking Rack after Dianna discovered he and Janie shared a past, he felt hopeful.

More than that, he felt understood. Accepted.

Loved.

When he told Amelie what happened she didn't judge him or seem let down. She didn't think he was a piece of shit for holding back the truth of who Janie was. She didn't think he was terrible for falling in love with Dianna when he was supposed to be being a dad.

She definitely saw him as better than he saw himself. Which was one reason he was here. To prove he was the kind of man his daughter-in-law believed he was.

Griffin straightened his shoulders and crossed the

gravel lot, going up the steps to the wide porch flanking the front of the bed and breakfast where he'd stayed when he first came to Moss Creek. He pushed open the door and stepped into the familiar space, hesitating just a second at the sound of female voices carrying into the front hall from the open kitchen. He barely had the door closed when Mariah, the chef who handled most of the meals, peeked around the corner, her brows lifting.

He raised a hand in greeting, feeling less comfortable around her now that he knew Janie'd probably given her an education on all his shortcomings as a man. "Hi." He glanced over her shoulder. "Is Janie here by any chance?"

Mariah slowly disappeared behind the wall and the voices he'd heard earlier lowered to soft murmurs that were most likely jabs at his expense. A few long minutes passed before Janie came around the corner, her glare trained right on him. "It's you."

He decided to move right past her less than encouraging greeting. "Can we talk?"

Janie's dark brows lifted. "*You* want to talk?" She snorted. "Never thought I'd see the day." Her scowl deepened, arms crossing tightly over her chest as she continued to stare him down. "What do you want to talk about?"

"Dianna." He'd relegated her to a level of importance in his life she didn't deserve. Convinced himself, and her, she would always be less important than his son. And that hadn't been fair of him. Not to her and, surprisingly, not to Troy.

Apparently, Troy and Amelie weren't thrilled to find

out they were the reason he'd been keeping Dianna at arm's length. And they were even less thrilled he was willing to give up on the possibility of a happy relationship of his own for their sake.

"I love her."

Janie's head tipped back a little, eyes displaying the full extent of her shock at his statement. "You love her?" She huffed out a little laugh. "I don't believe you. In order to love someone you have to have feelings, and I'm pretty sure you don't have any."

She wasn't cutting him any slack, which was fine. She had every right to still be mad at him for the way their relationship dissolved.

"I'm sorry for not being able to give you what you needed." He'd thought long and hard about what he would say to Janie. What she deserved to hear from him. "I've always been afraid of opening up to people because I didn't want them to see all the ways I was fucked up." The admission came out more easily than he anticipated. "I thought my only chance of someone sticking around was if I did everything I could to keep them from seeing how much I really lacked."

Janie eyed him, the set of her shoulders softening the tiniest bit. "It seems like you haven't learned though. You broke Dianna's heart."

"That's true. I did. I made the same mistakes I always do." He tipped his head at Janie, knowing what he was about to say next would go over like a lead balloon. "But you broke her heart too."

Janie's lips pressed tight together, the skin around

them turning white. For a second he thought he was dangerously close to seeing the anger he'd experienced from her so many times before.

At least she didn't have any of his clothes to destroy.

But then Janie sniffed, blinking hard as her eyes lifted to the ceiling. "I know. I didn't know how to tell her." She threw both arms out at her sides before bringing one hand up to rest against her forehead. "How do you tell your friend she's dating your ex-boyfriend?" She shook her head, hands going out again. "There's really no good way to say that. I thought maybe I could just save her from you and she would never have to know." She glanced his way. "No offense."

"None taken. I'm glad you were looking out for her." He and Janie didn't have a great history, but if she loved Dianna half as much as it seemed like she did, he was going to find a way for them to coexist.

Griffin stepped closer, needing to make sure Janie understood how serious he was. "But we've got to fix this. I can't live without her and I'm pretty sure neither can you."

Janie sniffed again, the tears she was trying to fight starting to slip free. "I love her too and I feel like such a piece of shit for not telling her."

"You're not a piece of shit." Griffin reached out to pat her arm, wanting to offer some sort of comfort but not knowing exactly what was appropriate or wanted. "Everybody fucks up."

It was what Amelie had said to him more times than

he could count. It must have finally started to sink in because it seemed like maybe it was true.

Like maybe he wasn't as awful as he'd always thought. Like maybe fucking up was bound to happen and what separated the assholes from everyone else was how you went about cleaning up the mess.

Janie sucked in a long breath, blowing it back out as she wiped at the corners of her eyes. "Fine." She lifted her eyes to his. "What do you have in mind?"

Griffin swallowed hard. Getting Dianna back would take more than just opening up to her. He couldn't dump his feelings on her and expect forgiveness any more than he could make Troy the only thing that mattered to him. So what he was about to request was a necessary evil. Hopefully his clothes and his paint job would survive.

"If we're both going to be in her life then the first thing we have to do is work our shit out."

TWENTY-SEVEN

DIANNA

THE KNOCKING ON her door didn't immediately register since it was nearly impossible to identify over the never-ending banging coming from the house next door.

"I'm coming." Dianna rolled out of bed, detangling herself from the covers before padding her way down the hall and through the living room. She flung open the door, not bothering to check who was on the other side because it didn't really matter, and she didn't really care.

At least she didn't expect to care.

Janie stood on her porch holding a box. She stretched it between them, looking uncertain. "I brought you apology scones."

Dianna's stomach rolled at the thought, the wave of

nausea bringing her hand to press against her lips. "I'm not really in the mood for scones."

Janie smiled weakly. "Are you in the mood for an apology?"

Dianna cringed a little as the steady air nailing picked back up again next door. "What I'm ready for is that freaking noise to stop."

Janie leaned back, peeking at the giant house. "It looks like your neighbor's doing some renovations."

Dianna snorted. "That's not my neighbor." She turned, leaving the door open as she walked to the couch. "That's Griffin's house." She dropped down onto the cushions, leaning back and closing her eyes. "And I'm pretty sure he doesn't live there anymore." The exhaustion she'd been fighting all week started to pull her under almost immediately.

"Am I allowed to come in?" Janie's question made her jump a little, bringing her back from the brink of sleep.

Dianna lifted one hand, waving it around before letting it fall back to her lap. "I don't care."

It was difficult to tell if her despondence was because of depression or the flu currently making her feel like complete and utter shit. She was willing to bet it was a little of column A and a little of column B. Add in the incessant noise of the work crew powering through Griffin's home renovations, and she was feeling about as awful as it got.

Her front door closed with a soft click and Janie's quiet steps padded across the carpet. "I know I came here to apologize and try to fix everything, but I feel like I need to point out that you look really, really bad."

Dianna lifted one lid and peeked at Janie perched on the edge of the chair across from her. "If this is an apology you're not off to a great start."

It wasn't the kind of bluntness she normally offered. Even after years of therapy and self-work she still tended to fall back into her people pleasing ways, but the past two weeks seemed to have cured her of that, which might be good and might be bad.

And was yet another thing she didn't care about right now.

"I know, but..." Janie's voice got a little closer. "You look like you are seriously ill."

"I've been throwing up for days." She grimaced as the scent of the sweetened biscuits tickled her nose, threatening to give Janie a front row seat to the hell she'd been dealing with. "I think I've got the flu." Dianna slouched down a little lower on the sofa, trying to get comfortable. "You should probably not even be here. You'll end up like this too."

Janie was quiet for a minute. Long enough that Dianna squeezed open her eyes again to confirm she hadn't hightailed it out the door in the hopes of saving herself from whatever contagion was floating in the air.

But Janie was still sitting in the chair, frowning at her. "Do you have a fever?"

"Not yet. I'm sure it'll be here soon." She'd felt this coming on for the better part of a week, but when it finally hit it brought her to her knees, making her close the bakery for the first time ever while she tried to recover. "It needs to hurry up and do whatever it's going to do so I can get back to work."

"I can run the bakery." Janie scooted closer. "You should have called me. I would have come down and—" She stopped, obviously realizing the flaw in her plan. Janie set the scones down on the coffee table, fidgeting with the artfully placed tatters on her jeans. "I didn't tell you I knew Griffin because I was afraid you wouldn't want to be my friend." She took a shaky breath, fingers twisting the loose threads of her pants. "And I wanted to be your friend, which meant I also wanted to help you realize you probably shouldn't date him."

Dianna shrugged, feeling less upset about Janie's secret-keeping tendencies now that she was in the throes of influenza. "I mean, you were right, so I guess it doesn't matter now."

"I wasn't right." Janie looked down at her lap before lifting her eyes back to Dianna's. "I should have told you right away. I also probably shouldn't have said everything I did about him because I know people can change."

"Just because they can doesn't mean they will." Change was a hard and never-ending task. One she was very familiar with. It didn't happen overnight and it didn't happen forever. It was something you had to constantly work at. Fight for.

And clearly not everyone was cut out for it.

"That's true." Janie stretched the words out, like she had more to say but wasn't in a hurry to get there. "But that doesn't mean they won't either."

Was she defending Griffin now? Maybe her exhausted brain just wasn't keeping up with the conversation. It didn't really matter either way. "That's fine, but I'm not waiting around while he gets it together." She sat up as the urge to vomit hit her like a wave. "I've spent too many years of my life unhappy. I'm not wasting any more of them."

No matter how bad it hurt, she would never again be with a man who wouldn't give her what she needed. No matter how handsome he was. No matter how kind or funny.

No matter how much she accidentally loved him.

Dianna jumped up from the sofa and rushed to the bathroom as the sickness overthrowing her insides came to a head. She hit her knees in front of the toilet just in time to empty out the tiny bit of coffee she'd managed to choke down.

When she straightened, Janie was standing in the doorway, watching her with a concerned gaze. "I think you need to go to the hospital."

Dianna wiped her mouth with the sleeve of her shirt, tipping back onto her butt and slumping against the wall. "I'm fine."

She was actually as far from fine as she'd been in a long time, and that was saying something.

Maybe she could have handled what happened with Griffin. She might have even managed to be okay with the Janie aspect. But add being sick like this on top of those things, and she was as far beyond not okay as she could imagine being.

Janie shook her head. "I don't think so. I think something is seriously wrong with you." She moved into the bathroom and crouched down, pressing her hand against Dianna's head. "You're not hot, but you are sweaty and clammy." She frowned as she inspected Dianna's face. "And you look a little gray."

"I just need to go back to bed and sleep this off." Dianna grabbed the sink counter, using it as leverage to hoist herself off the floor. About halfway up her legs gave out, refusing to support her.

Luckily someone else was there to do it.

Janie caught her as she started to wobble, pulling one of Dianna's arms around her shoulders as she carried the weight Dianna couldn't. "Okay. I think I've seen everything I need to." She pivoted, her free arm coming around Dianna's waist to provide an added layer of security. "We're going to the hospital."

"I said I'm fine." Historically speaking she'd gotten through worse things than this, so evidence suggested she would get through this too.

"Of course you are." Janie maneuvered her through the house, pausing at the front door to point to the slip-on shoes positioned for quick runs to the porch and the mailbox. "Put those on."

"I don't want to put those on. I want to go back to bed." Being upright was only making everything worse, and in this moment something had to get better or she was going to pass out.

Probably while throwing up again.

"You can go back to bed as soon as we get to the

hospital." Janie pointed at the shoes again. "Put your feet in there. The only way you're not going to the hospital is if you physically fight me, and right now you're not even able to stand on your own, so I'm not too worried you're going to be able to throw hands."

Dianna groaned, cutting the sound short when it came a little too close to making her heave. "You're overreacting." She didn't want to go to the hospital, but she also didn't want to prolong being vertical, so she shoved one socked foot into the fur lined slipper.

"Maybe. But I'm also pretty sure I'm not underreacting, so we'll see who's right when we get there."

Janie maneuvered her out the door and down the driveway. She left Dianna in her car, seat laid back, while she made a quick trip into the house to retrieve Dianna's purse and keys, locking the door on her way out. By the time she came back, Dianna was already dozing, the sound of the door closing and the engine starting barely registering.

She'd barely closed her eyes before Janie was forcing her to open them again. "Up and at 'em." Janie tugged at one arm, rousing her from the blissful peace of sleep. "Let's get you into this wheelchair."

"I don't need a wheelchair. I'm fine—" The sudden and overwhelming urge to throw up greeted her the same way it did every time she opened her eyes, sending her twisting in the seat as she bent out the open door, barely missing Janie with a retch that splattered against the blacktop. Dianna stared down at the tiny amount of liquid. "I guess I still had some coffee in me after all."

Just the thought of coffee made her grimace and threatened to force a gag.

"I should probably thank you for not doing that in my car." Janie hooked both hands under her arms, lifting her up and turning to settle her butt into a waiting wheelchair. "Not that I wouldn't have probably deserved it."

Dianna closed her eyes, lacking the strength to keep them open. "I'm not mad anymore." She managed to peek out at Janie from under one partially lifted lid. "I'm just disappointed."

"Ugh." Janie groaned, her head tipping back. "That's worse and you know it."

Dianna managed a little smile in spite of her current state. "I know."

Janie reached out to pat her on the arm. "I'll be in as soon as I get the car parked."

Dianna nodded. "You know where to find me."

She rested her eyes as a nurse wheeled her into the emergency room, taking her straight through the waiting room and into the back.

She did her best to help them transfer her into a bed and immediately pulled the blanket up to her chin, fully intending to go to sleep. Before she managed to doze off, another nurse was there, taking her temperature, checking her blood pressure, and forcing her to squeeze what little liquid remained in her body into a pee cup.

Janie came in just as she was getting back into bed, collapsing against the plastic covered mattress.

"Have they said anything yet?"

Dianna closed her eyes, wishing she was in the comfort of her own soft bed. "Only that they're disappointed in you too."

"Ha ha. Very funny." Janie pulled the chair beside the bed closer, reaching out to hold Dianna's hand. "Seriously though. I am so fucking sorry. I didn't want you to hate me just because I had dated Griffin before. I didn't know what else to do."

"You could have tried talking to me about it." Why was that so hard for everybody? They acted like opening up would kill them. Like it caused them physical pain to—

Hell.

Had she'd worked so hard and come so far that she lost sight of how it was in the beginning? Back when she sat and stared at her therapist for the better part of an hour, doing everything she could to avoid confessing the embarrassing, painful truth. To a stranger.

Dianna sighed, swinging one forearm across her eyes. "I'm sorry. Sometimes I forget how hard it can be to deal with your own shit." She'd been so focused on fixing everything in her own life—in her own self—she lost sight of how hard it was to get started. Because all she could focus on was how hard it was to finish.

And maybe that was because you were never finished. Maybe no matter how hard you worked or how hard you tried, you could never really be fine again. You could glue all the pieces back together, lining them up perfectly, but one wrong bump and that weak spot would give.

A lot like it had the day she found out Janie and Griffin were keeping a secret from her.

Dianna squeezed Janie's—her real friend's—hand. "Thank you for coming to see me today."

Janie gripped her hand tight. "You don't have to thank me for being your friend. That's all I really wanted to be, I just wasn't so great at it."

Guilt settled into her already upset stomach. "You were pretty good at it, right up until this morning when you dragged me here."

Janie laughed. "You say that now, but you'll be thanking me when they give you medicine to make you feel better."

Almost as if on command, the nurse strode back in carrying an IV bag. She gave Dianna a tentative smile. "So I have some news." She came to her side, hooking the bag onto the stand. "I think I know why you're feeling so crummy."

Janie lifted her brows. "I told you."

"Yeah, yeah." Dianna wiped at the line of sweat collecting on her upper lip as she tried to ignore the increasing urge to throw up again. "What plague have I been infected with?"

"The kind that can hang around for about nine months." The nurse cringed a little. "You're pregnant."

Dianna blinked at her. "That's not possible. I can't get pregnant. I have PCOS."

"PCOS can make it more difficult, but it definitely doesn't make it impossible." The nurse went back to messing with the IV. "And I can assure you, you are definitely pregnant." She collected some items and lined them down the tray. "When was the date of your last period?"

"I don't know. I've always been irregular." Irregular enough that it had never really been worth tracking.

"That's okay. The doctor's already scheduled you for an ultrasound, but we need to get some fluids in you before then so you start feeling better." The nurse went to work on her IV, but Dianna didn't register any of it.

She was pregnant.

All those dreams she'd given up on after trying to have them for so long just fell right into her lap. Her uterus, actually.

"So." Janie pursed her lips, lifting her brows as her eyes moved around the room. "Should I have the safe sex talk with you, or..."

"It might be a little late for that." Dianna let her head fall back to the mattress as she struggled to wrap her mind around everything. "I can't be pregnant. I tried for years when I was married before. Years."

"I promise. You are pregnant." The nurse taped her IV into place. "I also promise you should start feeling better really soon."

Dianna shook her head as the nurse walked out, overwhelmed and still a little disbelieving. "This is insane."

"Is it though?" Janie shrugged. "I mean, you tried to get pregnant with an asshole for years and it never worked. A few weeks with someone who maybe isn't as big of an asshole as he used to be and, boom." She exploded her hands, fingers flaring out. "Super pregnant."

"Oh God." Dianna covered her face. "Griffin."

The shock was significant enough it hadn't yet occurred to her that Griffin was a part of this.

"You've got to tell him." Janie's tone was gentle. "And you've got to tell him soon." She tapped the bed with one finger. "Like, right now."

TWENTY-EIGHT

GRIFFIN

*T*HIS COULDN'T BE happening.

Griffin screeched into the parking lot of the same hospital he brought Amelie to less than a month ago, whipping his truck into the closest space he could find. He opened the door as he shut off the engine, not even paying attention to whether or not he locked the doors as he ran toward the emergency room entrance.

When Janie called he assumed it was to let him know how her visit with Dianna had gone. Not for a second did he expect to hear she'd ended up taking Dianna to the hospital, dehydrated and lethargic.

He rushed to the desk, hand tapping the counter as he waited for someone to come help him. Finally a woman in scrubs came to give him directions, offering up the bay number Dianna was in before unlocking the door so he could go back.

The only thing that kept him from running was the fear he would pass her by. He walked as fast as he could while reading off the numbers, boots squeaking against the linoleum, until he found the one he was looking for. A curtain closed off the front portion, and he stood there for a second, unsure what to do.

What he had the right to do.

"Di?" He couldn't go straight in. Right now he was nothing to her. Not a boyfriend. Not a partner. Maybe not even a friend.

"Come in." Dianna sounded surprisingly perky considering the picture Janie had painted him, and a little of the fear squeezing his chest relaxed. Griffin pulled back the curtain's edge, peeking into the space.

Dianna sat upright, a tray positioned over her lap as she nibbled on the corner of a saltine cracker and took a sip from a can of ginger ale. Her skin was pale and there were circles under her eyes. Her dark hair was limp and tangled and her bright eyes were a little duller than normal.

And she was still the most beautiful thing he'd ever fucking seen.

She gave him a little smile. "Hey."

Griffin took one step in, pulling the curtain closed behind him. "Hey."

This wasn't how he planned to see her again. Nothing was ready. Not the house, not the sunroom, not the ring, not him. But there was no way he couldn't come to make sure she was okay. To see it with his own eyes.

He would've driven himself crazy otherwise.

Dianna motioned to the chair tucked close to her bed with the cracker still pinched between her fingers. "You want to sit down?"

He nodded, hesitating another second before moving to her bedside, his steps heavy and hard. He lowered into the chair, gripping the arms tight, not really sure what to do next.

He had a whole vision of how he was supposed to convince her to come back to him and this wasn't it. "I—"

"I'm pregnant." She cut him off, blurting out the words and leaving them hanging in the air.

He sat for a second, trying to digest what she said. "You're pregnant?"

Dianna's eyes moved over his face and she slowly nodded. "Yes." She picked up a strip of images from beside her on the bed and passed them his way. "They said about eight weeks."

Griffin took the pictures—the *ultrasound* pictures—being careful not to hold them too tightly.

"I know things are weird between us right now." Dianna paused. "I just wanted to tell you right away since —" She reached up to slide one hand down her hair, smoothing over the tangled mess. "I just knew you would want to know right away."

Griffin stared at the black-and-white blobs in front of him, straining to pick out anything identifiable. "This is our baby?"

Dianna softly smiled, reaching out to point at the center of one image. "You can't really tell, but that little thing that looks like a bean is the baby."

"Our baby." He couldn't keep himself from correcting her.

Dianna nodded. "Our baby."

It was barely more than a blip on the screen but had the power to change everything. Once again his whole life was turning upside down. Everything he thought he knew—the future he'd been working so hard to plan out—had changed again.

"How are you feeling about this?" Dianna's question was loaded and he knew that.

If he didn't answer this the right way there might not be any going back. Any repairing the damage he'd already done.

"Happy." It was the simplest and most obvious of the emotions he was currently experiencing. "Scared." Griffin lifted his eyes to where she sat in the hospital bed, looking weak and pale. "Worried."

"They promised me the baby's okay. I just got a little dehydrated from the nausea." Dianna tried to explain, but she was only picking up half his concerns.

"I'm not just worried about the baby, Di. I'm worried about you too." He reached for her hand but caught himself. He didn't get to touch her. Not yet. "I didn't know you were feeling so bad."

Finding out Dianna had been suffering alone threatened to drag him back down into the cycle of guilt and self-destruction he'd been spiraling through his whole life. And while he'd been working hard to move forward —to be better—this was pushing him to his limits.

"You couldn't have known." Dianna slid her fingers across his, offering the touch he was so desperate for.

Griffin latched onto the contact, lacing his fingers between hers before lifting her hand to his mouth so he could rest his lips against her soft skin. "I don't know what to apologize for first."

Dianna's lips barely twitched. "Probably for having such a weak pullout game."

She was teasing him. Trying to lighten the situation with a joke that would be remarkably well-timed under different circumstances. Or maybe just with a different man.

Griffin shook his head. "I won't apologize for that." His eyes dropped down to the ultrasound photos still gripped tight in his hand. "Not ever."

He came here unprepared for so many things. He wasn't ready to show Dianna how much he'd changed. He wasn't ready to show her all he'd done to create a life that included her. But he was ready for this. Ready for the opportunity to be a dad from day one.

A nurse whipped back the curtain, giving Dianna a bright smile. "Feeling better?"

Dianna nodded, dutifully taking another bite of her cracker. "I don't feel like I'm going to barf up everything in my stomach, so yes."

"Excellent news." The nurse came to Dianna's other side, unhooking the line connected to the IV taped to Dianna's hand. "I just got your discharge papers, so you get to break out of here." Her eyes lifted to Griffin. "Are you her ride?"

Griffin turned to Dianna, uncertain of the place he currently held in her life.

Dianna nodded. "Yes."

"Excellent. We will get you all situated and then you can go home and rest." The nurse went to work peeling away the tape from Dianna's skin and sliding the catheter free before covering the tiny dot of a hole with a Band-Aid. Then she went through Dianna's paperwork, explaining the instructions and the prescription for anti-nausea medication they gave her to tide her over until she got in with the obstetrician of her choice.

It wasn't long before Dianna was being rolled out the entrance and loaded into his waiting truck, dozing on the ride home.

They pulled past his house and he parked in her driveway, getting as close as he could to the front door without planting any of his tires in the yard. He rushed around to help her out, keeping her steady as her feet hit the ground. Dianna's eyes went to where the workers were milling around next door, coming in and out as they plowed through the remaining renovations. "Did you hire them so you wouldn't have to be close to me?"

Her question was quiet and laced with hurt. Normally he would have done anything to avoid answering her in the hopes of avoiding a conversation he didn't want to have. But that hadn't gotten him anywhere in his life. All it did was lead to a string of broken relationships and failure. And there was no way he was going to fail Di.

"No, I didn't." Griffin met Dianna's gaze, holding it as he laid out a little of the truth he'd planned to reveal once everything was perfect. But perfect was no longer an option, so he was just hoping for good enough. "I hired them so I could be close to you sooner."

Dianna's dark brows pinched together. "The math on that doesn't add up."

"It does, actually." He tipped his head toward the house that suddenly represented even more than it did when he woke up this morning. "Would you like to see why?"

Dianna glanced at the house behind him, barely hesitating. "Okay." She tried to take a step, but before she could get anywhere he scooped her up, carrying her princess style across their yards.

She let out a squeal of surprise. "What are you doing? Put me down. I'm too—" Her lips sealed together, pressing tight before she finished. "Too risky to jiggle up right now."

He gave her a grin, feeling lighter than he had in weeks. "I'll take my chances."

She could barf all over him if she wanted, as long as he got to keep her close. This might not be the way he planned all of this to go, but he couldn't find it in him to be upset that she rushed his timeline. It was taking everything in him to stick with it as it was.

One of the contractors he'd hired held the door open as he carried Dianna in, gently setting her down on the newly refinished entryway floor.

Her eyes immediately widened as they moved around the gleaming hardwood and shining staircase. "Holy cow." Her eyes snapped to his. "I knew there were a lot of people coming and going, but I didn't realize how much they'd accomplished."

He'd had people working almost around-the-clock for nearly two weeks straight, shelling out an exorbitant amount of money to push the project along at an epic pace. Because being away from her was fucking awful, but he wasn't willing to show up in her life until he could prove all he had to offer.

All he'd worked to be able to provide.

"They've been focused on certain areas." Griffin rested one hand on the small of her back, leading Dianna down the main hall, past the relatively untouched formal living room and den. "I wanted to finish the most important parts first."

And thank God he had. He might not have a completed product to show her, in any capacity, but at least she would see his intent.

Dianna stepped into the mostly done kitchen and sucked in a sharp breath. "Oh my gosh." She moved deeper into the room, one hand resting along the marble countertops he'd chosen. "It's beautiful." She gasped again, pointing at the line of cabinets stacked down the wall of windows. The ones he'd done his best to make sure looked exactly the way she wanted them to. "That looks so nice." She went to stand in front of them, resting her hands on the counter as she stared out into the messy backyard, confusion pinching her beautiful features. "Are you putting an addition back here?"

He stepped in beside her, looking over the corner farthest from her property. It sat back a little, the bulk of it blocked by the jut of the office, making it difficult for her to see well from her own yard. "I am." He focused on her face. "Would you like to go see it?"

Dianna immediately nodded. "Of course I would."

He turned her toward the mud room that now sat on the back of the kitchen, attaching the addition to the main house. Opening the door to the almost complete sunroom, he watched Dianna's reaction as she took it in.

She pressed her lips together, but not before her chin barely quivered. Moving carefully down the steps, she went straight to the custom-made swing sitting in the center of the space and sat down on the cushioned seat, leaning back against the pillows and blankets he'd piled up to make it as comfortable as possible.

Because he intended to spend every morning there for the rest of his life.

Griffin eased down onto the swing next to her, slowly rocking them back and forth as Dianna looked around the room he'd built just for her. Just for them.

"I've never seen anything like this." Dianna scanned the windows circling the space. "It's like being outside but still inside."

Griffin pointed to the removable panes. "All those come out and leave just a screen, so in the summertime the bugs won't bother you and in the wintertime you can still be outside without freezing to death." He gave her a little smile. "And now Snickerdoodle has a spot to hang out."

He hated that the space was still as empty as it was. He'd had a whole plan worked out. One he'd spent more hours than he could count organizing. He wanted it all to be perfect for her so Dianna would see how hard he was willing to work to have her back in his life. "I have a lot of plants on order so it will feel summery even in the winter."

Dianna's eyes came to his. "So it will be kind of like a greenhouse?"

"It will be whatever you want it to be." He'd researched all the options there were for an addition, settling on the one offering the closest likeness he could create to the mornings they used to spend together. "You said you were going to be sad when we couldn't sit on the porch for breakfast anymore. Now you don't have to be sad."

Dianna smiled at him. "This is really thoughtful."

"This isn't how I wanted it to be when you saw it for the first time." He took a deep breath, but it wasn't as difficult as he expected to explain what he'd been doing while they were apart. "I wanted to finish the house so you would know I was serious when I asked you to marry me."

Dianna's head tipped back a little. She opened her mouth, but he wasn't ready for her to respond just yet.

"I started going to therapy. Started trying to figure out why it's so hard for me to share how I feel. I wanted to have everything so much farther along before I came to you and begged you to forgive me." His eyes dropped to her belly, fingers itching to reach out and touch the spot that derailed all his carefully-laid plans in the best possible way. "I know I won't ever be perfect, but I wanted to try to prove I could be good enough to make you happy."

Dianna's dark eyes moved over his face. "You're going to therapy?"

He nodded. "Once every two weeks."

It actually turned out to be the easiest part of all of this. Certainly easier than finding enough people to finish the home he wanted to convince Dianna to make hers in record time.

"His name's Mike. He's about my age. Gets that this shit is hard for me, but he pushes me because he knows this is important to me." He reached out, letting his fingers slide across her face, finally giving in to the need to touch her. "He knows *you're* important to me."

Dianna's brows lifted. "He knows about me?"

Griffin smiled. "Everyone knows about you." He traced the line of her jaw. "I thought Troy and Amelie were going to throttle me when they found out what happened."

"Oh." Dianna's eyes went to her stomach. "*Oh.*"

Griffin spread his palm over the curve of softness protecting one of the most important things in his life. "Don't worry. They'll be happy."

Dianna chewed her lower lip. "But it will be weird. Their baby will be older than ours."

"Don't care." Griffin leaned in to rest his forehead against her temple, breathing deep, relaxing for the first time in weeks. "All I care about is having you with me, Di."

TWENTY-NINE

DIANNA

DIANNA SAT IN the chair she'd been directed to occupy, watching as mover after mover walked past, carrying in boxes and furniture and appliances.

"This is a lot of stuff." Amelie sat beside her, occupying a chair of her own. "And some of it looks pretty new."

Dianna watched a man walk past with what appeared to be a box with a drawing of a crib printed across the outside. "I didn't realize when Griffin was asking me if I liked things he was immediately purchasing them."

Griffin had clearly been collecting everything he needed to fill his home.

Their home.

From furniture to linens to plates and silverware, the

giant house was starting to feel a little less cavernous, and a little more like a home.

"He definitely makes shit happen." Amelie shook her head as a man carried in another box, this one displaying the picture of an infant swing. "He does realize people are going to want to throw you a baby shower, right?"

"I don't think he's thought about anything outside of making sure he is the best dad he can be." Griffin hit the ground running the second she told him she was pregnant, and he hadn't slowed down since.

He'd hired yet another crew to work on the house, determined to have the whole thing completed as quickly as possible so they could have plenty of time to get settled before the baby came in the spring.

"I might have to tell him to simmer down. We're going to have a bunch of pissed off people if there's nothing to buy for this damn baby."

Amelie scratched across her expanding belly, wincing a little as she stretched to one side.

Dianna watched her closely. "Everything okay?"

"I don't think you want me to answer that question honestly." Amelie wiggled around, angling her body in a slightly different position. "I'll just say pregnancy was pretty easy up until about a week ago, not considering the little scare we had." She blew out a breath as she settled into her new spot. "Now it seems like it's getting harder every day."

"I have not found pregnancy to be easy at all." Dianna struggled not to gag at the memory of how very sick she'd been in the earliest days of her pregnancy. Even now there were times when her stomach threatened to revolt, usually coming completely out of the blue. "So I'm not sure I'll be thrilled when I hit what you're calling the hard part."

Troy and Griffin came past, carrying the hutch she inherited from her grandmother, moving carefully as they took slow steps down the hall toward the spot it would occupy in the world's most beautiful kitchen. Griffin shot her a quick wink before disappearing from sight.

"Ugh." Amelie rolled her eyes. "I think he just got you pregnant again."

"God I hope not." Dianna adjusted the stretchy fabric of the leggings sitting a little tighter on her belly than they used to. "I'm having a hard enough time stomaching the one I'm dealing with now."

"That's what you girls get for messing with those handsome men." Muriel gave one of the movers a little wave as he passed. "Speaking of handsome men. You should've provided popcorn for the gun show. I could've sold tickets."

Dianna laughed as Amelie rolled her eyes. "It's chaotic enough here as it is. The last thing we need is the Bridge Bitches getting in their way."

She'd gotten to know Amelie and her grandmother a little better once Griffin realized he could be different things to different people and no one would feel slighted or left out. He no longer believed he had to keep certain parts of his life separate. And he no longer felt like one wrong move would doom everything.

At least not usually.

He still had days of doubt. Days of worry. Days of uncertainty. But now on those days he talked to her about it. She shared her own uncertainties and worries and doubts, letting Griffin know he wasn't alone.

And he did the same for her, because even now, so many years after all that happened, she still struggled with the lingering effects of the damage that had been done.

She probably always would.

It was a difficult realization to come to, but some things simply never went away. Some traumas stayed with you forever, changing you, lingering in the corners of your mind and waiting for a moment of weakness. But even on those bad days, she still woke up and chose to be the person she wanted to be instead of what everyone else tried to burden her with.

And Griffin was slowly learning to do the same.

Griffin came by again, this time stopping to give her a kiss, his hand lingering on her belly, before he went next door with Troy to collect more of her belongings.

Once everything was finally in place and the movers were all packed up and gone, she and Amelie and Muriel relocated to the dining room, clearing off the table just as their pizza arrived.

It was the kind of day she was still getting used to having. One filled with a different kind of family than she'd ever been a part of. The kind of family where everyone was kind and supportive. Uplifting and nonjudgmental.

Also the kind of family where kids were older than their aunts and uncles, but Griffin and Troy assured her it wasn't as big of a deal as she was making it.

Griffin sat down beside her as the pizza was being passed around, hauling his chair close to hers as he wrapped one arm around her shoulders and splayed one hand across her slightly fuller belly. "How are you feeling?" It was a question they asked each other often. One they'd both promised to always answer honestly.

"A little sad, but really happy at the same time." She leaned into him, resting her head on his shoulder. "I really love my little house, but I also really love this one."

Griffin's expression turned serious. "I'm still happy to connect them. I'll build a hallway across the yard so fast you won't even see it happen."

Dianna smiled because she knew it was true. Griffin wasn't lying when he said he liked to figure shit out. He'd managed to renovate the giant house she now called home in what felt like the blink of an eye. He'd made leaps and bounds with the help of his therapist, learning to open up in ways she never expected.

Because at the end of the day, Griffin still had the same singular goal that brought him to Moss Creek. He just wanted to be a good dad. And now he had another opportunity to prove how capable of it he was.

"No hallway." Dianna rested her hand on his leg, the diamond he put on it two days after Janie dragged her to the hospital winking in the light. "I think Evelyn will take amazing care of it."

She'd struggled with the thought of giving up her

little house. It still represented the first independence she found after leaving Martin. So when Amelie's best friend mentioned she was looking for a place to rent, it seemed like it was meant to be.

"I think so too." Griffin leaned into her ear. "And now Officer Staks can ask her out to dinner."

"Awe." Dianna pushed out her lower lip. "Don't give Cooper a hard time."

Griffin grinned, nosing along her hair. "It's a whole lot easier to feel bad for him now that I'm the one who put a ring on your finger." He pressed a kiss to the spot just beneath her earlobe. "And, I can't hate him too much because he has excellent taste."

"Stop bothering her." Muriel tossed a napkin at Griffin, the wadded-up ball bouncing off his shoulder before dropping to the hardwood floor. "It's a good thing she can't get any more pregnant than she already is."

"Ignore her." Troy slid a piece of pizza across the table. "She says the same thing to me every day."

"Well it's true every day." Muriel hid her smile behind I can of pop as she feigned taking a drink.

She liked to give everyone a hard time, but Dianna knew there might not be anyone happier on this earth about the way things were than her. She'd managed to inherit not only a grandson, but also his father. And from what Amelie had told them, Griffin was turning out to be a hell of a lot better at being her son than the ones she'd actually birthed.

They continued to tease and talk, enjoying pizza and

chips around the newly delivered dining room table, surrounded by boxes and piles.

It was absolutely perfect.

Once everyone was done, Dianna pushed up from her seat, rolling her eyes a little as Griffin insisted on helping her up. "I made dessert." She went into the kitchen—the kitchen that was done exactly the way she'd imagined it would be—and collected the treat she baked up early that morning.

She carried it out to the table, sliding it into place before peeling the plastic wrap covering it free and slicing it into chunks using a serrated knife. "This is my favorite cake." She dropped a piece onto a plate and slid it in front of Muriel as Griffin pried the lid off the chocolate whipped cream she'd made to top it. "My grandmother taught me to make this when I was a little girl and I have loved it ever since." She passed a piece to Amelie, continuing around the table until everyone had their own serving of angel food cake, some piled a little higher with the whipped cream than others.

Amelie took a huge bite, her eyes rolling back in her head as she chewed. "Oh my gosh. This is amazing." She took another bite, eyes closing as she savored it. "It's so light and tender." She swallowed it down, opening her eyes to focus on Dianna. "Can I have the recipe?"

Dianna smiled, a surprising amount of emotion tightening her throat. "Absolutely you can."

"WHAT DO YOU think?" Griffin moved in behind her, resting his hands on her hips as she looked over the shower in the master bedroom. "Still like it now that you officially live here?"

"I love it." She was a little in awe of Griffin's taste. The combination of deep green beadboard on the wall and marble tiles lining the shower and floors kept the room in line with the elegant but light-filled style of the house, managing to look both sophisticated and expensive, and masculinely feminine.

It sounded completely contradictory but made sense in her head. Then again, she preferred to wear men's cologne so maybe masculinely feminine was her thing.

"Good." Griffin stepped around the clear panel of glass serving as a barrier for the overspray and switched on the water. "I'm pretty sure I love it too." He moved in close and started to peel away her clothes. "Especially since we'll both fit inside it." His hands slid over her belly, caressing the barely noticeable fullness there. "With plenty of room to spare."

"I can't help but feel like maybe that was a little bit by design."

Griffin hummed against her skin, his hands moving to the waistband of her leggings and easing them past her hips.

"It was definitely by design." He dropped to his knees as he worked her pants to her ankles, pressing a kiss to her navel as she stepped free. He tossed them into the hamper then stood, sliding his hands up her thighs and around her ass as his lips worked their way up her body, pausing to catch one of her sensitive nipples before flicking it with his tongue.

Being pregnant was definitely an experience. Good in some ways, less fun in others, but always amazing.

Especially the increased blood flow part.

Griffin's mouth slid against hers as he made short work of removing his own clothes and pulled her into the shower. His slick skin rubbed against her, creating a slippery sensual sort of friction that amped up her already over invested nerve endings.

"Turn around."

She immediately obeyed, more than happy to do whatever Griffin asked in situations such as this. Muriel was probably right when she said it was a good thing he couldn't get her any more pregnant than she already was, otherwise she'd be carrying a litter by now.

Griffin's front pressed against her back, his dick resting against her ass as he reached around, one hand cupping her breast as the other slid between her thighs and began stroking her clit.

"Grab the handles."

She gripped the two small bars spaced under either side of the showerhead, holding tight.

"Good girl." Griffin thrust against her, sliding his cock along the cleft of her ass. "Don't let go. I want to fuck you until your legs shake without worrying you'll slip."

She'd been a little worried Griffin might treat her differently now that she was on her way to becoming a mother. That he might see her as something other than just his wife. But, as he was so capably proving, Griffin had the capacity to see her in all kinds of ways while still saying the dirty things that made her knees weak.

Dianna moaned as he changed the angle of his thrusts, the next one sliding his cock between the press of her thighs and along the seam of her pussy.

"Is that what you want too, Di? Do you want me to fuck you until your legs give out?" He wrapped one arm around her waist, pinning her body to his as he rocked against her again.

"Yes." She breathed the word out as his cock slid against her again, teasing her clit with the faintest of touches.

Griffin's hand pressed deeper between her thighs, forcing them apart just a little more. On the next thrust he pushed into her, filling her in one consuming stroke as the warm water sluiced down her front. "So fucking wet for me." He pushed into her again, the sound messy and obscene. "I think I like you pregnant, Di." His hips bumped her ass a little harder, making her bounce. "I might just keep you this way for a while."

Why was that so hot? The thought of him wanting to keep fucking a baby into her because he loved it so much had her ready to come almost immediately. "Griffin, I—"

"You aren't coming already, are you, Di?" Griffin

worked her clit a little faster as he continued to pump into her. "We haven't even really started yet. There's so much more I want to do to you."

The tension building in her body snapped as her climax tore through her, sending her sagging against him as everything went weak.

"Don't let go of those bars. I won't be able to fuck you like this anymore if I can't trust you to stay on your feet." Griffin's arm tightened around her waist as he shut off the water and snagged a towel. He wrapped it around her, the fabric fluffy and soft against her skin.

Dianna tipped her head back to his shoulder, reaching up to lace her fingers in his hair as he nipped along her neck. "Maybe you should take me to our new bed. See if it's just as fun to fuck me there."

Griffin groaned, thrusting into her one final time before sliding free. "You've got to stop the dirty talk. You're going to kill me."

Dianna slowly turned to face him, feeling relaxed and sexy and desired.

Feeling like a fucking goddess.

"You should probably get some life insurance then."

EPILOGUE

DIANNA

*J*ANIE GROANED. "IF that isn't the cutest fucking thing I've ever seen." She stabbed one finger in the direction of her open mouth. "Puke."

"Don't say puke." Dianna pressed her hand to her lips, willing her body to keep its shit together as Griffin walked in through the front door of The Baking Rack, their baby daughter strapped in a carrier across his chest.

"It's your own fault." Janie opened up the cooler, fishing out a can of ginger ale and passing it over, along with a teasing smile. "Don't expect me to feel sorry for you."

Dianna took the pop, cracking it open and swallowing down a little sip. "Thank you."

Janie was too distracted to notice her thanks. She was

already on her way around the counter, hands out, fingers making grabbing motions. "Give me that baby."

Griffin smiled, carefully extricating Nadia's six-month old wiggly body from the carrier before passing her off to Janie.

Janie hooked her on one hip, bouncing in deep, twisting sweeps as she kissed all over Nadia's drooly, chubby face. "Auntie Janie missed you. Have you been giving daddy shit?"

"She sure has." Griffin grinned, completely unbothered by his ex-girlfriend holding their daughter. "Literally. She's blown out three diapers already today."

Janie's smile widened, her mouth opening wide with the expression. "Good girl. Auntie is so proud of you."

Nadia kicked her feet and babbled, little fingers grabbing at the bright colors inked on Janie's arm as they continued to bounce around the shop.

Griffin came to the counter, the empty baby carrier still hanging across his broad chest. "We came to see if you needed any help getting everything ready for tomorrow."

She thought life was hectic before, but since getting pregnant and married and then having a baby and then accidentally on purpose getting pregnant again, life had become complete chaos.

Exquisite, amazing chaos.

Dianna glanced down the mostly empty cases. Like always, they were pretty ransacked. "I feel like I might need to figure out a way to produce more inventory."

She'd been dragging her feet on it, a little worried she

would eventually push the limits of how much the people of Moss Creek could buy in a day. But it was starting to seem like they didn't know any limits when it came to baked goods, so she was once again trying to come up with a way to up production.

"Makes sense to me." Griffin reached across the counter, resting his hand on hers. "Do you have any ideas on how to make that happen?"

Griffin was a great businessman. He'd built a thriving chain of car repair shops he still owned in Seattle, but rarely had to do much more than take the occasional trip and participate in a weekly zoom chat. That left him completely free to be the primary caregiver for Nadia and, as she expected, he was great at that too, juggling nap times and feeding schedules like he'd been doing it his whole life.

But while it was easy to leave their daughter in Griffin's very capable hands, she still fought the lingering fears that came with allowing him in her business. It was stupid. Ridiculous. Nonsensical.

But it was just how trauma worked. So she was learning, yet again, how to live with it.

"I've been thinking about some of your suggestions, and I think maybe it's time to consider finding a larger space." As terrifying as it was, she valued Griffin's opinion. Needed it. And he was always willing to offer it. Carefully and respectfully because he knew it was one of the ways she continued to struggle.

"The main issue is that a bigger space won't solve all our problems." She took another sip of ginger ale, taming down the tiny edge of nausea that followed her throughout the day. "I would also probably need to hire another employee."

It was actually a necessary evil either way. Not only would she need another employee when and if she expanded, she was going to need someone else to help carry the load when she was on maternity leave. With Janie on full time, she'd been able to expand her offerings so much that one person could no longer handle all the prep involved.

"Luckily you know people who can help." Griffin slowly stroked over her skin, offering up a reminder that grounded her in reality instead of in the past. "People who love you and people you can trust to guide you in the right direction. People like Mae and Mariah." He tipped his head at where his ex-girlfriend was now making their daughter belly laugh. "And then you have Janie."

"I heard that." Janie leaned closer to Nadia, rubbing her nose against their little girl's. "Auntie is going to feed you so many beans the next time she babysits and then send you home to stinker all over daddy."

"She can't have beans." Griffin smiled as their daughter continued to cackle. "But sweet potatoes do make her fart like crazy."

Dianna laughed, shaking her head. "Do I have to separate you two?"

Griffin and Janie had a complicated sort of truce. They'd each apologized for past bad behavior, but they would never be close. And that was fine. Because while they didn't have a friendship, they did have something just as important.

Mutual respect. Not that it was always apparent.

"Come on then." Dianna grabbed her pop and carried it toward the door leading to the back room. "You can help me back here while Janie and Nadia run the counter."

"Why do we even need to hire someone else when we've got you, huh?" Janie's sing-songy voice followed her into the kitchen.

So did Griffin.

His big body immediately crowded her back against the stainless-steel countertop. He leaned close, his nose skimming up the side of hers. "You remember this spot?"

She smiled as his lips brushed her mouth. "Of course."

His eyes held hers. "You still think that day was a mistake?"

Her chest squeezed at the uncertainty in his tone. There were still days it pushed through. Even though they had a beautiful daughter and a wonderful life together.

She laced her arms around Griffin's neck, pulling him so close the clips of the baby carrier he wore dug into her boobs. "No way." She smiled against his lips. "Except the part where I let you leave without helping me clean up."

GRIFFIN

"I CAN'T BELIEVE how warm it stays out here." Dianna sat beside him on the swing, curled up among the pillows and blankets, their daughter nursing at her breast. "I was a little worried all these windows would let the cold air come right in, but it's perfect." She sighed, the sound content and relaxed. "And I freaking love this swing."

Griffin held out a bite of the French toast he'd put together while she showered, feeding it to Dianna so she didn't have to juggle both baby and breakfast. "I'm glad."

He'd drawn up the plans for it himself. Cut every piece and assembled them all, carefully sanding, staining, and sealing so it would last for years. He'd even figured out how to do basic upholstery, thanks to Nora Pace. She'd spent an afternoon helping him with foam and fabric, happily offering her assistance even though he'd snatched some of the most prime real estate in Moss Creek right out from under her.

And to think he'd done it in the hope that it would keep him away from Dianna. Luckily, it had done the exact opposite. It brought him right to her doorstep.

And ultimately her to his, making it theirs.

"What do you have planned for the day?" Dianna's

voice was a little sleepy, which would definitely be a determining factor in any plans he made.

She'd been working her normal hours even though she was exhausted from being newly pregnant, still breastfeeding, and almost continuously nauseated. Luckily, her normal hours weren't nearly as long as they used to be, thanks to Janie's help at The Baking Rack.

"I haven't decided yet." He offered her another bite of breakfast. "I might just hang out around here."

His Sundays looked a little different now than they did before. He no longer worried about dedicating the entire day to Troy, thinking he had to continuously prove how much he cared. How much he wanted to be the dad Troy deserved.

Now he took a more relaxed, but still just as dedicated, approach to their relationship. They both had young babies and wives taking up most of their days, so he and Troy had to squeeze in time together whenever they could. Sometimes they met up in town for a quick lunch, just the two of them. Other days they got together as a big family, taking the babies and Muriel to the zoo or a museum. The time they actually spent together might be a little less quantity wise, but it was just as gratifying. Maybe more so.

Before, the pressure to be a perfect father made him feel like every interaction with his son was somewhat of a life-or-death situation. One wrong move and everything would crumble around him the way it had so many times before.

But now he knew that wasn't the case. Troy didn't

expect him to be perfect. He just wanted him around. The realization allowed him to breathe and actually enjoy the time he spent with his family.

Extended and convoluted as it was.

Dianna yawned, leaning back into the thick cushion of the swing as she closed her eyes. "I might hang around here too."

Nadia started to wiggle around so he carefully lifted her from Dianna's lap, tucking their daughter's small body against his shoulder as he pulled Dianna's shirt and nursing bra back into place. "Why don't you go upstairs and take a nap?"

Dianna blinked her eyes open. "But I just got up."

"So?" He stood up from the swing and held his free hand out. "The laundry's all done. The house is clean. There's nothing else to do. Might as well catch up on the rest you need."

Dianna chewed her lower lip for a second as she mulled it over.

She felt guilty relaxing. Like it made her lazy. It was a scrap from her past that she'd confessed still bothered her. Still affected the way she lived her life. And while he did his best to remind her how untrue it was, he understood that sometimes there just wasn't any reasoning with the way you felt.

So all he could do was wait. Give her time to work through all the truths she knew before settling on what she wanted to do.

"I am pretty tired." Dianna reached for his hand,

letting him help her up. "I think this baby is sucking all my energy."

She was reasoning her way through all the voices that lingered in her mind, reminding herself they were wrong. It was something he did often. Something he would probably do forever.

"Both our babies are sucking your energy." He cuddled Nadia a little closer as he rested his free hand on Dianna's lower back, angling her toward the mudroom. "I can't do much about the little one, but I can keep the big one occupied while you rest."

He and Nadia took Dianna upstairs, getting her all tucked into bed before quietly making their way back to the first floor. He settled his daughter into the highchair they kept in the kitchen, passing her a set of plastic keys laced on a ring to play with while he worked.

The word brought a smile to his face.

Working looked a hell of a lot different for him now than it did a couple years ago. A lot did. He came to Moss Creek lonely and broken down, dreaming of a second chance. Hoping to be a father. Hoping to find what he thought passed him by.

Never once realizing just how true that dream would become.

Made in the USA
Monee, IL
11 February 2024